MURDER
IN THE
PINEBELT

A BISHOP BONE MYSTERY
BY
ROBERT ROGERS

Electronic Prepress and Workflow design by:
Tishomingo Tree Press
606 Bay Street
Hattiesburg Mississippi 39401
www.tishomingotree.com

ISBN: 978-0-615-40318-2

Printed in The United States of America

10 9 8 7 6 5 4 3 2

I acknowledge the comments and suggestions made by all those who have read the story and add my thanks to all. Also due for well deserved thanks, are the mill owners who generously took their time to escort me through their mills in Brookhaven, Mississippi and Monroeville, Alabama, and explain mill operations from log yard to shipping bay. In particular I want to thank Patrick Harrigan of Harrigan Lumber for not only conducting the tour, but for reading the book afterwards.

I especially want to thank my late wife, Carolyn, for never doubting that the book was good, for never letting me give up. I dedicate this book and any others I write to her. Thanks also to Lantz Powell, my agent, for his help and support.

Robert Rogers

Chapter 1

Old Judge Chancellor shoved his cell phone into his pocket. His face bore a satisfied smile. "Bone's not the only one who can smell out a problem," he said to himself. He had just asked Bishop Bone to join him to "kick around" a possible flaw in their auction procedures. More a possibility than real as far as he was concerned, but one that had troubled him since the liquidation auction of timberlands owned by an out of town investor syndicate. "Gotta give him credit, though. He was on the scent first."

He stared out at the small lake nestled in a hollow, just yards from where he stood. He had been coming there for years to fish on his afternoons off. When she was alive, his wife came with him. She didn't always fish. If berries were in season, she spent her time in the undergrowth picking blackberries or huckleberries for a cobbler the old judge loved. There was never a time now when he stared out across the lake that he didn't think of her and wish she had not gone without him. Things were not the same without her. Still, he cherished the memories the lake brought back and fought back the tears that came with them.

A dense growth of hardwoods, pines, dogwoods and lush magnolias grew to the lake's edge. Birds chirped here and there in the trees. Clear water lapped gently over the black mud in the afternoon breeze and made like a faint smacking sound as it withdrew. Little bubbles formed and popped in the mud behind each receding wave. They always had, he remembered.

For the day, he wore his new fishing vest and a broad-brimmed hat to keep the sun and bugs off his balding head. His office staff gave him the khaki vest on his last birthday. He picked up a fly rod from the weathered old picnic table behind him and let it dangle from his right hand as he ambled closer to the lake. His face was chalky white and he moved with the slow fragility of an eighty-two year old. But, that mattered little to him. A big fish was out in the lake waiting for him, ready to do battle. That's what he thought. He always had.

Since his retirement, he limited his fishing trips to two hours every Monday from three to five, when the weather permitted, so he could get his nap in after lunch. He paused at the planked pier that extended some ten feet into the lake. His eyes darted between the boat on the bank and the pier. Fish from the pier, or the boat?

He pushed the boat into the water, then stepped gently in as it cleared the muddy bank. When it drifted to a stop, he stood with his back to the sun and flicked the slender rod back and forth to lengthened the line so it would drop the fly near the branches of a fallen tree at the far shore. The line "swished" as it cut through the air. A mockingbird edged forward on its magnolia limb perch to watch, as if the brown and yellow bristled thing with a shiny glint was a tasty bug.

The judge dropped the fly onto the water, a few inches from a branch that poked up from the surface of the lake. Its waters looked green-blue in the sun's rays. Pleased with his cast, he began to pull the fly toward him with an easy, fluid motion to move the fly like a desperate bug. The fly hadn't moved more than three inches before a silver flash broke the surface to grab it.

He smiled, yanked his rod to set the hook, and began to reel in. "Got one honey," he almost called out, as he once did when they were together, but caught himself in time. She can't hear me, he reminded himself.

He was so involved in the battle to land his catch, he didn't hear the movement along the shore of the lake behind him. It wasn't that loud, just the soft whir of a lure launched at his back. It hit with a light thud. A quick yank set the ganged hooks of the lure into the shoulder of the judge's vest. The judge scarcely felt the thump when the lure hit him. But, he did feel the hooks bite into his shoulder, the tug when the lure was reeled in and the cold water on his face as he was yanked backwards into the lake.

He thrashed about with both arms to keep his head above the water, but he was weak and his clothes and boots got heavy as he was dragged backwards. Each gasp for breath brought more water into his lungs and his desperate attempts to stay alive grew more and more feeble and soon ceased altogether.

Chapter 2

Days earlier, with no idea of what I was about to put into motion, I pulled off a dirt haul road, parked my jeep in front of the headquarters of the Pitts Lumber Mill and hurried to get inside. It was summer hot. Across the road were half a dozen metal buildings strung together like a giant metal snake. A log bumped along a conveyor belt into a building in the distance. Inside the mill, men shouted to be heard over the sounds of logs chewed into lumber.

"I'm here to see Mr. Pitts," I told the young receptionist and handed her my card. The inside cool was a blessing.

"He's expecting you, Mr. Bone," she said. I shoved my floppy hat into the back pocket of my dungarees and followed her to Burl Pitts' glassed-in office at the rear. I soaked beads of sweat off my forehead with my handkerchief after a miss on the short sleeve of my shirt. Men and women at desks took a brief note of my intrusion into their workday then resumed whatever they'd been doing.

Burl stood to shake my hand, his hard and callused, a matching gaze with no softening smile. He was a big man, with broad rounded shoulders and a hard, ruddy face marked by a graying beard in bad need of a trim. I was certain he could see the top of my head and I was six feet tall. His khakis were frayed and stained. Hanging on the wall behind his chair were black and white charts and a number of yellowed newspaper stories.

"You've come to check the new system," he said. "Never should've let Jimmy take that loan. Didn't need it. Don't like strangers nosing around my business."

The lawyer in me jumped at his last remark. I understood that the mill was owned by Burl and his brother Jimmy. I dismissed it. What did it matter anyway? I was only there for an inspection.

Pitts Lumber borrowed money to convert the mill from natural gas to wood chips, which they burned to power a turbine. Their lender asked me to report on how the new system worked; a report to a committee, a piece of paper for a file. Their due diligence. It's how I made a living, consulting with banks. I brought a note pad and camera. Banks liked reports with pictures.

I opened my mouth to speak, but he cut me off. "Let's go." He picked his yellow hard hat off the floor and slapped it on, said I'd get one up front.

Outside, the smell of cut pine filled the air and grew stronger the closer we got to the mill. The mill noises did too. We paused at the road to let a tractor pass. I stepped back to avoid dust swirls from its tires. Burl didn't move.

As we continued, I offered small talk. "Newspapers say that investor group will auction off their timber holdings … TRS." TRS was the short name for Timber Resources South, an investor group out of Chicago. Though somewhat small in terms of dollars invested, they nevertheless had timber holdings in Louisiana, Mississippi and Alabama. They also owned a small lumber mill in Lawton County where I lived. Pitts Lumber was in Sampson County about 30 miles east. The local newspaper had run several stories on the decision to liquidate and, in effect, go out of business.

"About time!" he said.

"You guys going to bid?"

"Don't know," he said. "You in on it?" He paused for half a step to check my reaction.

From the tone of his question, I was glad to answer, "No."

"We might bid. Might not. We got plenty of prime timber, but I reckon I wouldn't pass up a bargain."

"What'll happen to the mill?" I asked.

"Reynolds's looking for money to buy it," he said. Morgan Reynolds managed the mill for TRS before it closed. It was in the newspaper story. Morgan's picture as well. "Trying to get Lumberman's Bank to lend him the money. Be a big-assed mistake if they do."

He glanced sideways to see if I had an opinion. I didn't. He continued. "Should have bought it myself and tore it down. Never been enough business for two damned sawmills around here. Reynolds knows it!"

Burl opened the door to a shack near a small metal clad building that spewed brown steam out roof top chimneys. The smell of something burning wafted past my nose. Inside the shack, at a desk, a man with a thin, dark mustache smiled at a pretty young woman. Her flirty giggle ended when Burl poked his face through the door.

"Mae Belle." Burl frowned, and made a sharp gesture with his thumb. "Time you got back to your desk."

She sprang to her feet and hurried out. The man with the mustache found something interesting to read on his desk.

"Jimmy," Burl said, "Bishop Bone's here from that development bunch. Wants to see how we made out with that damn low interest loan you arranged. I told you they'd be in here snooping! Tell him what he needs to know, then get over to the office!"

Burl's abrupt command brought Jimmy's face up with an angry frown.

Joint owners maybe, but Burl sure as hell acted like he was in charge. From the look on Jimmy's face, I was sure he didn't agree, but he said nothing.

Burl told me, "This is my brother, Jimmy." I parked next to a chromed Harley in front of a sign that said, "Jimmy's Place." It fit the image of the man who deemed himself important. Even if Burl evidently didn't.

I figured Jimmy for the mid-fifties, but with a line-free face, he could have passed for less. Burl wasn't so blessed. He was probably sixty but would have passed for more. There was not much, looking at the two men, to link them as brothers. Jimmy was not as tall as Burl or as rough looking, though there was a toughness about him. Like Burl's, his muscles showed, just not stacked as high. Both had a predatory hardness in their eyes, like they were always sizing up what they saw, to figure its worth … to them

Burl did not wait for a reply. He stepped out the door. Jimmy stared him out, then offered his hand, all smiles, no calluses. His dark hair rippled in waves. His pressed denims could have come off the rack. He was what my grandmother would have called a "Dandy."

"Burl gets a little excited now and then," he said.

I handed him my card and explained my connection with the bank. "Lawyer, huh."

"I don't practice," I said. "Just work for banks." I'd passed the Mississippi bar when I came back from California, not to practice, but to add a little status to my consulting practice.

"Tell 'em it's the best thing we ever did. I don't care what Burl says. We run half the mill off hogged lumber scraps. Save enough off our gas bills to nearly 'bout make our note."

I asked what he meant by 'hogging.'

"Hogging's grinding lumber scraps into chips small enough to burn," Jimmy said. "Used to sell 'em to a pulp wood plant. Come on, I'll show you where the money went."

We exited to see Burl Pitts with two men. An older one was as tall as Burl, had a broad, handsome face, silver hair and a neatly trimmed beard. He looked fit enough to hold his own in a Saturday night fist fight, though not with Burl. Not many would. The younger one was thin and tall with a head like a marble covered with a thin layer of sun bleached hair. He smiled politely and listened … not the boss.

"What brings you out here, Caleb?" Burl asked the older guy.

Jimmy slowed to catch the conversation, not easy with the mill noises.

"Skinny cruised some of that last tract of timber I bought for y'all. I got to thinking we should scale a few loads in the yard to double check our estimates. No extra charge, Burl," Caleb answered.

"I wouldn't pay it anyway. How'd he do?" Burl asked. He began to stride toward his office.

"Okay," Caleb said as he and Skinny fell into step. "Right on the 'effn money. Like always."

"Caleb Washington and Skinny Dearman," Jimmy told me. "Caleb buys a lot of timber for us. Skinny's his assistant."

"Uh huh. He said 'cruised.' Is that like a drive by appraisal banks use to get the quick value of a house?" I asked. I didn't figure the comparison made much sense, but that's what came to mind.

"Ha. No, nothing like that." Two men on the mill's catwalk waved. Jimmy waved back.

"Foresters don't measure all the timber in a tract of land for an appraisal. It'd take forever," he said. "They stake out a small section, the cruise area, and measure the timber there. They multiply that timber by the number of sections in the whole tract to come up with an appraisal. Some art, some science."

"A sample?"

"That's right. The bigger the sample, the better the estimated value."

We stopped beside a noisy conveyor belt trailing yellow pine dust and debris. Chip lines showed on the ground on both sides of the belt.

He pointed upward and shouted to be heard. "The belt takes sawdust and chips from the mill to storage silos up there. From there, it's burned to power the turbines that run the mill."

I snapped a couple of pictures and made notes for my report.

"Me and Burl, uh, more or less divide up the work in the mill. My office is back there." He gave a head gesture at the shack we'd left. "I run the two kilns ... do other stuff too. I mainly monitor what comes in and what goes out of the kilns," Jimmy said. "That one's loaded." He pointed at the building with brown steam, the one with the burnt smell. The chimneys on its twin had none.

"Getting ready to load that one." He pointed to a cart stacked with freshly cut lumber at that kiln's open door.

"Hot air blows through the stacked lumber. Over two hundred degrees to get the moisture to about twenty percent. Lots cheaper to do since we converted from gas."

I snapped a couple more pictures.

"Dry lumber's stronger. It won't warp like green lumber." He pulled at the front of his shirt and turned toward his office. "Whew! Let's get out of this heat."

No argument from me. My shirt was soaked.

Inside his office, he touched a row of numbers on a computer screen. "A sensor measures the temp of the air blowing into a stack of lumber in the kiln. This is from a sensor on the other side. When the temp on both sides is about the same, takes about twenty hours, the stack is ready for the planer mill … where it's smoothed, graded, sorted and stacked for shipment."

I thanked him for the tour and left.

As I backed out to leave, a white compact car pulled in. A fresh faced young man with dark hair and glasses got out. A briefcase dangled from one hand. He put on his working smile and hurried toward the door.

My report to the bank was in the mail before the end of the day.

* * * * *

I owned an old log cabin and twenty-two acres not far from downtown Lawton. Bought it when I decided to make Mississippi my home. It sat on timbered columns on a bluff overlooking Indian Creek.

The creek almost divided the property into equal parts. On the far side, beavers had built a dam across a small branch that emptied into the creek. The damn formed a little pond for their stick-mud mounds. A waterfall down the creek marked one boundary of my plot, the interstate the other. I often relaxed on my back porch with the newspaper and something cold and watched the beavers work. A screen kept out mosquitoes and bugs.

I'd showered and changed into dry clothes, shorts and T-shirt, when I heard a car coming down the driveway. My winding driveway, flanked by a dense growth of trees, funneled car noise directly to the cabin. I didn't get many visitors and liked it that way. Kathy Sullivan, my best friend in Lawton, was coming out to grill steaks, but it was too early for her.

It was Seth Campbell. I'd worked for his company the year I moved to Lawton, even helped in his unsuccessful campaign for governor. We became friends, fished and played tennis.

"Bishop!" he shouted. Like me, he drove a jeep.

He took the front steps two at a time. His was a broad handsome face—ever smiling—with dark, alert eyes and salt and pepper gray layered hair. He was a couple of years older than I was, but looked younger. Something to be said for clean living, I supposed. I was closing in on social security.

"What brings you out?" I asked.

"I was on my way to the farm and decided to take a chance," he said. "Should have called." He stuck out his hand and asked, "Got anything cold? I'm thirsty."

I went to the fridge, got each of us a beer. We drank them on the back porch and stared down at the creek. An overhead fan twirled with a steady thump and fanned us with a cooling breeze. I told him about my visit to the Pitts' mill that morning.

"I know the Pitts. Knew Buford, their father. A hard man. Burl takes after him. Big … tough. Absolutely no patience."

I agreed with his assessment.

"Buford died in the mill. He climbed onto a conveyor belt to free a piece of lumber that jammed the belt. Didn't stop to cut the power. Damned belt slipped and threw him to the concrete floor. Killed him."

Seth's family came to Mississippi to participate in the timber boom at the turn of the last century. His first job was in the mill TRS later came to own. Seth's dad and Buford Pitts were competitors until the senior Campbell's health forced him to close the mill. Seth became a developer of factory outlet centers and later went public as Campbell Enterprises. I became a shareholder, small, when I worked there. The dividends helped balance my budget.

"Buford left the boys well off, but they didn't sit on it. They've done very well. Both are worth millions. Jimmy lives like it, but Burl, well, he still lives in the old house Buford built. Will until he dies."

I said. "Not a hell of a lot to tie them as brothers. They're about as different as night and day."

"Jimmy always tries to outdo Burl. Never has."

He tilted his bottle up for a drink. "Well, why'd I come by? You've heard about TRS, the investor bunch out of Chicago?"

"They're liquidating. I read about that."

"That's right. That reminds me! Something else I need to ask you." "What?"

"Let me finish this first. Some of the investors are 'old money.' But some went in tight and got tired of money calls from the managing partner. They're the ones that forced the liquidation. Gonna be a sealed bid auction. The bids will be opened in public though. High bid wins. John Prozini's the managing partner. He's uh—"

"A bullshit artist?" I asked, an intuitive guess based on what I knew about people who dealt in investments.

He smiled. "As good a description as any. Smart as hell, but full of it. Can talk the legs off a running rabbit."

"Prozini asked me to recommend somebody to watch for anything the investors could bitch about. He wants to show how diligent he was, in case they sue him for mismanagement. I gave him your name. Small fee, but easy." He shrugged.

"Hell, Seth, I know a tree when I see one. That's about it."

He waved away my objection. "He wants somebody with a keen eye and no ties to timber. No conflicts of interest. Just to watch for anything odd or suspicious. I told him you'd be perfect. You'll get a letter."

He finished his beer and stood.

"You wanted to ask me something," I said.

"Right. Almost forgot again. Rooster wants you to talk to Morgan Reynolds. Reynolds needs a loan from the bank to buy the mill from TRS. Rooster's at a conference in New Orleans this week or he'd have called."

Rooster Matthews, a feisty little man Seth had known since they were kids together, was Chairman of the Board of Lumberman's Bank.

Seth owned a big chunk of its stock.

"Burl Pitts said something about that this morning."

"Word's out then. Not surprising," he said. "The mill did okay until housing starts dropped. They shut it down last year and voted to auction off their timber holdings. If Morgan can't buy the mill, they'll get rid of it, too. Rooster says the loan is Morgan's last hope." Morgan, he told me, was well respected as a mill manager and in timber circles. Last year, the Governor appointed him to the Timber Commission.

"You know him?" I asked.

"I've run into him around town now and then, business functions. A good man, hard worker, as far as I can tell. Has a degree in Industrial Management from Jackson State. Graduated with honors. So, he's well qualified, just needs a boost."

"Burl said there's not enough business around here for two mills."

Seth said, "The Pitts never liked competition. The mill's not state-of-the-art, but it's still competition according to the Pitts. Burl in particular. The shape the mill's in, Morgan'll have to scrap around to make it. That's what worries the bank."

"Before this morning my knowledge of sawmills was limited to old movies where the heroine is tied to a log headed toward a huge saw with fast, doom-music playing. I don't think I'm qualified to give an opinion."

He laughed. "Rooster wants an opinion of Morgan's grit. Will he fade under pressure or stick it out if things get rough? Banks loan money, whether they say so or not, to the person as much as to their net worth. I've given him mine, but he wants yours too. He figures you have a good sense about people."

I laughed. "I don't know about that."

"I agree with Rooster. So do the banks you work for," Seth said.

Rooster was Seth's campaign manager when Seth ran for governor the year I worked as project manager for Campbell Enterprises. I got dragged into the campaign when the governor's backers smeared Seth with the scandal that had chased me out of California and cost me my marriage and my consulting practice. After the election, I returned to California to clear my name, and did. But, with my marriage gone, I came back to Mississippi. Rooster provided the banking contacts I needed to start over, with a strong endorsement. I didn't make as much money as I had, but I didn't need as much, and I had time to enjoy the view from my back porch. And, there was Kathy.

"An opinion's about all I can promise," I said. It seemed a simple enough job.

"I'll let him know. He'll be back Monday." He thanked me and left.

I glanced at the clock in the kitchen. Still too early for Kathy so I walked to the porch to spy on the beavers. The pond's surface was cast in an orange sheen from the afternoon sun. A beaver dragged a limb into the water and began an effortless paddle to the dam.

The sun was little more than a glow in the trees when Kathy drove up. The grill's briquettes were a red-orange, ready for the steaks. I raced down the steps to embrace her as her lips flashed the smile that always hit me as seductive. It gave me a lift on the worst of days. I'd had a few. Her face was more round than narrow, but pretty, and it didn't come with an ego. I liked that. I pulled her close to enjoy the intoxicating fragrance that only a woman has and hers was the best. I kissed her and we stood like that, her eyes locked with mine for one of those intervals that seems to have no limits. I kissed her again.

"Good to see you," I whispered and walked with her up the steps. Like me, she wore shorts and a tennis shirt. "You look great!" Her shoulder length hair snuggled the contours of her face. She was a brunette but the beginnings of gray lightened it a shade. Her eyes were a golden brown.

I first met Kathy during my probate of a young woman's estate. She had worked for Kathy in the library, which Kathy managed. Since then, I got all my reading material from the library. Didn't cost as much and I enjoyed the visits. Unlike me, she always seemed so damned happy. Although I still fought depression, I overcame my apprehension and introduced myself. I was older, but our age difference didn't seem to matter. We liked the same things and liked to be together. She too had suffered through a divorce and after the final decree, came to Lawton to care for her mother. I came to escape my past.

"You do too," she said, touched her hand to my face and looked into my eyes. They were green. "I like your haircut. Little gray makes you look distinguished."

She was right. A little gray had begun to show at the temples. The rest was light brown. I let it lay where it fell after a shower unless I had a business trip to make and had to comb it. Half the time I wore an old floppy tennis hat to cover the spot that had begun to show in the back. My face showed some lines with a sag here and there. I tried not to spend too much time in front of a mirror.

I told her about Seth's visit.

"I'm a little leery about giving an opinion on somebody's chances to turn around a closed sawmill. I saw my first one today."

"Don't worry," she said. "Just tell him what you think. It'll help the town if the mill reopens."

When it was good dark, I switched on the outside lights that turned the woods around the cabin into silvery images and the creek into ribbons of green. We sipped wine on the porch and listened to a tumultuous chorus of nature compete with Mendelssohn's violin concerto that came from speakers I'd hung on trees in back. Since she had arranged for a friend to stay with her mother, there was no pressure for her to leave. It was a night I cataloged under "B", for beautiful.

Chapter 3

I called Rooster Monday morning to get more details on the Reynolds' loan. It'd be well secured by a first on the mill and a second on Reynolds' home. A sixty five percent loan to value so long as the mill was a going concern. Good at any bank.

"But, we don't want to have to liquidate, Bishop, if he defaults. That brings out the bottom feeders, and we lose money no matter the loan to value," he said. "We want to know if Morgan will cut and run if he hits a bad spot."

I'd give him my impressions of the man.

Morgan asked me to "come on out" when I called. The sooner the better. "Up to my eyeballs in grease right now," he said and added a laugh. I'd be out in the afternoon.

John Prozini's letter was in my post office box. I was to attend the auction and watch for anything suspicious. The letter had no specifics, other than a suggested fee, higher than I expected, so I called him for details.

"John Prozini," he said, when his secretary connected us. I told him who I was and why I'd called.

"You just want me to sit there and watch?" I asked. "No investigation ahead of time?"

"No, Mr. Bone. Judge Chancellor and his team, Mr. Rose and the rest of them, have done an excellent job."

"Why hire me then? I mean–"

"Ah, well, you should know that some of the investors have threatened to sue me for mismanagement. I want to be able to stand up in court and say that not only did I hire the best liquidation team in Mississippi, I also hired an independent observer to watch for anything untoward. What more could a prudent man do, Mr. Bone? I ask you."

I couldn't think of anything. "So, you want me to take notes as the properties are sold? Is that about it?"

"That's it. If you see anything suspicious, write it down. That's what I'm looking for. Seth Campbell said you had a 'suspicious eye.' I'm paying you a fee to use it. However, I hope to hell you don't see anything!" He laughed.

I understood. I was to watch the auction and take a note of anything to suggest it wasn't on the up and up. A waste of time, I thought, but a fee is a fee. And, it'd look good in court if Prozini ended up in litigation.

* * * * *

I parked on the gravel beside two cars and a pickup truck in front of a trailer office that faced the mill. Bodies moved along the shadowed catwalks in the mill, but unlike the Pitts mill, no "lumber" sounds came from inside.

Morgan Reynolds, a diminutive black man dressed in grease stained dungarees and a short sleeved shirt met me at the door. I recognized him from a recent picture in the local newspaper. He smiled and extended his hand. If he had any worries, they didn't show on his face. He was not much more than five and a half feet tall, with quick dark eyes and words pushed by nervous energy. His face was a study in concentration, but always with a smile.

"Morgan Reynolds," he introduced himself. "You must be Mr. Bishop Bone. I remember reading something about you awhile back. Some newspaper story."

I said, "Bishop's fine."

"I answer to Morgan!" he replied. "So, the Rooster sent you to eyeball me, is that about it?" he asked.

"That's about it," I said.

"Well, come on in! Let's get to it."

I followed him into a small office at one end of the trailer, sparsely decorated, if I wanted to be generous. Desk and a couple of chairs. Scuffed linoleum flooring. "I want to hear the sound of two by fours roll along conveyor belts out there," he said. "I surely do miss that noise! Music to my ears!" He sat in the padded desk chair and gestured for me to sit down.

"I can imagine." I took the sturdier looking of the office chairs. It shuddered when I sat down, but didn't collapse.

"I believe Mr. Rooster's worried I won't get this thing off the ground long enough to make it fly," he said. "You're supposed to listen to what I have to say and tell him what your gut tells you?"

That was it.

"Look here!" He waved a stack of papers he took from his desktop. Half a dozen owners, he said, agreed to let him cut their timber on "spec." They'd get paid when he did.

"Some people say there's not enough market to support two mills so close together," I said. "The Pitts mill in Sampsonville?" I gave him a dubious look. "They have lots of business."

"Remains to be seen what the market will support. Fact is, both mills are here, and have been here for ages, right in the middle of the pine belt where pines grow like weeds. I know every square inch of it."

I glanced through the window at the mill. Kept my concerned look. "The mill is..." I bobbed my head in the direction of the mill.

"Uh huh, I know. It's shut down. Deader than a doorknob. 'A few upgrades,' Prozini said and we'd be competitive. He didn't know Burl Pitts. We needed more than a few. Too much overhead and not enough upgrades. That's what killed this mill, but I can make it go! My overhead's low!"

"Okay. Back to your situation," I said, "Lets suppose you get spec support from some of the timber owners, without paying customers, that'll dry up in a hurry. You can't have many customers with the mill shut down."

He took a letter from the in-box on his desk and held it out. "This is from a new discount lumber outlet. They sell to weekend handymen. They want my lumber."

"Won't the Pitts go after them?"

"I'll sell junk lumber with knots, stains and imperfections, pine and hardwood, cheap stuff Burl won't let in his yard. Even if he did, Bishop, he can't match my price. I'm low overhead. I get paid last. Eatin' money's all I need! I work for food!" He grinned.

"But low overhead or not, the mill's not running."

"Look out there." He pointed out the window to a young man on the mill steps. "That's my boy, Scooter, almost ready to graduate. Half his engineering class at Jackson State came down here to get the mill ready. Volunteered! I'm gambling we're gonna get that loan. Working on the come, you could say." He added a gambler's smile. Confident a seven was coming up. "Hell, we could saw logs tomorrow if we had to! Nearly 'bout. Tell Rooster to fund that loan!"

"How're you gonna make it if you don't get paid on time or you're late with a shipment? Weather may hold up timber cutting. All your money going out, none coming in. Doesn't balance, does it?"

"My hands'll work for chits till I get paid, Mr. Bone … Bishop. I can work any station in the mill if it comes to that. Night shift if I have to, right by myself. Me and Scooter. That'll stretch my working capital."

"Working capital? Where'd you get working capital? Rooster said the bank eliminated working capital from your loan request."

"It did, but I cashed in my 401k. That and my savings gave me a lot of what I need. Then, out of the blue, some outfit asked me to bid on a big piece of TRS' timberland, a listed company. They want their interest in the timber to be secret. I agreed to front a bid for them and they gave me a big fee regardless of how it comes out."

"A lucky break."

"You got that right. With my fee already in the bank, I have all the working capital I need. Money'll start to come in within two or three weeks after we cut the first log. Rooster has my pro forma. I sent it over early this morning. I mean to succeed!"

I believed that he would, or die trying.

"Come on, I'll show you around."

I followed him through the plant. He showed me a machine that ground the bark off a log, a "debarker." An operator cut off the bad ends in an operation called "bucking." I didn't ask why they called it that. It was too damn hot to stand around talking about something I'd forget by morning anyway.

After being "bucked," a conveyor belt carried logs through a number of stations that transformed them into lumber. Not much was wasted. Unlike the Pitts who burned chips to power their mill, Morgan sold the bark and shavings to be made into particle boards and pulp.

I met Scooter and his friends. Scooter was small, like his father. I saw the resemblance in their faces. The big difference was that Scooter's was more relaxed.

"Dad's taking us to Landrum's Country tomorrow. Wants to show us how things used to be, how they used to saw logs," he said with a smiling glance at Morgan.

Morgan gave him one of those "yeah" smiles in return.

Landrum's Country was the re-creation of an old farm settlement, including a country store, water driven sawmill, a quaint church where young people loved to get married and all sorts of other buildings and implements of the period that brought back memories of the way people once worked the land to make a living. It was a popular favorite for locals and visitors. Families came for the day and the night when entertainment was offered.

Kathy and I had strolled through the grounds a number of times. It was hard to see it all in one day.

* * * * *

I called Rooster with an interim report. "If anybody can make it, he can."

"That's our judgment as well. Just wanted a backup opinion." They'd make the loan.

Morgan Reynolds opened the mill on Saturday and shipped lumber three days later. I attended the ribbon cutting ceremony. Morgan, the mayor, and other dignitaries had their pictures taken under a just painted black and white sign, "Reynolds Sawmill."

I never saw anybody prouder than Morgan when he cut that ribbon. From a catwalk inside the mill, we watched the "official" first log sawn into a "cant." For those of us who didn't know, Morgan described it as a piece of lumber with two flat sides and two rounded sides. Morgan worked one of the stations, Scooter another. Scooter said that a computer and laser scanner determined how many pieces of lumber could be cut from one log. I didn't stick around to verify the count.

That evening, Kathy and I celebrated nothing in particular with dinner at the Pub, a building near the center of old town. It was re-named "Pub" after the owner got a genealogy report that said one of his ancestors "might" have run a public house in Ireland before immigrating to the US. The name caught the fancy of the local restaurant goers immediately and the place became a popular eating place in town. Inside, patches of red brick showed where plaster fell off the walls. A patina of worn stains marked its heart pine floors. Wobbly fans on black, rough sawn beams stirred the air. Along one wall was a gleaming, copper covered bar with stools and bare wood tables in front. Mugs hung from racks over the bar. Bottles of spirits from all over showed in slots and shelves behind it. And, levered taps offered mugs of cold beer to those with that preference.

We elected to sit outside, away from the crowd, more privacy and cool enough for comfort.

We talked about the opening of Morgan's mill and the boost it'd give to Lawton's economy; and my "appointment," for lack of a better word, to be at the auction and watch for odd things.

"Seth told Prozini that I had a suspicious eye," I said.

"Your reputation's caught up with you," she said. It was one of those things you laugh about and embellish when you're having a good time.

She caught me up on her mother's health—it was good—and her two children, a boy and girl. They jointly owned a small gift shop in Sante Fe, New Mexico and were doing well. I didn't talk about mine. I hadn't heard from them lately and didn't know how they were doing. We became estranged after my divorce, but had made some progress since. I was content, as were they, to let the rift heal itself over time, nudged along by what would have been family events, Christmas, birthdays and the like, where old memories are revisited, the good ones, and new ones made.

The Pub featured blackened catfish that evening. We chose that with a bottle of Zinfandel.

Though I didn't know it, my "suspicious eye" had also attracted the attention of those more directly involved in the auction.

* * * * *

A brass plate at the porch steps of an old Victorian said, "Daniel Rose and Associates, Law Offices." The old house was within an easy walk to the Courthouse.

Caleb Washington leaned against the hood of his gray van parked in front, and watched the approach of Rose's new Cadillac. He glanced at his watch. Seven thirty. The sun was a golden rim over the horizon.

Over the years, he'd become known as the dean of timber appraisers in South Mississippi. That's why he'd been assigned the task of directing the appraisals of the TRS tracts of timberland to be auctioned and that's why he'd been summonsed to Rose's office … at such an early hour.

After his meeting with Rose, Caleb was to look at a tract of timber for Burl Pitts and had dressed for the job, faded dungarees, lightweight jacket and boots. Considering the distance he had to drive, he would be late if the meeting lasted too long.

Rose parked, got out with a briefcase. His lawyer's poker face showed nothing. A slight man with brown hair, bald at the crown and thinned over the rest of his scalp, he looked born to sit behind a desk. His dark suit, white shirt and tie were right out of the attorney's dress code manual.

"Morning," he said.

"Too damned early, you ask me," Caleb replied.

Rose glanced at his watch. "I told you eight." He climbed the wooden steps to unlock the front door. With lips pursed, a deep crease marked his forehead.

"Well, hell's bells, your message said it was urgent. I've been here since seven. Something wrong with the damn auction?" Why else was he called for such an early meeting? He cursed under his breath.

"I'll tell you," Rose said. He entered the front hall remodeled into a waiting area then paused at the receptionist's desk to flip a switch that lit the room and highlighted a wall hung picture of Rose as he shook hands with the governor. "Let me get the coffee started."

A sofa, easy chairs and a number of tables with dog-eared magazines provided seating and amusement for clients, though most came there for relief not entertainment. Spiked plants placed about completed the décor. What was a living room, on the left, was now a conference room. Its door was closed. Rose glanced briefly at his picture, then went into a small room down the hall to start a pot of coffee. Caleb lagged a step behind.

"So, what the hell's going on?" Caleb asked. "You going to tell me or what? Is it some kind of damned secret?"

Rose spooned coffee into the basket and shot him a hard look.

"Keep that fucking lawyer look to yourself!"

Rose said, "I'm tired of the dirty, smutty language you use, Caleb. You curse in front of my receptionist … in front of my clients. They don't like it. I don't like it! It shows disrespect. I want you to cut it out! You understand?"

"Don't give me that Baptist holier-than-thou bull shit, Daniel. You're not so pristine pure. I've heard you rant and rave in court, bull shit and all."

"I'm a lawyer. I rant and rave on cue. It's what I get paid to do."

Caleb thought "shit" to himself. He reached into his pocket and flipped a quarter onto the counter. "I'm paying you to get the hell off my back. That should do it."

Rose stared at him for half a second, then pointed a finger at his face. "Whose name do you see on the bottom of your checks?"

Caleb realized he'd gone too far. His face lost the arrogance that fueled the coin flip. Contrition replaced it. "Aw, hell, Daniel, I'm sorry. Wife gave me hell this morning. Getting up so early. Don't marry a young woman. Drive you crazy."

"I don't intend to."

"Umm. Can't sleep worth a damn either. I'm just cranky. I'll keep a lid on it."

"See that you do."

Rose reached into a cabinet for two mugs and handed Caleb one. The smell of brewed coffee began to fill the room. "Prozini hired a guy to act as an independent observer when we open the bids. Bishop Bone. You know him?"

"Yeah, I know him. He was in the news awhile back. Causing trouble. Saw him at Burl's mill the other day."

"He's going to be looking over our shoulders."

"What's to see? 'Sides, Jimmy says he doesn't know shit about the timber business."

Rose shrugged. "Prozini says the investor group wants to sue him. He needs to show he took every precaution. The way I see it, Bone's mostly window dressing. However, Chance got a little upset when we got the letter. You know how careful he is." "Chance" was Judge Chancellor, Rose's law partner. Prozini hired the retired judge to chair the auction liquidation. Since his retirement, the judge came into the office until noon. He probated wills, but if offered something challenging, like the auction, he took it.

"Too careful, if you ask me."

"Too careful or not, Chance ordered another review of the bid packages. Wants to make damn sure we don't leave ourselves open. I reviewed the legal documents last night. Your appraisals—"

Caleb interrupted, "Hell, Daniel. Appraisals are just estimates! Everybody knows that. It says so in every bid package. Even so, they're better than most. We increased the size of the cruise areas we ordinarily use."

"I know. I also know there are a lot of calculations when you do an appraisal. All that Bone guy has to do is find one error and every appraisal is suspect. Recheck your math," Rose said.

Caleb glanced at his watch and sighed. "Look, Daniel, I've checked them twice already. Bone couldn't find shit, even if he knew what to look for." He stared at Rose for a second. It was clear that Rose wasn't going to change his mind. Meant a late working day. A bitchy wife. Damn it. "Ah, hell, I'll do it again. I don't want a law suit any more'n the next man." He held his mug under the flow to fill it with hot coffee.

"Everything's on the conference room table. I'll unlock it. Chance wants you to re-certify everything."

"In writing?"

"Yeah."

"Huh," Caleb said.

"Chance and I want to show snoops, like Bone, if he pokes around, that we know what we're doing."

"Waste of 'effn time, but I'll do it." He took his coffee and followed Rose to the conference room.

"There they are," Rose said of the documents stacked on the table.

"See you," Caleb said, then pulled out a chair to reexamine appraisals of the timber and land of all the tracts to be auctioned off. Two and a half-hours later, he emerged and met Rose in the hall.

"I can't see a damn thing for anybody to complain about, Daniel," Caleb told him. "You know I didn't do any of the cruising. Skinny did the stuff around here. I picked good appraisers for tracts away from here. You know how that goes. Put three appraisers on the same tract and you get three different values."

"I know that."

"I won't put my butt in a sling to say the valuations are completely accurate. I'll certify that qualified foresters did the appraisals in accord with established methods used to value timber on the stump. The math's okay. I can't certify the maps or legal descriptions. They came from you. I don't know if they're accurate or not."

"Not from me, Caleb, from Prozini."

"Well, it was you who handed them to me."

"Yeah, but you are the one qualified to understand them."

Caleb said, "I ain't arguing that, but I can only be as accurate as the shit, sorry 'bout that, the STUFF I was given."

"Okay. As far as you're concerned, there are no errors in the appraisals?"

"Yeah. You know. Based on what you gave me."

"Did you check the big maps?" State maps where TRS timberlands were located had been blown way up and marked to identify each tract put out for bid.

"How many times do I have to say it? Everything looks okay! Damn it to hell! What the fuck! "

Rose's hard look interrupted him.

"Okay, okay. I apologize! I didn't know this place had turned into a church." Caleb signed the re-certification. The auction would proceed as scheduled. When he was some distance away from the office, he said, "Fuck you, Rose! You ain't my damn mama. Tellin' me what I can say! Son of a bitch!"

The outburst satisfied him. He smiled.

Chapter 4

A vacant courtroom was sequestered for the auction. I showed up in my black suit, note pad in hand, and took a seat along the center aisle behind a rail at the front.

I watched a slightly built man with thin brown hair, and middle-aged woman, push the Plaintiff's and Defendant's tables together. I didn't know Daniel Rose, but the man at the table had the look of a lawyer so I decided that's who it was. His movements were quick and nervous, his face trial-day somber. He removed his coat. The gray-haired woman, a few pounds overweight, worked at an even pace. She wore a gray suit and white blouse with a lacey frill. She set up a tape recorder with mics at one end of the tables. Large maps of what I assumed to be the tracts being auctioned were on tripods to the left of the tables.

The silver haired man Jimmy Pitts had told me was Caleb Washington pushed through the gates at the front. He said something to Rose and sat down in one of the soft-backed chairs behind the tables. While he waited, he twirled about in the chair to shift his attention between Rose and people in the courtroom, some of which he acknowledged with a wave of his hand. When he saw me, his eyes blinked. He nodded in my direction like he knew who I was and maybe he did. I'd been around or maybe he'd seen me that day at the mill. It didn't matter.

By eight o'clock the room was filled with people who made nervous, clipped comments. Talk ceased when a man in black robes, I took to be Judge Chancellor, came from the judges' chambers to sit in the elevated judge's chair. Alert eyes were wide-set in a pasty white, bloodless face. He welcomed the assembly and identified Daniel Rose, then Dora Lee, Rose's assistant, the gray-haired lady with him, and Caleb Washington. Rose slid into his coat.

The judge called the meeting to order and said with a hand pointed at Caleb Washington, "Mr. Washington coordinated the valuations of the various tracts being auctioned off today." His voice was raspy and loud due to his loss of hearing. At least eighty, I thought.

He continued. "If there are any questions about appraisals, they should be directed to Mr. Washington before we open the bids. Mr. Washington, do you have anything you'd like to add?"

Caleb pushed back his chair and stood to face the courtroom crowd. "The summary appraisals, the ones y'all got in your bid packages, were not intended to give an exact indicator of value. I want everybody to be clear on that." He glanced at Rose first, then panned the room to look for raised hands. There were none.

"Y'all know the only way to really determine the volume of timber is to scale it in the log yard." He looked at me with a half-assed smile and said, "That means we measure the volume of the logs, Mr. Bone. To figure their worth."

That's when I figured him for an asshole. No measurement needed.

He turned back to the courtroom and continued. "There's a disclaimer to that effect in each appraisal. Some of the parcels showed a lot of valuable veneer timber. Some pulpwood, not worth much. And a lot of top grade saw timber."

He paused again for questions. "Okay. Where fee ownership of the land is included, an estimated value is shown for the land. Now, y'all know that full appraisals, not the summary appraisals in your bid packages, were available in the offices of Judge Chancellor and Daniel Rose. They showed everything, legal descriptions, acreage and a detailed breakdown of the timber. Any questions?"

There were none. Any bid below the already low minimums set by TRS and specified in the summary appraisals, he said, would be automatically rejected. Bid deposits would be returned when all the successful bidders were determined. I noted the gist of the opening remarks on my pad for my report to Prozini.

The judge asked, "You have anything to add, Daniel?"

The man I'd decided was Rose stood. "Yes, sir. Bid amounts and bidders will be entered on bid sheets as they are opened. High bids will be announced after all bids are opened. If a bidder drops out, the next highest bidder will be selected."

"Thank you, Daniel. Now—"

Rose waved him off. "Almost finished, sir. At the end of these proceedings, the bids will be shredded and burned for privacy purposes.

The bid sheets and a recording of the proceedings will be mailed to the partnership offices of TRS in Chicago along with the final accounting."

I added a scribble to my pad.

Rose looked around the courtroom. "I understand that the partnership has sent an independent observer. Would the observer please stand."

I stood when he looked in my direction. "Bishop Bone," I said.

"An observer?" the judge asked Rose.

"Yes, sir. I gave you the folder … with the notification. We talked about it. You had remarks."

The judge put on his glasses and opened the folder in front of him. "Oh, I remember now. Please take a seat in front, sir."

I approached the conjoined tables.

"No, not there," the judge said. "Up here." He pointed to the witness chair. "You'll have a better view."

I did as he requested but felt odd as hell, like I was a witness skewered on the stares of everyone in the courtroom. I preferred a seat at the attorney tables doing the skewering.

"So, do you have any questions about the process so far, Mr. Bone?" To those present, the judge added, "Mr. Bone is an attorney, I understand."

I said. "I don't have any questions. However, instead of shredding the bids, I prefer to take possession of them along with a copy of the bid sheets."

"Do you suggest there's some irregularity already?" the judge asked. "If you are, speak up! I'll stop it right now. I mean for this liquidation to be completely above board!"

Murmurs filled the courtroom. People leaned forward to catch every word. Every eye was on me.

"I second that," Rose added. "Why do you want to keep the bids, Mr. Bone? We'll have the pertinent data recorded on the bid sheets. We'll have a tape recording of the bids as they're opened. What more do you need?"

Air conditioning came on with a tremor and sent waves of cool air into the room.

"I'm not suggesting any irregularity, gentlemen," I said with a look first at Rose, then at the judge.

The judge opened his mouth to speak, but I continued. "However, there is an ancient law that rules complicated transactions such as these.

Murphy's Law. I'm sure you've heard of it. If it can go wrong, it will. I'd feel more secure if nothing was destroyed until TRS has its funds, the deeds recorded, and mailed to the buyers."

Rose began, "That's absur—. Uh, Judge, what do you think?"

"I think what Mr. Boone, or whatever his name is, is asking … is adding an unnecessary complication, but this letter says he has the right to take such action as he deems appropriate to insure the integrity of the liquidation." His hand unconsciously touched the gravel as if ready to rule me in contempt.

Rose said, "It's tantamount to an implication of impropriety, sir."

"Not at all, gentlemen. I—"

Rose interrupted. "In the interest of acting with an abundance of caution, your Honor, why don't we keep the bids and other documents in a secure cabinet at the office until we mail out the final report. Mr. Bone can have them then, along with our final report."

The judge stared down at me. "Will that satisfy your fear of Mr. Murphy?"

I suppose I'm cantankerous, overly suspicious and cynical, but when somebody objects to what I consider a simple request, it makes me dig in my heels.

"My knowledge, your Honor, not fear. I see no reason to put Mr. Rose to that trouble. I'll just take possession after the winning bids are announced. I also need a copy of the final accounting. No tape recording, but I reserve the right to ask for a copy."

The judge slapped the top of the bench. "You're dictating how I run my court, uh, I mean this liquidation! I won't have it!" He raised out of his chair momentarily.

"I agree with the Judge!" Rose said. "If you have a complaint, spell it out! If not, let's proceed. A lot of these folks have come a long way."

Whispered exchanges rippled through the crowd. I saw a couple of faces I knew at the back, Jimmy Pitts and the one Jimmy had identified as Skinny Dearman the day I visited their mill. Also the studious young man with glasses who parked next to me as I left. I had a passing thought. What did he have to do with it? Since he was at the Pitts mill, I supposed he must have some connection.

"I only want the documents you were going to shred. What's the problem?"

The room filled with a din of multiple conversations. Judge Chancellor sighed, rapped the gavel for quiet and said, "Okay, Mr.

Bone. When we finish here, hopefully before noon, the bid packages and relevant documents will be placed in the courthouse vault we use to secure evidence. It is not open to the public and someone is on duty here at all times. Nothing will be destroyed, if that's your concern, and the packages will, as a matter of fact, be in the custody of the court. Will that be satisfactory?"

"I think you are being more than accommodating, your Honor," Rose said.

I could be a regular asshole when provoked. I said, "To maintain the integrity of the chain of possession, your Honor, I'd like to be there when the packages are stored. Likewise, I'd like to be present when they're taken out."

Rose looked toward the judge for a response.

"You try my patience, sir, but in the interest of progress, you can be present. Now can we proceed?"

I acceded and made an appropriate entry on my pad. Opening of the bids began. Rose pulled envelopes from portfolio cases and opened each. As far as I could see, all envelopes were sealed and that's what my report to Prozini would say. Maybe I should have examined the bid envelopes ahead of time, but Prozini said "attend the auction and observe," nothing more. My request for documents exceeded my authority also, but I didn't care.

As envelopes were opened, Rose called out the names of the bidders, the tract numbers and bid amounts. Mrs. Lee made entries on the sheets in front of her. Many of the bids were well over a million dollars. Caleb Washington periodically removed maps from their racks to replace them with new ones as tracts were sold. The judge sipped water from a glass and watched. Now and then a hush came over the crowd for one bid or another; particularly the one made by Morgan Reynolds on the tract of timber in Lawton County, and the competing bid by Pitts Lumber. Morgan's bid beat Pitts' by less than a hundred thousand dollars. I didn't imagine Burl would be pleased. I knew a listed company had paid Morgan a good fee to be a straw bidder, but it was a shock to some that he had the money to bid. It was common knowledge that he was strapped for cash.

After all bids were opened and the high bidders announced, the judge said, "Are there any questions about this auction? Anybody? Anything?" He searched the room for hands and stopped at me. I shook my head.

"None. Let it be known that there are no objections. Let it also

be recorded that the observer appointed by TRS has no objections."
He rapped his gavel and said, "I certify that the high bidders have been lawfully selected and declare this sealed bid auction concluded."

Sounds grew as interested parties grabbed their belongings to leave, some smiling, those with the winning bids, some not, the others.

The judge rapped his gavel for quiet. "I see representatives of the newspaper at the rear. I have a story for you. I hired Daniel Rose out of law school and made him my partner before I took the bench. Well, I'm proud to say that Daniel has been nominated to fill a vacancy on the Mississippi Supreme Court."

Rose looked at the judge in shock.

"That calls for congratulations," the judge continued. "How about a round of applause for Daniel?"

He stood to lead the applause.

"All that remains is for the Mississippi Bar Association to send an endorsement and that will be done after its next meeting. Congratulations, Daniel," he said.

Rose bowed slightly, first to the judge, then to the crowd. He looked up at the judge and mouthed a "thank you." Mrs. Lee beamed with pride and whispered into his ear. He hugged her.

Many lawyers passed the bar exam with dreams to get elected to a well-paid public office, or to be appointed to a prestigious judgeship. The Mississippi Supreme Court qualified as prestigious. Rose stood at the edge of his dream.

The crowd poured out through the double doors at the rear. Skinny Dearman waited for Caleb Washington, who exited in full stride up the aisle.

Rose turned to the judge and said, "If you want to go on, sir, I can put the documents into the vault."

The judge opened his mouth as if to agree, but looked at me, frowned and said, "No, Mr. Boone might find that unacceptable. We'll do it together."

"Bone, Sir," I said. "Bishop Bone."

His eyes switched toward me for an instant.

"What about the location maps?" Rose asked nobody in particular about the tract maps that had been on the tripods. "They just show the general locations of the tracts sold."

I glanced at the tract maps left on the two tripods. They didn't appear to be of any real value. Kind of a picture view of where properties were located.

"I don't want them," I said.

In that case, they'd take them back to the office.

Mrs. Lee shoved the opened bid packages into the portfolio cases, snapped the tops shut and lifted them onto the table. I picked up the closest and she handed me the other one. Rose lugged the bid charts and other documents and lagged a step behind as we made our way to the vault. The judge told the uniformed bailiff to open a room-sized vault. I slid the cases onto a shelf inside. Rose did likewise with his load and the bailiff closed the heavy door behind us.

"Satisfied?" Rose asked.

I opened my mouth to answer, but the judge cut me off.

"I can tell you this, Mr. Boone "

"Bone."

"Bone then, damn it! You'll get old one of these days! I remember you now, Bone. You were in it with the chicken growers last year, causing trouble. I don't like your grandstanding," he said all the time poking a finger into my chest. I could see the top of his almost bald head. It still had a few curly wisps here and there. I didn't like to be poked, but decided nothing would be gained if I objected.

"You have a good day, sir," I said. "Please have someone call me when it's time to pick up the stuff."

He stared at me for an instant then stumbled off without a reply. His face was lined with fatigue.

I congratulated Rose on his announced appointment and hurried toward the courtroom door. A gray-haired man stood at the rear of the courtroom and watched me approach. His suit was wrinkled as if it had been slept in. He wore no tie. His face didn't look much better. It showed a sadness that I took for depression. I saw that look in my mirror for a long time so it was easy to recognize.

He said, "Mr. Bone, my name is Jonas Osstrum. I'm one of the investors in TRS. I want to thank you for standing up to the judge."

Ah, the "representative" of disgruntled investors. Seth said they might send somebody. From his appearance, I thought he must have driven all night. The man was nearly my height, probably my age, with a broad executive's face that showed authority, or once did. What hair he had left was a blend of salt and pepper gray, mostly gray. His stomach strained at his belt.

We exchanged a handshake.

"I've practiced long enough to know that things can go wrong and when they do, you wish you'd anticipated them," I said. "The judge thought I nit picked, and I suppose I did, but that's the way I am."

"It's a good idea. If nothing else, you let them know they'd better dot their i's and cross their t's."

I invited him to the Blue Plate Café near the train depot where, for not much over five bucks, you could get their special, Monday through Friday. You sat in a ladder back chair with a cane bottom and waited for a plate full of whatever was fresh that day, vegetables, a serving of meat with cornbread, biscuits and iced tea, plus a piece of cake or pie for dessert. Nobody left hungry or broke.

Smells of hot food greeted us at the door. Waitresses hurried from the kitchen's door laden with plates of hot food on trays. The place overflowed with customers and conversations. Eating implements banged on plates and spoons tinkled against glasses of tea or cups of coffee. Three fans clung to the bead board ceiling and stirred the steamy air. I spotted a small table and angled toward it. Osstrum stayed close.

"Bishop!" Chief Jenkins called from the table where he sat with a couple of uniformed policemen. Jenkins was Lawton's Chief of Police. Like mine, his rough, broad face bore deep worry lines. He was approaching retirement.

I told him that the fish had bit "real good" since the last rain. He said he'd be out. We'd had a run in right after I'd moved to town, but later became friends. Being friends of the Campbells didn't hurt. They had the clout that comes with "old money."

Osstrum's comments about the liquidation, as we ate lunch, came with a bitter edge. He told me of the recent death of his wife and placed the blame on his TRS investment.

"I thought I'd be okay, but to hear some of those bid numbers, it almost made me sick. Prozini said appraised values, the bottom end appraisals, in the bid packages would stimulate competition. I think it stifled it."

"Hard to predict something like that," I said.

"Before we put in our money Prozini told us that trees in a plantation added wood each year, 'like a bank account adds interest,'" he said. "Turned out to be crap, like a lot of what he said. The rough numbers I took down in the courtroom sounded like some of our plantations had starved."

"Like some of my investments," I said.

"I doubt I'll have much left after I pay what I owe. I interviewed for a job in Mobile. Middle manager for a shipping company. I was in charge of two hundred people at one time, Mr. Bone. Now, I'll be happy with a job that pays peanuts and I do my own typing."

I could relate to that. Like him, I was on my butt and burdened with depression when Seth Campbell offered me a job.

"Sometimes it's best to forget the past," I said. "To have something to do, anything, seems to help, I think."

"I suppose you're right. Could I get a copy of your report to Prozini?" he asked.

"I don't mind," I said. "Except for my cover letter, all I send to Chicago will be public information. Why not ask the judge for a copy? His would be official."

"Right now, I don't know who to trust," he said. "If you don't mind, I'd rather get it from you."

He added, "Some of us didn't like the way Prozini ran things and we got an audit. Turns out that over the past few years, he was the only one to make money. Our lawyer said that under our agreement, he could do practically anything, short of fraud! Damn it to hell!"

He began to sound like trouble.

"Everything always looks rosy at the front end of an investment," I said. "I don't suppose you have any evidence—"

"No, but I haven't given up. The only thing I know is that he was guilty of greed. Maybe we all were. We wanted the big payoff he promised. Prozini couldn't lose. He played with our money."

"To keep me from a conflict, Mr. Osstrum, I need to disclose that fact to Mr. Prozini, but otherwise, I don't mind if you look at what I get from the judge or at my report. Call me." I gave him my card.

He glanced at it and said, "My son is an accountant."

"Around here?" I asked.

"He was born in Oxford, Mississippi, but we moved to Chicago when he was young."

I bought lunch over his hesitant objections, and wished him well. He said he'd call.

Chapter 5

A sharp knock brought a young man to the door of his Lawton apartment.

"Dad!" he said. His step dad, actually, Jonas Osstrum. The young man, Bob Fitzgerald, went by his father's name who had died when he was young. "I didn't know you were in town. You weren't sure."

"Hello, son," he said and gripped the young man's hand. "It was a last minute thing, kind of. I saw you at the auction, but you got away before I could catch you."

"Sorry I missed you. We could have had lunch. Come on in." He motioned him in. "Not much to look at, but it's comfortable."

"Looks fine, son. I ate with Bishop Bone, Prozini's observer," he said, as he passed. "Someplace by the train station. Good food."

"Yeah." Fitzgerald agreed. "I've eaten there."

"For a minute or two, I thought Bone would contest the auction," Osstrum said and took a seat in an easy chair. "I half wished he had."

Fitzgerald filled two glasses with ice for scotch and soda, their usual, and sat down to face him.

"You settling in down here okay?" Osstrum asked and took a sip.

"Pretty much," the young man said. He shoved his glasses back against the bridge of his nose. "Burl Pitts says he'll 'try me out' on their books. As soon as I can, I'll call on Morgan Reynolds."

"Don't know why you didn't come back to Chicago. Lots of firms looking for accountants there. Could make good money. I still have a few contacts."

"I know and I appreciate it," Fitzgerald said, "but since I met Edna at school and … well, you know, I love her." Edna Dodd lived in Lawton with her parents. They had oil interests and lived on Trace Avenue, near the Campbells. She and Fitzgerald worked at the same firm. They were engaged, but Fitzgerald wanted to wait for marriage until he established himself.

"Yeah, I understand, I loved your mother." He emptied his glass.

"I like Mississippi. Lots to enjoy. What's happening with you? How've you been managing?"

"Hell, I've gone from one depression to another. After your mother died, I wanted to crawl into a hole and die myself. Gained weight. I guess you can see." Osstrum slapped his stomach. "I may come out of it."

Fitzgerald's mother had committed suicide. Inoperable cancer and the hard financial times after TRS's failure were more than she could take.

Osstrum retired reasonably well fixed, but TRS came along, a chance to make money in the timber business, a hedge against inflation. Housing starts were high with timber in demand, but the bottom fell out of the timber market and Prozini began to make cash calls. Cheap Canadian imports exacerbated the slide. Osstrum had to borrow or be cashed out at a fraction of his investment. They sold their home and moved into an apartment.

"Talk is that the auction brought out the buzzards. You, uh, might not get as much as you thought." He made a palms-out gesture.

"Hell, I'm not surprised," Osstrum said. "It's nature's way. Feast on the wounded. God damn it to hell! Killed your mother! I know it did! Sometimes, I want to—" He threw up both hands. "What the hell! I don't know what I want to do."

Fitzgerald refilled Osstrum's glass.

"People around here know about me?" Osstrum asked.

"No. I haven't even told Edna. She knows I grew up in Chicago. That's about all. I didn't figure it mattered."

"Didn't want to be associated with a loser. I don't blame you."

"No, not that. Not all investments pan out. You know that, Dad. I just wanted to approach prospective clients without any prior affiliations."

Osstrum fell back against the cushion of his chair. "You're right, of course."

"I have to make my place in the firm. I make cold calls on prospects twice a week. Sometimes I just show up, most times I call first. I've picked up a few clients. The biggest is Pitts Lumber."

"We knew you'd be successful, your mother and I," Osstrum said.

"You want to stay here for awhile? I have an extra bedroom."

"Tonight, if you don't mind. An outfit in Mobile offered me a job. Not much, but I don't need a hell of a lot at my age. That's really why I came to the auction. It was on the way."

During the night, Fitzgerald slipped six twenties into his

stepfather's wallet. It would make the eleven dollars already there last a lot longer.

Osstrum left the next morning.

* * * * *

Willie and Elsa Patterson, an older black couple with a place on the outskirts of Lawton, needed to sell some of their timber to get Elsa a new washing machine and to pay a couple of bills that had popped up unexpectedly. They hired Caleb and Skinny Dearman to appraise the timber.

Caleb left Skinny to do most of the work. "I have a couple of chores," he said. "Be back in awhile."

Skinny finished and sat on a stump beside the Patterson's driveway to wait for Caleb's return. "Hot out here," he told his boss when he showed up. "Finished an hour ago. What took you so long?"

"Huh? Yeah," Caleb mumbled. "Sorry. Got tied up." He stared at the western sky. "Clouds coming in. Supposed to rain. Cool things off."

"Won't take back what I sweat out an hour ago," Skinny said. It didn't help that he detected beer on Caleb's breath.

Caleb swallowed his reply, but Skinny caught the last. "… bitching."

They loaded the equipment into the back of Caleb's van.

"You drive," Caleb said. "I want to check your numbers before I sign off."

Caleb threw something into the glove compartment as they drove away and glanced at Skinny's notes, but only for a second. He stared out the window, lost in thought.

As they neared the shotgun home of Dinah Patterson, Willie and Elsa's granddaughter, Skinny looked at him and said, "I thought you were going to check my—" He hit the brakes. "Look! Dinah's front door's open. Wonder why?"

Caleb said, "Most likely taking in groceries."

"No. Something ain't right, Caleb! Her car's parked at the back door. I'm gonna check." He wheeled the van onto the dirt driveway.

Both men got out, hurried up the steps and looked into the front room. Their alarm was made all the greater by the window air conditioner being full on and the front door open. The house was covered in the shade of tall oaks and pines, so the front room was dark.

Caleb entered first. "Hello," he called. "Dinah!" No answer. He called again. Still no answer. They heard running water at the back of the house. A whimper?

"You may be right, Skinny. Something's wrong. Stay here. I'll check." He hurried toward the back.

"Dinah!" Caleb craned his neck for a look inside the bathroom, the source of the running water. "Oh shit!"

The young black woman was in the tub, her head tilted to one side. One arm touched the floor. A mongrel dog lay with his nose against her hand, his head on his paws. The dog turned toward Caleb at the door and released a low pitiful moan.

A bottle of rubbing alcohol and a bag of gauze pads sat on the floor within easy reach of the woman's hand. Water poured from the tub's spigot. The raw smell of fresh blood in the bottom of the tub brought his hand up to cover his mouth. On the tub bottom beside her thighs, lay a sharp pointed instrument. He backed away quickly.

"Call 911," he shouted to Skinny. "Tell Chief Jenkins we got a dead girl out here."

Caleb called Willie Patterson as soon as he was outside.

Skinny sat in a chair on the front porch and stared into the front yard. To know that a dead woman was inside threatened to empty his stomach. To make it worse, the woman was someone he knew.

Willie's old pickup pulled into the driveway within minutes. The gray haired black man got out and bolted through the front door. Elsa, grim faced, stayed in the truck. Over Caleb's admonitions to wait, Willie pushed past into the bathroom.

"Oh, Lord!" he cried out. "Oh Lord, God almighty, why'd you go and let this happen? This sweet, beautiful child ain't never done no wrong to nobody." The dog whimpered again.

He walked head down back to his truck to tell Elsa.

"She was born Chandra," Willie told Chief Jenkins when he arrived. "Dinah was the name she used with white folks. We ain't seen her mamma since right after she was born. Ain't got no idea who her papa is. Got a older brother, Otis. He stays in Atlanta."

"I know Otis," the chief replied. Otis was in trouble with the law before he left town.

"Do what you can to find who done this to this poor girl," the old man said. "Ain't done no wrong to nobody. Now she's dead. It ain't right. No, sir. It ain't right. Me and Elsa ain't gonna sleep this night. No time soon. It's the baddest thing I ever seen."

He walked away, his head bowed.

"I'll do every thing I can," Chief Jenkins said. "I'm damned sorry."

The old man waved but didn't stop.

"Gonna have to let Otis know," he said over his shoulder, almost as an apology.

"Just as soon you didn't," the chief said.

"Ain't got no choice," Willie turned and said. "Boy ain't gonna like it, though. Ain't gonna like it one bit."

I doubt I'll like Otis being here either, Jenkins thought. He felt a rain drop on his face. A bright flash and loud clap of thunder made him look up. More rain was to come.

* * * * *

Beads of water dripped off my rear porch eaves in soft "plunks." The rain had fallen steadily since sundown. The weather reporter said it came from the remains of a big storm that veered off toward the west. The "ding ding" of the front doorbell called me to the door. I was at the computer catching up on reports. Chief Jenkins stood outside.

"Come in," I said. "You been chasing bad guys in the rain?"

"Don't I wish." He shook the rain off his jacket and cap and had a look of sadness on his face that I'd not seen before. Hung both on a peg by the door.

"Got a cold one?" He dragged out a kitchen chair and sat down. "Sometimes this job is the shits, Bishop. 'Fore God."

I handed him a beer, in a bottle; found what was left of mine, and sat down to listen.

"Worst thing I ever saw, Bishop," he said. He told me about Dinah Patterson's death. He'd just left her house.

"I hope I never have to see anything like it again." His hand wrapped itself tightly around the bottle as if to squeeze away the thought. "We found five hundred dollars in an envelope in her car. Three hundreds and four fifties."

"Money for an abortion?" I asked.

"I guess she thought she could save the money and do it herself. Maybe she didn't want to drive all the way to Jackson to get it done."

"Money likely came from the father?" I asked.

"Yeah. That's what we figure. Old man Patterson and Elsa, her grandparents, looked like somebody'd cut their hearts out. They raised the poor girl. Damn crying shame!"

"Any idea whose baby?"

"I didn't get into it. They didn't volunteer. I doubt they know. She lived alone."

He sighed and took a long swig of beer. "Not really my jurisdiction come to that, but they called me. Since the sheriff's busy, he asked if I'd finish it up. I wish he hadn't.

"I'll go back out there when things settle some to see what the Pattersons know. The father needs to bear some responsibility. Damn it to hell! Knock a young woman up like that and tell her she's on her own. It really pisses me off, Bishop!"

"You'll run lab tests?"

"Yeah, autopsy too, but I can't see how to nail anybody. Not against the law to bed somebody. Man's law, anyway. She waitressed at the Pub. You might have seen her."

I did recall seeing a young black woman there.

"Pretty girl, friendly, maybe too friendly if you know what I mean," he continued. "Went to JC part time." JC was the local shorthand for junior college a few miles south of Lawton. "Who knows who she took a liking to? I'd sure as hell like to meet the bastard! Off duty."

He walked toward the door, reached for his cap and said, "Got another problem. Otis Patterson's the girl's brother. They were close. He'll be in town looking for the father whether he broke the law or not."

"Trouble?"

"Yep."

* * * * *

Otis pulled into Willie and Elsa's front yard before the sun was full up the next morning. Brakes squealed his old car to a stop near the front steps. Like many in rural Mississippi, wood block columns held the wood house off the ground to let air circulate underneath. A deep porch spanned the front. Two cushioned rockers and a small table sat at one end.

A screened front door kept flies and mosquitoes outside. Oaks and pines surrounded the house to shade it from the harsh summer sun. Last night's rain clung to their branches and dripped onto the ground. Scattered around were beds of shrubs. The fresh rain brought a cluster of roses to full alert.

Otis leaped onto the porch and stormed to the back of the house where Willie and Elsa sat. An angry scowl covered his face, his hands clinched into fists. He wore jeans and a sleeveless shirt that showed tattoos on the meaty parts of his arms. He was medium height and sturdily built with broad shoulders, big hands and muscular arms.

"Otis!" Elsa said. They were half way through a pot of coffee and platter of biscuits. The smallish, white haired woman stood and gave him a hug.

"Come on in, boy," Willie said. "Get yourself some coffee. Fresh made. Plenty in the pot. Must've drove all night."

"Drink some coffee and let your nerves settle a mite, son," Elsa said. "Reckon you be tired from all that driving."

"Ain't thought about it," Otis said. "Been thinking about Chandra."

Willie said. "The Lord's looking after the poor chile now. For sure, uh huh."

"But he ain't looking after the one who done it to her, is he?" Otis said. "That's my job."

"Best to leave that alone, son," Elsa said. "Ain't no good gonna come from you in trouble with the law again."

"Ain't me troubled the law the last time. Wasn't me done anything," Otis said. "Wasn't no proof. Just got me 'cause I was black. 'He's a nigger! He did it!' White assed bastards!"

"Uh huh," the old man said. "Things been changing 'round here, Otis. Ain't like they was. Changing for the good."

"I bet." Otis pulled out a chair and sat down with a cup of steaming coffee.

"How you able to get off work, Otis?" Willie asked.

"Got in my car and left soon as you called. Just warehouse work. Move freight around. Warn't no kind of real job no how. This's all they need." He flexed his muscles. "Won't have no trouble getting back on. If I want to."

"The old mill's gonna be putting on hands," Willie said. "They say Morgan Reynolds ain't got no money though. Has to buy timber on credit. Asked me. Uh huh. Reckon I might."

"Chandra worked there, didn't she?" Otis asked.

"Till they cut back," Elsa said. "Had a good job too. Office work."

"Who's she been seeing?" Otis asked. He split a biscuit, spooned in jam then got up to refill his cup. As he did, he glanced at his grandfather's worn leather whip curled on a nail in the wall and recalled stories of how the old man trained mules when he was young, before tractors replaced them both.

"Skinned 'em good." The old man had told him. "First thang is to let 'em know you're smarter 'n 'em. I knowed where ever one of their hurtin' spots was and I could lay the end of that whip right on top. Uh huh. I worked that leather strap like it had eyes, boy. Ole mule never knowed when it was comin'." It was a good memory. Otis looked back at the old man and smiled, but only for a second.

"I said who's she been seeing?"

Elsa looked at her grandson and said, "We don't know, Otis. Scooter Reynolds called her now and again while she was at the mill. Don't reckon anything come of it. She never said nothing and he quit calling."

"She didn't tell us anything, Otis. And we ain't heard nothing," Willie said.

"I'm gonna see Scooter," Otis said.

"Don't you go causing no trouble, boy!" Willie said. "Ain't gonna do no good for nobody for you to end up in jail. I cut timber to pay your fine last time. You'll go to the pen next time. You hear me! Dinah's gone! No amount of trouble you stir up's gonna change that!"

A snarl formed on Otis' lips. "Dinah! Is that what she called herself?"

"Said it was gonna be her stage name," Willie said. "Her white name. We didn't like it much, but Chandra had lots of spirit."

"Uh huh." Otis shoved away from the table. "Gotta get me some sleep. Scooter in town?"

"Yeah," Willie said. "He'll be finishing college right soon. Could be you, boy."

"White man's game, Grandpa. Get uh education and work for the white man. 'We'll get you some credit! Buy a car, buy a house and work the rest of your life paying notes.' Chasing the white man's rainbow. That's what it is. Slaves all over again!" Otis said.

"Nothing wrong with working for a man that got a payday for you." Willie began.

"Come on, Grandpa! We done got rid of our leg irons. Damned if

I'm gonna put them back on for the few dollars some white man promises. 'Here it comes! Here it comes, boy!' It never comes, Grandpa. White man always gets the big end of every dollar. We get just enough to think there'll be more. They ain't never no more."

Otis slept until Elsa called "supper" later that afternoon. Afterwards, he got into his car and drove to the Reynolds' house, located in a better part of town. It was craftsman styled, built in the early part of the century, a white two-story with a wide front porch that held chairs here and there and a swing at one end.

Scooter, in a white shirt and pants, sat in a straight-back chair tilted back against the wall to wait for his buddies from the mill. He had left early to finish a correspondence homework assignment. His goal was to graduate after the fall term. He could finish the last of his requirements by correspondence.

When Otis drove up, he tilted forward and bounded down the steps.

He called out, "Hey, my man, what—"

The intense frown on Otis' face and clinched fists interrupted the rest.

"What's wrong with you, man?"

Otis grabbed Scooter by the front of his shirt and threw him down. Scooter rolled and bounded up all in the same motion. Scooter was much shorter than Otis and not nearly as well built.

"What the hell's going on?"

"Slipping it to Chandra. Left her to die! You gonna pay for that!" Otis stepped toward Scooter.

"Come on, I didn't have anything to do with your sister!" Scooter jabbed out with his fists to hold Otis at bay. Otis ducked and lashed out with a right that missed. Then a left grazed Scooter's forehead and left a cut.

"The fuck you say!"

"Truth is, she wouldn't have anything to do with me, Otis! I swear!"

Otis charged with his head down, arms in windmill motion. Scooter jabbed out at Otis' face, but all only slowed his charge. Scooter caught most of Otis' fists on his shoulders and arms but one hit him high on the head and knocked him to his knees. Scooter blinked his eyes to clear the buzz from his head. He shoved his hand into his pocket and when Otis drew back to hit him again, Scooter jumped up, switchblade in hand.

"I'll cut you, man! I swear!"

Otis stepped back. "Mother fucker!"

"Listen to me, Otis."

Otis circled, tensing to charge.

"Chandra told me to piss off! She wasn't interested in me."

"You did it. You fucked her up and left her to die!"

"I never touched her. If you heard anything different, it's a lie. A damn lie!" Scooter wiped at the blood from the small cut on his forehead. Otis frowned as if considering what Scooter had said.

A siren caused both men to turn as a police car screeched to a halt in front of Otis' car. Scooter shoved the knife into his pocket.

"What's going on here?" The policeman asked. His hand touched the butt of his holstered automatic. His partner stood a pace away with a black club.

"Nothing," Scooter and Otis said together.

"Just horsing around," Scooter said. "Me and Otis were clowning, catching up on news. That's all."

"Call said you were fighting," the policeman said.

"No, sir," Otis said. "It's like Scooter says. We was clowning."

"Best not to clown in public," the policeman said. "Especially you, Otis Patterson."

Otis' jaw clinched, but he kept his mouth shut. The two men watched until the police car disappeared around the corner. Scooter shoved his hand into his pocket, ready for another charge from Otis, but none came.

"Reckon I ain't mad at you no more, Scooter," Otis said. He straightened his clothes. Scooter brushed at the grass clinging to his shirt and pants. "Now that I think about it. Don't reckon it was you. I just got mad. Ain't no more gonna come of it. 'Far as you."

"No reason to be in the first place, Otis." He dabbed at the small cut on his forehead.

"I'm still gonna get the mother fucker who done it! I swear to God!"

"I'm sorry, Otis. I really liked her, but it wasn't me. After she left the mill, she worked at the Pub. I haven't talked to her since."

The Pub's where Otis went next. He learned from the Pub's kitchen staff that "Dinah" didn't talk about her love life much. However, she did flirt and carry on with some "white dudes." They knew their faces, but didn't know any names.

"You see them in here again, you find out their names," Otis told them. "It's worth five bucks."

"I'll get them names, Otis."

Chapter 6

Chief Jenkins drove out a couple of days later and parked beside the back porch. It was close to five thirty. He had new fishing tackle to break in.

"You about recovered?" I called down. We hadn't spoken since the Patterson girl had been found dead.

"Yeah, pretty much," he said and continued toward the creek. "Like always. You try to put it behind you. Fishing helps. Makes me think I'm doing something productive anyway."

I grabbed my tackle from under the porch and joined him. He pulled in a good mess of bream and a two-pound trout within thirty minutes. With my half dozen bream, he had enough for a decent fish fry. Not all creek fish had a lot of meat on their bones so quantity was needed. We cleaned them at a little spring that fed the creek.

"Heard you made a real spectacle of yourself at the auction the other day," he said as we scaled our catch.

"Who told you?"

"It's all over town how you raised hell with the Judge and Rose. Sometimes it's hard for me to tell folks that I know you, let along claim you as a friend."

"You could call me a step-friend if that'd help."

"I'll try to remember that. You rubbed old Judge Chancellor the wrong way."

"Yeah? I figure he needs to cut down on his eggs."

"He's getting old, forgets things. I can tell you this," he continued, "Judge Chancellor's about as honest as they come."

I laughed. "Hell, Chief, I didn't know enough to suspect anybody of anything odd. I certainly didn't see anything irregular. One thing, though." I told him what Jonas Osstrum said about cash calls and the partnership's decision to liquidate.

"Never saw a sour deal end with everybody happy," he said. "He'll get over it. Rose told me the judge said you showed your ass."

"I thought he said 'grandstanding.' Hell, I only asked for the documents Rose said they'd shred. I got my back up when they made a big deal out of it. The judge's used to having his way. When I objected, his feathers got ruffled."

"I told Rose that's just the way you are. Look for trouble under every rock."

"Thanks for the vote of confidence," I said.

He picked up the fish to leave. "We got the forensics back on Dinah Patterson."

"Saw a story in the paper about it. Didn't say much," I said.

"We're trying not to make a big deal out of it. Looks like that fetus she tried to abort had a white father. Puts a slant on it I don't like."

"Any ideas who it might have been?"

"No. We asked her coworkers what they knew."

"They tell you anything?"

"Not a hell of a lot. Just said … she was evidently active, you know. Flirted with the men. Nobody remembered any names. She got good tips. We asked her classmates at JC if she'd been seeing anybody special. No one could recall if she had."

"Looks like a dead end."

"Yeah. We won't release the report. No crime was committed by the father, whoever he was. We've closed the file. It goes down as an accidental death."

"Any chance it was murder?" I asked. Wouldn't be the first time.

"Looks clear cut to me. Accident."

"Too bad selfishness isn't a crime."

"Yeah. Her brother, Otis, I told you about him, is in town making noises. If he finds out who the father is, I hate to think what he might do. We've got pretty damn good race relations around here. I mean to keep it that way."

I agreed.

"I told him to cool it. Awhile back, he got into a scrape and had to leave town. Said he didn't do it, but they all say that." He shrugged. "Judge Chancellor worked a plea bargain with Milty to keep him out of jail." Milton Bush was the district attorney, but everybody called him "Milty."

"He leaving any time soon?" I asked.

"Doesn't look like it. He took a job at the mill."

"Morgan's mill?"

"Yeah. Morgan says he's a hard worker." He gave a wave with his hand. "Who knows?"

* * * * *

A day or so later, Judge Chancellor called to tell me the auction papers and documents were ready. He'd signed off on everything and made a copy of the final report for me. Rose would meet me at the courthouse at three.

"I hope I didn't cause you too much trouble," I said.

"It just seemed aggressive, the way you lit into us."

"When a lot of money's at stake, you can't be too careful. Anything goes wrong, I don't want people looking at me."

"Murphy's Law?" the judge asked.

"O'Leary's corollary. When it does go wrong, it's always my fault."

I hung up and checked my email for new bank assignments. None. I was bored. If something didn't come in soon, I'd have to caulk my shower, a job I hated.

With nothing better to do, I decided to go to the courthouse early. I hoped Rose would do the same. We could get the hand-over done with. Mostly, I didn't want to be late for the afternoon paper. I never had anything to drink until the paper came. Now and then, when one problem or another kicked the shit out of me or I was bored, I waited for the paper by the road. The paper lady somehow knew. If I stood there with my hand out, she'd say, "Had a bad day, Mr. Bone?"

* * * * *

Rose wasn't early so I cooled my heels.

"He was here," the bailiff, a lean young guy told me. "Got here right after two. Told me the Judge wanted him to get that stuff out of the vault, the portfolio cases and stuff y'all left after the auction."

"Uh huh. What'd he do with it?" That son of a bitch, I thought. Supposed to wait for me.

"It's still in the vault, just where y'all put it. He didn't have the judge's written authorization. I wasn't going to release anything without the judge's okay."

"Good" I said.

"It'd be my ass if I did. The judge is a stickler for things like that. I called him, but he was already gone for the day. Mr. Rose went back to the office to see if he'd left an authorization."

Uh, huh, I thought. I imagined Rose could sign the judge's name as well as the judge.

"He says wait in there if you showed up before he got back." He waved in the direction of a conference room with a table and chairs. Its walls were lined with shelves of law books.

I took a chair and saw Rose when he came through the door, breathing hard. His thin hair was blown over to stand straight up on top of his head, gray tie swept back over his shoulder, and shirt drenched with dark splotches. He saw me and glanced at his watch.

"You're early, Mr. Bone. I hoped to get everything together before you arrived. If you don't mind waiting, it won't take a minute to put everything together," he said.

"I don't need it organized. Put it in a sack for all I care. I don't expect to do more than glance at anything anyway. I thought it was a well-run auction. Except for the crap you threw at me."

His facial expression disagreed, but he said nothing. He handed the bailiff the sheet of paper. The bailiff studied it for a second, then opened the vault.

Rose said, "The judge was positive about the way I was to hand the files over. You know how he is."

I said, "Yeah. Well, you can tell him you organized the hell out of everything."

He shrugged.

"There they are." The bailiff pointed to the cases and documents. They helped load everything into my jeep.

Afterwards, I asked Rose. "The final report?"

"Oh, here." He pulled a thick envelope out of his briefcase and handed it to me. "By the way, we seal our files as of today."

I didn't really give a damn. I had the judge's final report and after a last look at everything, I'd write a cover letter with comments and send it to Prozini.

Once home, I sat down to read it. It was clear, without contradictions or inconsistencies. I glanced at the bid charts and picked up a number of bid packages to see if the data matched the chart entries. I saw nothing amiss.

The high dollar bids on three tracts in Lawton County and one in Sampson County caught my eye. Morgan Reynolds made his "straw bid" on one of the Lawton County tracts while two women, a Ms. Kitchens out of Atlanta, Georgia, and a Ms. Gibbs from Montgomery, Alabama, made the other "high dollar" bids, all in the four million-dollar range. At the auction, I was too busy to pay much attention to bidder's names or dollar amounts. As I looked at the final report, I concluded that some people had a hell of a lot of money to risk.

I finished my report and faxed it to John Prozini, along with a final bill. My cover letter said Jonas Osstrum had asked for a copy and that I didn't object since everything in it was available to the public. Prozini called me almost immediately to thank me for my "prompt report and very reasonable bill." A low overhead confounded people who lived in large metropolitan areas.

"Mr. Rose has already sent the official documents and tape recording. You made yourself heard at the auction, Mr. Bone."

"The liquidation team was a bit uptight. I understand, but I still had a job to do."

"Good job too. Thanks," Prozini said.

"What about Jonas Osstrum? He wants to review the report and my files."

He said, "Are you aware that Mr. Osstrum is digging around to sue me for mismanagement? Did he say anything at the auction?"

"No. I saw him afterwards. I gathered he wasn't happy. So?"

"You do what's legal, Mr. Bone. However, I recommend that you shred what you have ASAP. You don't need to get into our dispute. If you don't have the papers, you're less likely to be deposed. I'm sorry, another call is coming in."

Do what's legal? It's not illegal to disclose public information, for the most part anyway, to Osstrum. But then he said I shouldn't get involved in their family squabble. "You can do it, but you shouldn't." Clear as mud! To cover my backside, I sent Prozini a fax to document our call and to confirm that he had not vetoed or forbidden me from allowing Osstrum to review my files.

Maybe Osstrum wouldn't call or he'd call after I'd thrown the stuff away. Often angst like his vanished after a good night's sleep. His hadn't. He called right before lunch and asked if he could come out. Damn it! I gave him directions.

* * * * *

Otis picked up the phone. "Yeah."

"Otis?" a woman's voice asked.

"Yeah," he replied.

"Some of them white men you asked about's been in here again. Come in right after that auction they did at the courthouse last week," the woman said.

"You got names?"

"Willie Bea got some for me. She waits tables. She say it ain't all of 'em, just some. You want 'em anyway?"

"I'll come get 'em."

"You bringing that money you promised?"

"Uh, can I give it to you payday?"

"You best do or I'll send my man to that mill to wait on you, Otis Patterson."

"You'd best send two men if you do."

"Man I be sending already is two men, Otis."

"Payday, okay?"

It'd be okay.

* * * * *

I picked Saturday to cut my grass. It went dormant during our mini-drought, if brown is an indicator. Rains brought it back to life, but the brown layer smothered the fresh growth and had to be cut and cleared away. I dragged the mower from the shed, filled the tank and yanked the cord until its rusty old motor coughed blue smoke to rotate the blade. It needed to be sharpened, but that meant I had to take it off, a dirty job. The filter was also dirty. Another job I vowed to do very soon. I made the same vow the last time I cut the grass.

Birds, mostly robins, followed me around the yard like chickens, to peck at morsels and bugs the machine kicked up. The work was the equal of at least two round trip jogs to the waterfall. Lawton's summer humidity can make concrete sweat and humans melt. I distracted myself with plans to ask Kathy to dinner that night at an all-you-can-eat-buffet with a huge dessert bar. The thought sustained me.

Finished, I sat on the top porch step with a glass of ice water to admire my great accomplishment and to watch birds finish off what I flushed out. The smell of freshly cut grass still hung in the air when Osstrum pulled up in an old compact. He was dressed casually, a short sleeved shirt and long pants, freshly pressed. It was an improvement from the slept-in clothes he wore the day I met him after the auction. He looked rested too, ready to face the world, not beaten as he had at the Blue Plate Café when we ate lunch together.

I offered him a drink. He asked for coffee so I put on a pot and showed him the worktable where my notes, the bid packages, appraisals and my report to Prozini were arranged.

"Let me know when you're finished," I said.

While he studied and made notes, I puttered around outside, pruned dead wood out of bushes and pulled weeds. I aimed to keep the slope between my back porch and the creek cleared of obstructions so as not to spoil the view. I was at the creek when Osstrum strolled up.

"Nice view," he said. "I haven't seen a beaver in, hell, I can't remember. Since I was a kid, I guess. They never stop working. I wonder if they ever get tired." He picked up a pinecone and tossed it into the creek. The splash sent the beavers scurrying for cover. "You a fisherman?"

"Now and then. I just watch what goes on most of the time. If I catch a fish, I have to clean it. Reminds me of work. You finished?" I asked.

"Yes. I made copies of some stuff, a lot of it in fact. Hope you don't mind. I wrote you a check for five bucks."

"Not necessary," I said as we walked up the slope toward the cabin.

"It's only fair."

Five dollars wasn't enough to argue about one way or another.

He said, "Morgan Reynolds bid on a huge tract of timber in Lawton County. He was so strapped for working capital that he asked us for money. How'd he get four million dollars to bid like that? Did the bank increase its loan to cover the bid?"

I knew, but Morgan told me to keep it confidential. "Can't say. He'd be your best bet for information like that."

"Hmm. Might have picked up an investor. I know we turned him down. No money. Besides, I've invested in my last timber venture. I'll call him, but I doubt he'll tell me much. When we voted to close the mill and liquidate, in effect we fired him."

"I don't think he sees it like that. He understands business."

"Uh huh. Your handwritten notes," he said, "showed acres for some of the tracts and not for others. Any reason?"

"I relied a lot on gut feel in my review, looked for anything odd in the numbers, but I did check a few detailed appraisals to compare bid amounts with appraised values. I scribbled notes as I switched back and forth to keep my thoughts straight."

He said, "Prozini only sent us summary appraisals, not the detailed ones you have. Not that it made much difference. None of us, except Prozini, knows a hell of a lot about timber. Good lesson. Don't invest in anything you don't understand."

"Can't know everything. Sometimes you have to rely on who recommends it."

"That's our problem. We relied on Prozini. Our audit came up with a lot of information about what was done, but no obvious evidence of wrongdoing. We're still looking."

"Me, too. I was anyway, as an observer and during my review. I didn't see any."

"I wish I'd brought a copy of the audit. I don't like loose ends."

"What loose ends?"

"I'm not sure," he said. "When I say loose ends, I really mean money. I want to understand why we lost so much. We expected more from the auction."

He promised to stay in touch. It was a promise I hoped he'd break. I didn't want his troubles to become mine. Prozini's "family squabble" found a place in my memory. I wished it'd go away.

A newspaper story the following Monday caught my eye. Reynolds' Lumber Mill suffered a fire over the weekend. "No substantial damage," the story said. I never felt altogether secure about the loan, so anything that might cause a default was of interest to me. I made a note to drive by and take a look.

Chapter 7

My phone rang. It was Daniel Rose. "What have you been up to?" he shouted.

"What the hell are you talking about?" As I had learned to do, I shouted back. Once that got his attention, I could begin to act civilized.

It did. "You've been harassing auction bidders!"

"I haven't harassed anybody," I said. "I don't know what you're talking about."

"You're the only one with access to their names and phone numbers. Have you ever heard about invasion of privacy? You're about to be sued!"

"You're about to piss me off! I haven't called anybody. I— " Uh oh, it hit me. Osstrum had made copies. Names and phone numbers! Damn it!

"What?" Rose asked.

"Jonas Osstrum, one of the TRS investors, asked for permission to review the bids. While he was here, he copied some of my files. Wanted to get a handle on why they'd lost money. That's most likely why he called the bidders. Nothing sinister in that. He had a legal interest in the auction."

"My clients didn't catch the name, exactly. I figured it was you."

Clients? "You figured wrong. All I did was let him look at the files."

"Did you have that authority? John Prozini said he only authorized you to attend the meeting as an observer."

"Don't give me that legal bull shit!"

"It's not bull shit, Mr. Bone! My clients have been harassed, accused of fraud! Their wives as well. Very upsetting!"

"Don't they live in the real world? I told Prozini about Osstrum. He didn't object." It pissed me off that Prozini let me catch his flack, and I wasn't pleased with Osstrum either.

I continued, "The names and addresses of the bidders were read out loud by you at the auction. Osstrum was there and he's a TRS investor with a valid interest. Also, recorded deeds, public information as you know, show the legal owners. So, don't give me that crap about lawsuits."

"Not the telephone numbers. Those weren't public."

"Good God, Rose. They make phone books you know."

"They also have listings for regular lawyers. You might want to look one up."

"If you have a bitch it's with Osstrum."

"It depends on what you told him! You set him in motion. You're both liable."

"I didn't tell him shit!"

He hung up.

Not my day. He's still pissed at me from the auction. And, damn Osstrum! What the hell did he do? I called Prozini.

I said, "Seems I got crosswise between Rose and one of your investors, Jonas Osstrum. I'm catching flack from both sides and it's not fun. Maybe you can tell Rose to back off. He just hung up on me."

"Yes. Daniel Rose. He's quite upset. Called me earlier. I did tell you to stay out of it, Mr. Bone. You're a lawyer, you know about the good Samaritan doctrine. No good deed goes unpunished."

"I don't see myself as a good Samaritan. Osstrum is a partner with an interest in the auction results."

"I did warn you about him. In fact, I told you to shred your files and stay out of our little dispute. You chose not to and, well, you see how it goes."

"Don't get fancy with me. I told you Osstrum wanted to read my files. You didn't object. I confirmed that with a fax."

"I don't recall that conversation and I never received a fax. I never gave you authority to invade anyone's privacy or let anyone else. You're on your own, I'm afraid. Sorry."

"I have telephone records and a memo of our conversation. It may come down to my word against yours, but guess who gets the benefit of hometown decisions?"

"Don't threaten me, Mr. Bone! You made a mistake and you want me to pay for it. It's a measure of a man's character to take responsibility for his actions."

"That cuts both ways," I said, but he never heard. He'd already hung up. The fee wasn't big enough for this much aggravation, I thought.

Damn it to hell. I found Osstrum's check and called the number on it. No answer. I'd call in the evening.

I called Rose back. "Prozini's had a convenient lapse of memory, but I have telephone records and a memo of my call. I have no reason to lie, no financial gain. I've disclosed nothing that wasn't public. Even a nominee to the Supreme Court should know that I have absolutely no exposure."

"I'm—"

"If I hear anymore about this, I'll file an action for declaratory relief and tell the world about your champertous activities. The bar association will be interested in that. I know the media will."

"What? You say I encouraged this potential legal action for a fee? If you are, you'd better be able to back it up."

"I don't know what you're doing, Rose. I know that you have no case. A good lawyer would tell his clients not to waste their money."

He hung up on me too. It was my day to piss people off and to be pissed off. I didn't like being threatened with a lawsuit when I hadn't done a damn thing wrong. The last time somebody sued me, I lost my family and the practice I worked long and hard to establish. I had to get out of the house or kick out a wall. I called Morgan to see if I could inspect his fire damage.

"Come on," he said over the sounds of metal against metal. "A break'll do me good. Had nothing but trouble all day."

* * * * *

I broke out in a sweat as soon as I got out of the jeep. It was hot as hell and the mill was noisy and dusty. I wore shorts and a tennis shirt, but it made no difference against the heat and humidity. Morgan jogged toward me from the mill, his khakis spotted with sweat. He hit his cap against his pants leg. A plume of sawdust flew out. I extended my hand. He did too, but drew it back to wipe off the black grease with a rag from his back pocket.

"Chain broke, but we caught it before any damage was done. So, you want to see our charred embers? Did Rooster ask you, or you just volunteering?"

"I'm a volunteer today. I needed to get out of the house."

"Come on," he said. I followed him to the log yard.

"There." He pointed toward the blackened ends of half a dozen logs. "If I hadn't come back to the office, the entire yard would have gone up in smoke, everything." He said he worked till about ten that night. Halfway home, he couldn't remember if he turned off the coffeepot and came back to check.

"Hell, I was afraid of a fire in the office. When I drove through the gate, the whole damn end of this stack was afire. I grabbed a fire extinguisher and had it mostly out before the fire truck got here. Caught it just in time."

"Deliberate?" I asked.

"Had to be. Smell of gasoline all over. Chief Jenkins and the fire department are investigating. You can still smell it if you get down close."

"Damage?"

"The burned ends you see here. Easy to trim. Not much of a loss. As soon as I can, I'm going to patch the old fence and keep dogs in here. Can't afford a night watchman yet. Until then, I'll use a drive by patrol."

"Good idea."

"Uh, mind coming into my office?" he asked. "I have a couple of things I'd like to talk about … in private."

I didn't argue. My shirt was sweat-dark, front and back.

The office cool felt great. I thought I'd freeze as the air hit my sweaty body, but I didn't complain. Better that than melt. The wall behind Morgan's chair was decorated since I was there last. Framed newspaper story of the ceremony when the mill reopened, and letters of congratulations from politicians. The wooden chair I sat in leaned to one side. Like one of my repairs, I thought.

He sat down, stared out the window at a young man driving the loader to the log pile. Morgan said, "That's Otis Patterson. His sister died awhile back. You may have read."

"Yeah," I said with a look out.

Otis wore a sleeveless shirt and shorts. No hat protected his head even though the sun roasted everything it touched. He had the look about him, like, "Don't get in front of me."

"He won't come right out and ask, but I'm certain he thinks I may have had something to do with Chandra's death. Actually, from what I hear, he suspects half the town. He's like a fire under a pile of leaves. Smoking now, but with a little wind, he could blow up in a minute."

"The chief said she worked for you."

"She did. Did a good job, smart as she could be. Made good grades on her classes at JC. She went part time. She switched around the office friendly like if you know what I mean. I lost my wife years ago, but hell, no way was I going to take her on. I had a failing mill to run."

"You think Otis might have set the fire for revenge?"

"A possibility. He's a hard worker, but I don't need him around here with a hidden agenda."

"You talk to him?"

"I don't know what to say. I don't want to fire him. His grandpa, Willie Patterson, asked me to put him on, and I want to buy timber from Willie and his friends. Truth is, that girl wasn't carrying a black baby."

"Where'd you hear that?" I asked.

"It's all hush, hush around city hall, but one of the sisters told me. I'm not of a mind to spread it around, but I don't want Otis gunning for me either. Scooter says he's already calling around, accusing every white man she flirted with at the Pub. Making threats, Scooter says."

"Puts you on the horns of a dilemma doesn't it?"

"Hmm. Not a fun place to be."

"Seems like he would have said something to you."

"That's the way I see it too, but I can't be certain. He might not want to lose his job. People get pissed, they don't think too clearly."

"Is anybody else mad at you?"

"That's one of the things I wanted to talk about," he said. "I think the Pitts are doing a number on me. Burl's behind it, most likely."

He said timber owners were asked, on the phone, why they'd want to deal with an outfit that "will shut its doors in six months." They were told that after "Reynolds closes his mill," they might not find buyers for their timber. Morgan did not say that the Pitts had somebody torch his logs, but the implication was there.

"Could be somebody wants to speed up the process," I said.

"I don't know." He sighed. "I know I have a mill to run, Bishop. My profit margin is already damned thin. I don't need anymore problems and I don't have time to watch my back and run the mill."

So, why tell me? I had my own ass to cover and Daniel Rose was all over it. The answer came next.

"Uh, I wonder if you'd have a talk with Burl. I think he'd listen to you. You helped the chicken growers awhile back."

"I got roped into that because of a couple of bank loans. I try to avoid conflicts. I haven't mediated since I stopped handling divorce cases.

Sleep better too."

"Damn it, within twelve months, I'll mostly cut hardwood. Lots of market niches for hardwood. Could be, we won't even be competitors!" He exhaled loudly.

"I doubt Burl would give a damn what I said. He has a one-track mind. It begins at one end of his mill and ends at the other."

He laughed, half-heartedly and patted the top of his desk with the fingers of his hands. He looked up and said, "I'm not sure the fire and the phone calls tie in, but a year or so ago, there was a rumor that a big lumber outfit from the state of Washington wanted to buy a mill down here, one of those stock-for-assets things. Nothing ever came of it, except for the straw bid I made. It crossed my mind that some outfit might still be looking."

"I can't see Burl Pitts selling his mill. Can you?"

"Hell no! He loves the damn thing, most likely'll be buried out in his log yard."

"So, as a practical matter, that just leaves your mill."

"Yeah and Burl might be happier if my mill wasn't here to sell." No mill, no competition.

"The thought crossed my mind too, but I'm not as certain as you that Burl would do it. He tough, but I don't see him burning you out. Not his style."

"Who else? Not Jimmy. He's more interested in getting laid. No, Burl's the big winner if this mill closes. Not that it will, Bishop! It closes when I do, if you get my meaning," he said.

I got it. Not a pleasant thought. "Why not write Burl a letter and tell him what you plan to do? Or, call him."

"Folks 'round here like to deal face to face. Burl, more than anybody. That's what you do … for a living."

I told him I'd think about it. Protocol required me to tell Rooster first. If he didn't object, I'd give it a try. I didn't see Burl Pitts as an easy man to negotiate with under the best of circumstances and Morgan's mill didn't fit under that heading.

"By the way, did Jonas Osstrum call you? He raised hell with a lot of bidders. Splashed some shit on me in the process."

"He called. Wanted to know where I got the money for my bid. I told him I made a straw bid for a third party and I wasn't authorized to disclose anything else. Where would I get four million bucks? He hinted, hell, almost said, I was part of a conspiracy to underbid the property. Like I caused him to lose money. It raised my dander, but he seemed so upset, I let it go."

"Who did you bid for, if you don't mind? You said something about a listed company first time we met."

"That's what I was told, a listed company. No name. A courier brought the bid and I signed it in blank. Also I signed a document that assigned any rights I had, if my bid was the high bid."

"Somebody must have asked you to bid?"

"I agreed to keep it secret." He drummed his fingers on the desk. "Hell, I don't see how I can keep it from you. I want you to do me a favor. You'll keep it to yourself?"

"It's what lawyers swear to do."

He laughed. "Oddly enough, it was a lawyer. New Orleans office. He said he'd been hired by a client to find a straw bidder."

"I'll be damned."

"I have his name and number around here someplace. Swegman, I think it was."

"He say anything else?"

"No. Just said his client wanted to establish a presence in the region, but wanted it kept secret in case they wanted to buy more timber. Didn't want to jack the prices up. I called a friend in Jackson to make sure a straw bid was on the up and up. He didn't see anything wrong with it.

"The fee was wire transferred into my account and all of a sudden I had a chance to get the mill running. Now, if you can talk sense to the Pitts, Burl in particular, I have a damn good chance to keep it running."

"Why would a listed company buy a chunk of land down here without plans to use it? Hard to believe a big timber company would speculate with four million dollars, but I don't know the business. Maybe it's done all the time."

"I was curious too. I asked Skinny Dearman if Caleb had said anything about a company wanting to move in. Skinny scales my logs if I don't have time. Works for Caleb the rest of the time. Said he hasn't heard anything."

A car pulled up outside. "Sounds like you've got company," I said.

Morgan walked me to the door where we were met by a blast of hot air and a young man with glasses and a black briefcase. I'd seen him at Pitts Lumber the day I was there. He drove up as I left. I also remembered his face at the auction. Young, enthusiastic, and upwardly mobile.

"Mr. Fitzgerald," Morgan said. "Come in."

He told me, "This young man has offered to update my financial statements. A show of good will, he says. I like good will!" He smiled.

Fitzgerald did likewise and stuck out his hand.

"You were at the auction," I said. I felt it prudent not to mention that I'd seen him at Pitts Lumber.

"Yes. You were rattling the judge's cage." He smiled.

That's how everybody saw it. Funny thing is, I thought, the judge and Rose rattled mine.

I stopped at Chief Jenkins' office on the way home to tell him about the "leak" of Chandra Patterson's lab results. I walked in to the blare of gospel music from the radio that Irene, his secretary, kept on all day long. She was middle aged and on the dumpy side. No matter how many times I showed up, the look on her face always said, "Who are you?" The chief was out so I wrote him a note, troubled Irene for an envelope, and asked her to put it on his desk.

Next stop was the library to see Kathy. She was in a meeting. Damn it. She also got a note. I checked out two books and drove home. I got two in case half way through one, I'd remember it, or if I got a hot streak and finished one on Saturday and needed one for Sunday. A few pages at night put me right to sleep.

I picked up the paper at the road. Something cold to drink seemed in order. I was on the back porch, a beer in one hand, newspaper in the other when the phone rang.

"Who in hell told you?" the chief asked.

"Morgan Reynolds," I said. "It was a confidential disclosure to me, but I figured you needed to know. Somebody in City Hall had to leak it. Can you keep his name out of the flap I know you're gonna cause?"

"I'm gonna call him for damn sure! I don't want him to tell Otis Patterson shit. That boy's already at every back door in town. Flap's not the half of what's gonna happen! I'm gonna chew some ass around here!"

I warned Morgan. He took it in stride, like he expected it.

I called Osstrum the next morning.

"You've been harassing people," I told him. "That's your business. But, using information you got from me makes it my business. Daniel Rose threatened me with a lawsuit. And don't think for a minute he won't sue you as well."

He apologized without conviction, but defended his right to call on much the same grounds as I had; the names and telephone numbers were virtually public information.

"That might be one of those questions of fact a jury decides. Do you want to pay a lawyer to prove you're right? I don't."

He didn't either. "Our audit lists TRS properties by date of acquisition and purchase price. The auction listed them by tract numbers assigned by Caleb Washington. So, it's been hard to make side by side comparisons, but it appears we'll have big losses. We think that gives us a right to investigate."

"That doesn't mean you won't end up in court if you accuse bidders of fraud. People don't like it," I said.

"The last place I want to be."

I asked, "By the way, did you find out anything? Just curious."

"No. Bidders who took the time to talk said they based their bids on the appraisals and personal knowledge of the timber and land. If they bid low, it was because they were looking for a bargain."

"It may be time for you to accept the fact that you lost money and move on."

"Yeah," he said. "You're probably right."

Maybe Rose would feel the same way. Fat chance, I told myself.

Chapter 8

I picked up two new bank assignments from the post office. Each required financial statements and personal visits to borrowers in the Jackson area, a day trip. It was a relief to be productive. I called both for appointments. They were as eager to get the visits over with as I was to get out of town for the day.

I saw both the next day. The businesses appeared strong, customers all over, phones rang while I was there, the help stayed busy. I reviewed their financial statements on site, saw nothing amiss and headed back to Lawton in the afternoon.

On the way home, I stopped at a roadside place for a pulled pork barbecue sandwich and a glass of tea. People waited to get in. Once I bit into my sandwich, I could see why. It was worth the wait, even if it did put me late.

The security lights around the cabin were on when I got back. My job had a tendency to make some people mad and some very mad. That's why I put them up. After a quick check for shadows in the bushes, I turned off the engine and bounded up the front steps. A gust of air hit me in the face as I opened the front door.

What the hell! The back door was wide open. Damn, did I go off and leave it open? I took two steps, saw a pane gone from the door and my work area rifled. Computer and printer gone! Except for a shotgun, the computer and printer were the only things of value in the cabin and they weren't worth much. The shotgun was still in the closet. Having survived the crash of one hard drive, I stored most of my files on discs and hard copies. The discs were in a box in a back room, untouched, as were the hard copies.

Osstrum's check was gone. "Five bucks?" A handful of loose change was taken and the documents and portfolio cases of material Rose gave me. The cases weren't worth much, but maybe the thief didn't know. Then it dawned on me. It was the contents of the cases the thief was after. The rest was a feeble attempt at a cover up. I called Osstrum at his office in Mobile with the news. "Somebody has your address and phone number. It may not be anything, but if I were you, I'd be careful. You may have pissed somebody off."

He said he'd move to another apartment as soon as possible. So, maybe he was onto something. Another thought nagged me as well. Somebody didn't want me poking around. I wondered what might happen if I did. It wasn't a pleasing thought.

I didn't sleep much that night. Outside noises that ordinarily provoked a roll over in bed and resumption of sleep, brought me upright for a careful listen. Morning coffee was a welcome relief.

When I knew the chief would be in his office, I called. "Guess what?"

"You've got yourself in another mess?"

"Maybe." I recited details of the break in.

"Bone, damned if you don't need a separate police department to watch after you." He always called me Bone when he was pissed.

He exhaled. "Okay, I'll send somebody out there. For a thousand dollars worth of damage, you tie up half the force. I suppose we need to fingerprint the place."

"I'm sorry, Chief. Send somebody who isn't busy. Now that I think about it, why don't you come out?"

"Kiss my ass, Bone."

He brought backup. They dusted for an hour, then searched around outside. They found nothing useful. I replaced the door pane that afternoon.

I'd read the missing auction files. Nothing seemed out of order. Had I missed something? Everybody at the auction, half the town it seemed, knew I had them. I turned it over in my head for a couple of hours with no success. Around one, I gave up and sent the puzzle to my subconscious for a try.

* * * * *

Osstrum called Fitzgerald. "Moving to another apartment, son," he told him. "Figured I'd let you know. I'll keep my telephone number."

"Why?" Fitzgerald asked. "You're close to your office."

"A couple of bidders threatened to kick my ass if I called them again. Somebody broke into Bone's cabin and took a check with my name and Mobile address. Thought I'd better play it safe. Now that I'm getting paid, I can afford a better apartment anyway." Osstrum said. He gave him the new address.

"Thanks," Fitzgerald said. "Sorry you have to move."

"It's okay. Change'll keep me from getting bored." Depressed was what he wanted to say, but didn't want to worry his son. He felt better of late, now that he had work to keep his mind off things.

"How about you? You heard anything else about the auction?" he asked.

"Only what I told you. People saw it as a distress sale and bid low. Nothing suspicious."

Osstrum recited his theory that a group with an interest in a particular tract of timber may have agreed to let one bidder prevail with the understanding that afterwards, they'd all share in the profits. "I didn't find anything to back it up. Maybe I was way off base," he said.

"Could be, Dad. By the way, Edna and I may get married next spring," Fitzgerald said. "I am picking up clients. I'm pretty sure the Pitts will use the firm. Burl Pitts called Mr. Dawkins, the senior partner, and said I did a good job with their financials. I also got good feedback from a couple of others I called on."

"Congratulations, son."

"One thing I'll tell you about. Kind of funny. Oddly interesting anyway. Last time I was at Pitts, I asked about a huge safe in their file room. More like a vault. The woman who helped me said that Buford, their father, used to keep his 'moonshine money' in it. She said Burl and Jimmy still refer to it as "Pa's moonshine money.'"

During the dry years, the Pitts cooked sour mash out in the woods and sold the moonshine all over south Mississippi. Kept proceeds in that safe. That was when Buford was young. They owned a large chunk of the county. Buford later opened the mill. If he sold lumber for cash, he also threw it into the safe, "tax-free" money.

"I'm surprised somebody hasn't tried to steal it."

"They have a security system and a night watchman. That safe must weigh a ton, anchored in concrete and secured inside a block wall room. It'd take an army.

"You think they used some of that moonshine money for their bid … at the auction?" Osstrum asked.

"No. I found entries for their check. It came back anyway since their bid wasn't the high bid."

"Doesn't matter. I was curious about how they think."

"Burl's the one who does the thinking over there. Jimmy keeps close to the kiln shack."

"Reynolds was the high bidder on the tract Pitts bid on," Osstrum said. "You know how he managed that?"

"I know he deposited twenty thousand dollars in the mill's checking account before the auction. He told me he got it as a fee to act as a straw bidder in the auction. Said he couldn't tell me anymore than that."

"He wouldn't tell me either," Osstrum said. "How do you think he's doing?"

"Scraping by right now. He's buying timber on credit. Doesn't have a lot of cash."

* * * * *

In the country a few miles outside of Lawton, Skinny Dearman and his wife, Claire, waved goodbye to Caleb Washington from the doorway of their doublewide mobile home. Skinny put his arm around his young wife's shoulders. She was thin, like Skinny, with dark brown hair, matching eyes and a pretty face.

"It pisses me off," he said, as they cleared the dinner table, "the way Caleb stares at you. All through supper, he sat there with a damn smirk on his face staring at you. He can't keep his damned eyes off your bosom."

Claire said. "Come on, Skinny! He's an old man. And, your boss."

"I don't care. I don't want him getting ideas. You laugh at every damn thing he says. Corny damn jokes. I've heard 'em all ten times."

"You asked him to stay for supper."

"What the hell could I do? He sat in the front room while it cooked and talked about how good it smelled. He acts like he doesn't have a home to go to. He has a wife! The other day he let it slip that he's been by here during the day. You didn't tell me that!"

"I didn't think a thing about it. He came by to see if you'd come in yet."

"He always knows where I am. 'Sides, he has my cell phone number."

"Well, he didn't try anything, if that bothers you. I gave him some ice water and he left."

"What'd he talk about?"

"Just said we'd done a good job with the place."

Their mobile home sat in the middle of a cleared area on five acres of wooded land in the country with a pond out back. They bought calves to graze the land and to sell when they were full size.

"I don't trust him a bit. He flirts with every woman we run across, young and old. I can't stand going into a café with him."

"He's as old as my daddy, Skinny. Don't be jealous," Claire said and slapped at him with a dishtowel.

"It hasn't reached his brain yet. Another year, I'll be ready to go out on my own. Now, I do his work and he gets all the money. Bootlegging jobs on weekends to make ends meet. He got some kind of bonus for that TRS auction! I heard him tell his wife on the phone. You'd think he'd put a little in my pocket. Especially since I did all the work." He stared through the back door into the twilight.

"Why don't you ask for a share?"

"I did. You know what he said?"

She shook her head no.

"He said I got paid for the work I did. And he got paid for the work he did. He didn't do any, as far as I'm concerned."

"Well, we're getting by." Claire put her arms around his waist and squeezed. Then she kissed him hard. "You're my man Skinny, not that old man."

She pulled at his arm. "Come on, Skinny, I need some cuddling. You've been neglecting me."

Lost in thought as he was, he hardly heard her.

"Skinny! I'm talking to you! Where are you?"

He turned his face toward hers. "I'm sorry. Just thinking. Something's been gnawing at my guts."

"What in the world are you talking about, Skinny?"

"After the auction, a man, Osstrum I think he said, called me. He said he was one of the investors in that timber they auctioned off at the courthouse. He was bitching about the money they'd lost on the parcels around here. I appraised every damn one of those parcels he was going on about."

"Was he claiming you made a mistake?"

"Yeah and worse. That I may have deliberately rigged my numbers."

"Skinny!"

"They said appraise low. That's what I did. I don't like being accused, Claire."

"Next time you tell that man to call me. I'll set him straight. My man doesn't make mistakes." She squeezed him. He pulled her close and kissed the top of her head. "I love you, Claire." She squeezed him hard and smiled.

"The judge called me too. That Bone guy got him riled up. He asked me a lots of questions. Like I was on trial. Just like with that Osstrum guy, like I'd done something wrong. Finally, though, he thanked me and apologized for taking so much of my time. It didn't leave me with a good feeling though."

"I'm sorry. I didn't know."

"Yeah. Just did my damn job. Anyway, that's what been on my mind."

"You got some notion about it?"

He shook his head, no. "Can't say that I do, Claire. Can't say. Just did what I was told. Mr. Rose … ah … I gotta think 'bout it. I don't like being accused. Ain't no fingers been pointed at anybody else."

"Do your thinking tomorrow when you're at work. You're … with me now." She smiled and pulled his arm.

Chapter 9

I rang Kathy's doorbell for our Saturday dinner date. She and her mother shared a Queen Ann cottage in the historic district of Lawton, north of downtown. Participants in the timber boom at the turn of the century built most of the houses in the district. A landscape architect was hired out of New York to plan the streets and parks. Railroads were built to accommodate the shipping of lumber and the city prospered. Children and grandchildren of the original settlers still lived in some of the fine old homes.

During those early days, the tragic death of the son of one of the participants resulted in the construction of the Lawton Museum, Lawton's cultural centerpiece. It hosts art exhibitions, musical events, activities that kindle the imaginations of children, young and old. Tour buses regularly stop to allow tourists to enjoy all the Museum has to offer.

Kathy opened the door. "Come in for a few minutes. I'm almost ready." She smiled. She was the only person I knew who never seemed sad. It worried me that I might do something to change that. A failed marriage still haunted me.

"You look great!" I said. A light tan blouse and slacks showed all her curves. Her shoulder length hair was pulled back to spotlight her face. Her brown eyes sparkled in the porch lights. That, with the look on her face when she smiled, got me every time. She played in a tennis league and stayed in good shape. I played too, but it didn't work for me like it did for her. I had to jog to stay even. I had a glass of white wine with her mother in their patio room at the rear while Kathy finished up. Her mother had resumed her interest in painting. We talked about that.

When Kathy and I walked into the Pub, practically every table was full, but I'd reserved a table on the patio so it didn't matter. The sun was gone and the evening air was pleasantly soft and moist.

As we strolled past tables, I heard Seth Campbell call, "Bishop!" We went over to say hello. Seth and his wife, Beth, sat along the bricked wall. Beth greeted us cordially. Her face had added a few lines and her hair more gray since I last saw her, but she was still attractive.

Seth said, "I won't hold you up. I left a message on your phone. John Prozini's in New Orleans talking to investors about some new venture, but is coming through Lawton tomorrow afternoon to pick up the rest of the auction files. He wants yours as well." Seth said Prozini was reluctant to call me directly since we'd crossed swords over the Osstrum business. Rose and Judge Chancellor would be there.

I told them what happened to my files.

"Hmm," Seth said. "Rather than have him run all over the county, picking up this and that, I said we'd meet at my house. Three o'clock. Even if you don't have anything to hand over, it might be good to meet anyway. Good time to air your differences."

I'd be there.

Kathy and I found our table on the softly lit patio and ordered Chianti. The central fountain beside us bubbled with rhythmic sounds as water cascaded downward. An easy breeze bathed our faces. Pink blooms in the perimeter beds danced in the flicker of the gaslights and painted Kathy's face in a warm glow. The prime rib was outstanding. Anything I did with Kathy always was.

I asked, "How about an after dinner drink on the back porch? I haven't seen enough of you." I covered her hand with mine.

"Of course."

"You have a sitter?" Someone usually came in to be with her mother if Kathy was going to be late.

She smiled.

"Great."

We drove along the red bricked streets of Lawton's old town on the way home. It had the charm of a quaint old mill town. Antique streetlights lit the downtown much as they had a hundred years ago. Most of the buildings in the business district were two stories with just enough ones and threes to give the skyline architectural interest. Over the years, many were restored or converted for use by banks, professionals and locally based companies such as Campbell Enterprises.

We sipped a liqueur on the back porch and watched bats swoop up and down in the night to compete with fish for hapless insects caught in the waters of the creek. Cries of wild creatures filled the night. Amber glows of lightning bugs danced in the dark around the cabin. Crickets and frogs added their serenades.

We saw a herd of deer slip to the creek's edge to drink their fill without fear. Beyond the marsh on the other side of the creek, the beavers' pond was as quiet and still as black ebony, dotted with rounded bubbles that shone like silver in the moon's glow.

"Beautiful sight," Kathy said. She reached over to touch her hand to my face.

"You should see it in the morning."

She smiled. "I have."

"Not tomorrow's morning."

* * * * *

I pulled up to the Campbell's Tudor house at three exactly. The hundred-year old home had a turret entry, diamond pane windows and a Gothic arch doorway. Tall magnolias and live oaks flanked the sides. Azaleas, camellias and countless other shrubs and plants I couldn't identify filled well tended gardens. A tall wrought iron fence with spiked tops and a gate, left open, surrounded it all.

Beth showed me through the foyer to the library. I was the last to arrive. The room opened via paned doors to a rose garden in full bloom. Bookcases filled a wall behind Seth's desk. Oriental rugs covered a planked floor. A drink cart sat to my right along a paneled wall.

Daniel Rose sat in a dark leather chair next to the garden wall; the judge in a chair next to him. The judge looked tired and frail, but managed a smile. Both wore dark suits. A slender man with tan skin sat on the edge of Seth's desk. One hand held a cigarette, the other a drink. If the give-me-your-money, with an all-teeth-showing smile on his face was any indication, he was in the middle of a good time. He wore an off white suit, fitted to show he was no ninety pound weakling, had a broad handsome face with just a trace of mustache. Had to be Prozini, I decided. Seth hadn't mentioned that Prozini was black, but Seth was color blind.

"Get yourself a drink, Bishop," Seth said, with a gesture toward the cart. No beer or wine was displayed so I defaulted to my back up, a Manhattan.

"I think you know everybody," Seth said. "Well, maybe not John

Prozini."

"Only by name," I said. "We've talked."

He shoved his hand toward me. "Shocked that I'm black, Mr. Bone?" he asked.

I replied, "I wouldn't say shocked. Surprised hits closer."

"You know what they say, we've joined the mainstream," Prozini looked at my empty hands. "Where are your files, Mr. Bone? That's the main reason I'm here, to pick up files."

Seth turned toward me and began, "I haven't had a—"

"My files were stolen," I said.

"How convenient," Rose said.

"For whom?" I asked, with a head gesture in his direction.

"Somebody with something to hide!" he replied.

"That's what I was thinking," I said.

That set Rose off with claims on behalf of clients of mental anguish and invasion of privacy. I didn't let a charge go by without a rebuttal, but mindful of Seth's hospitality, I looked for a way to quit and found one. I turned to the judge and asked, "This could be a hairy case, wouldn't you say, Judge?"

All eyes turned toward the judge. His martini glass jiggled.

"You're asking me for a ruling, counselors?"

"I think we are," I said.

He drew in a deep breath, focused on the floor for a second then said, "I believe there's merit on both sides." His voice was tired, his words strained.

Rose's eyes widened.

The old judge took a breath. "I sat in on a couple of interviews Daniel had with his clients. I also called some of them myself. For the most part, they objected to having been called. Maybe they were accused, maybe not. It wasn't totally clear."

"No damages." I said. Maybe punitives, but I didn't want to raise that issue.

"No. This Mr. Osstrum who made the calls, in sum, asked how the bidders determined their bids. Some thought he worked for you. Did they get together and pool their bids? Were they coached? Daniel's clients, to a man, swore they'd bid on their own."

Rose opened his mouth to speak, but the judge waved him off. "Let me finish, Daniel! Mr. Bone will certainly keep TRS and Mr. Prozini on the hook. The deep pocket rule we all know about."

The judge rubbed his wrinkled face, sipped his martini and added, "I'm not even sure how we, me and you Daniel, can avoid being defendants. We might very well stand in pari delecto with Mr. Bone and Mr. Prozini."

"What!" Rose said. "How do you figure that?"

"Well, did you make it clear to Mr. Bone the files were confidential? You and Mr. Prozini may have alluded to confidentiality, but would that convince a judge with an open mind? It hasn't convinced me. 'Course, lots of folks here about claim I've never had one." He laughed.

Prozini said, "If I may put a word in. Nothing's to be gained by going forward. Who wants to pay out legal fees for nothing? Your clients had no real damage. I think it's dead, Daniel."

Yeah, I thought and litigation to a promoter is a huge no, no. Next time he solicited investors, skittish to begin with, he'd have to answer why.

"I'm willing to let a jury decide," Rose said.

Seth set his glass on top of his desk. "Mr. Rose, you remind me of the man who sat in the pew in front of us at church this morning." Seth said the preacher had asked the congregation to stand and sing a hymn. A man in front of Seth and Beth rocked back on his heels and sang with zeal, easily the loudest voice in church.

After the service, Seth heard him tell a friend—his hearing was bad so he had to shout—how much he enjoyed that hymn, his favorite. "Thing is, he was the only one in church who sang it." The rest of the congregation sang the one the preacher announced.

"Mr. Rose, haven't you been listening?" Seth asked. "You don't have a case! Let it go!"

Seth Campbell had spoken. I respect a man who speaks MY mind.

Rose sank back into his chair, stared at Prozini and Judge Chancellor, and said, "I'll consider the facts carefully."

I hoped that was a surrender.

Before adjournment, Prozini dangled an investment. "Low budget movie in Mexico, Gentlemen," he said. "High yield and low risk." There was no mention of budget controls or distribution rights, but investors could be present "for the shoots." They could meet the stars and even get bit parts.

"Some of you might become movie stars!" he said with a toothy smile.

We passed. I was afraid the judge had literally passed. He could hardly keep his eyes open. Martinis will do that.

Seth offered Prozini their guestroom.

"Thank you, Seth," Prozini said, "but Daniel has offered to put me up at his place."

I went home and microwaved dinner, some greasy frozen thing in a colorful box out of my freezer. To take the edge off, I opened a fresh bottle of wine and ate outside on the porch, where it was cool.

I considered it a productive day.

* * * * *

Otis shouted into the phone. "You fucked Chandra around. Dinah, you son of a bitch! As good as killed her and you ain't gonna get away with it!"

"Who is this?" the man asked.

"Don't make no difference who I am," Otis answered. "I know who you be, and I'm gonna get you."

"I don't know what the fuck you're talking about, but if you call again, I'm going to have the law on your ass. You understand that?" The man slammed the phone down.

Threats didn't bother Otis. Sooner or later somebody would slip up and tip him off, and then he'd have the bastard.

The man stared at the phone with a concerned look. "Otis Patterson," he mumbled. "Otis fucking Patterson."

* * * * *

The next week Morgan's request to talk to Burl Pitts reached the top of my to do list. It was not a task I wanted to do. Had to cut the grass. The damn shed leaks. In heavy rains, water dripped onto my woodpile. It was important to have dry wood for my annual Christmas fire.

But, billable things first. Banks want an immediate response with new files, so I drove into town to the post office to see if anything had come in. Burl would have to wait. I learned long ago to prioritize. That way, I avoided procrastination. No billable letters in my box, damn it.

Resigned to my fate, on the way home, I stopped at the hardware store for a tube of roof patch. Jimmy Pitts roared into the parking lot on his motorcycle as I threw my purchase into the passenger seat. It was a sign. I reintroduced myself and stuck out my hand.

"No need." He laughed and said, "Everybody in town knows you since the auction. Of course, I know you from when you checked our new system for the bank. Burl's still bitching about it."

"You ever been in a situation where somebody asks you to do something that you don't want to do?" I asked.

"Are you kidding? I'm married."

"Well, I'm in that situation and I'm not married. I wonder if you can help."

He pulled back with a frown.

"You see, Morgan Reynolds asked me to talk to Burl "

"You can stop right there. If it has anything to do with Reynolds, you can forget it. When Reynolds closes that mill, Burl will most likely give everybody half a day off. Well, at least an hour."

"I know that you guys don't get along with him."

"You ain't even close, Bone. Especially Burl."

"Here's my problem." I repeated Morgan's request.

"I hear you. Listen, Burl might talk to you or might not. Like as not to hit you up side the head."

"I doubt it'd take more than ten minutes. What's the sense of a grudge? Let the market place decide who'll stay in business."

He shrugged. "Getting down to the short strokes, you want me to ask him?"

I did.

"Hell, he's likely to hit me up side the head."

"Stand way back."

"Uh huh. Whew. Ask Burl to make peace with that ni—"

My sharp look stopped him.

"Uh, that Reynolds guy. Uh huh. And, most likely Burl'd be sober when I did. No give in 'im a'tall when he's sober. Uh huh. Man, oh man."

He shook his head this way and that, then said, "Okay, I'll see. I might need a favor from you one of these days. You'll owe me. Give me a day or two. I'll have to wait till he's liquored up. Or yeah, catch him after church." He'd let me know.

That's how to handle procrastination. Meet it head on or run into it accidentally.

I cut grass then caulked a split seam in the shed's roof. I was just out of the shower when the phone rang. Close to three o'clock, my mind was on the newspaper.

"Bishop Bone," Judge Chancellor said. "I guess you wonder why I've called?"

I held the phone out from my ear. His voice came through loud and clear.

"Missy, my house keeper, says I don't have enough to do, but to hear you and Daniel go at it made me to rethink our bid procedures. I turned them inside out, to look for holes."

"I appreciate the position you took at Seth's on potential litigation," I said.

"I hate to rain on Daniel's parade, but I also hate to see him spin his wheels. He's always for the underdog. No real damage suffered by anybody. Why waste time in litigation?"

No question about it! My esteem for the old man increased immediately.

"Tell you why I called. Today's my day to fish, Bishop. You don't mind if I call you Bishop, do you?"

"Not at all. I call you Judge."

"I have a small place out from town. I'm there now as a matter of fact. Missy just dropped me off. Chief Jenkins tells me you're a fisherman."

"We do a little creek fishing," I said.

"He also says you're a good man, butt headed like me, but okay."

"Thank you." I guess.

"Can you join me? Missy picked up a six pack on the way out. The chief says y'all don't fish without a six pack."

I chuckled. "Did you find out anything?"

"I can't say for sure. Mostly I want to brainstorm a couple of thoughts in my head. There may have been a loophole in that liquidation. The chief says you thrive on turning rocks over to see what's under them. He had another word for it."

I bet he did. Making a mountain out of a molehill was what he liked to say. Hell, the paper could wait. I wrote down directions to his place, grabbed my tackle and took off.

Chapter 10

I braked to a stop in an open space off the narrow dirt lane the judge told me to take. I jogged toward the pier. The judge was nowhere in sight, but I saw his boat in the lake. He wasn't in it. Then I saw him, face down in the water! His hat, partially submerged, upside down beside him

Son of a bitch!

I waded in to drag his lifeless body onto the shore. I felt for a pulse and began pressing on his chest to revive him. It didn't work. Damn it to hell, the old man was dead! I stared at his pale blue face and tried to comprehend what I was seeing. He was dead! And, I'd just talked to him. It didn't seem real.

I called an ambulance and the chief. Both rolled up about the same time. Med-techs removed his vest and continued the resuscitation process with no more success than I had.

"What do you think?" Chief Jenkins asked.

"Looks like he fell in and drowned. May have had a heart attack. Poor bastard. He'd hooked a good-sized trout, too. Still on the end of his line."

We pulled the judge's boat onto shore and retrieved his gear.

"He called me. Asked me to join him," I said.

"He said he might. You got his curiosity up."

"I kind of liked the old man. He said what was on his mind. I respect that," I said.

"Me too."

We hung around for a few minutes after the ambulance left, mostly to stare into the water and to curse the judge's bad luck.

"Mind writing a report?" he asked.

"Get it to you in the morning."

"Damned shame," he said, then drove away.

I retrieved my fly rod to leave.

"Hell," I said. They had left the judge's vest and beer cooler on the picnic table. I loaded both into the jeep and drove home.

The next morning, a bank officer called to order a couple of loan inspections on the Coast. She'd fax me the details. I welcomed the diversion. Money problems were easier to handle than ones where death was involved.

I prepared the report the chief asked for and dropped it by his office with the cooler and fishing vest. He was out. Irene's gospel music was in full throttle. I couldn't say the absence of the chief was related, but I did muse about it.

"I brought the judge's cooler. Six beers inside," I told her. "And his fishing vest." As I placed it on her desk, I noticed tears in its shoulder. There were two, with pink smudges on the underside, one of those things you see and dismiss.

* * * * *

I signed the visitation register at the funeral home, then made a pass by the judge's coffin. His face looked too white. The dead all do, I thought. You'd think after all the years they'd been doing it, funeral homes would be able to put a little pink in the faces.

I retreated into the hall to find Chief Jenkins. On my right, Rose held court with Caleb Washington, Skinny Dearman and Burl Pitts. Burl stood a head above everyone but Caleb. I didn't see Jimmy. Burl's hard facial expression hadn't changed since the last time I'd seen it. John Prozini, also in the group, listened intently to Rose; his lustrous smile subdued. They didn't see me and I didn't care to be seen.

Ah, there the chief was, beside a gray headed, middle-aged lady in a dark suit. A man with a Bible edged in to comfort her. Must be somebody close to the judge, I thought. Of course! Missy, the judge's housekeeper. She was stout enough to handle the judge should he need it. She dabbed at her eyes with a white handkerchief. The chief patted her arm then moved away. The man with the Bible stayed.

Chief Jenkins headed in my direction.

"Bishop," he said. His face reflected the sadness of the others who had come to pay their respects. "Still can't get over it." He glanced back at the casket flanked by stand after stand of flowers. More stood in the hall outside, a testament to the respect the judge commanded in the community.

"Missy" he gestured almost imperceptibly at the housekeeper, "has looked after Judge Chancellor for five years, like a second wife. It hit her hard." His voice cracked a bit. "She said the judge was like a kid with a new toy. Wearing his new fishing vest. It was a birthday present."

He was ready for a beer. I was too. We went to the Pub for a pint of their finest.

A motorcycle roared up outside. Jimmy Pitts walked through the door and turned toward us. He looked tough in a black leather jacket and boots. "Mr. Bone … Chief Jenkins." He headed toward our table. He waved to the bartender and held up a finger. The bartender grabbed a mug.

"Jimmy," the chief replied.

"'Supposed to meet Burl," he said. "He went to the funeral home … visitation. Rose and Judge Chancellor 've been handling our legal business since I don't know when. If y'all don't mind, I'll just hang out here till he shows up. Not much for funerals. Too damn sad." Jenkins motioned at a chair. He pulled it out and sat down.

He looked at me and said, "I mentioned to Burl, you know, what you said about Reynolds."

"What'd he say?"

"You want the short version or the long one?"

Short would do.

"He said, 'Tell Bone to kiss my ass. If Reynolds wants a handout, he can go to the welfare office. If he can't meet the competition, tough shit.' I think that about covers it. Of course, when he comes in, you might want to ask him yourself." His face broke into a cross between a smile and a smirk as he smoothed his mustache.

Well, I had tried. I dreaded having to tell Morgan, but figured he hadn't counted on Burl saying much else. I was a long shot that hadn't paid off. Few do.

Jimmy's beer arrived. He made a suggestive comment to the young waitress who giggled and rushed off. His slap at her behind missed. I wondered how waitresses reconciled having two lives, their faux lives as play-thing-objects to people like Jimmy and their real lives as wives or girl friends. Were they able to keep them separate? Chandra Patterson came to mind. Fortunately, I didn't have long to ponder the question, because just then, Burl pushed through the door with Caleb Washington and Skinny Dearman. He came in like an avalanche.

"Well," Jimmy said, "speaking of the devil. Burl, come over here a minute!" He waved at his big brother.

"Yeah," Burl said. "Chief." He bobbed his head. "Bone."

"I told Mr. Bone what you said." Jimmy smiled.

Burl stared at me for an instant with hard eyes and said, "I wouldn't care if Reynolds was in the emergency ward. He's a competitor and as far as I'm concerned, a competitor is my enemy."

"He plans to concentrate on hardwood as soon as he can. You—"

"So what? Hardwood's a lumber market. I may expand. We have a lot of forty-year old hardwood we can harvest, a hell of a lot more than he'll ever have. Better grade too."

"He says you undercut him with timber owners," I said. "Seems to me you could back off and let the market place decide who's going to make it."

"I make the market in these parts, Bone! The sooner that damn play like mill of his closes, the better I'll like it. Every day it's open costs me money. I figure that bunch already owes me a million dollars."

Jimmy frowned, like, "Part of that damned million is mine."

I said, "You mean you have to watch your prices? If he wasn't there, you could up your prices or pay less for your timber? Hell, Mr. Pitts, you want a monopoly. You want to be king!" Unreasonable people pissed me off.

Burl stepped toward me with clinched fists. I tensed to stand and instantly calculated how I was going to survive the next three minutes. Maybe kick his knee, knee to the groin might be better … . The chief pushed back from the table a few inches to remind the man of his presence. Burl's eyes caught the movement. His fists relaxed. I settled back into my chair. Safe for another day. A head butt might have worked.

Burl looked at the chief and said, "People should keep their mouths shut about things they don't understand!"

I didn't offer a rebuttal. Best to leave well enough alone.

"You coming, Jimmy?" Burl headed to the patio where Caleb and Skinny sat. Jimmy picked up his beer and followed.

Rose and Prozini walked in later. They sat alone, leaned forward over the table, and talked with their faces close.

The chief asked for an explanation. I filled in the details.

"Burl's not somebody you want to make too mad," he said, "unless you're quick on your feet."

"Unreasonable as hell," I said.

"You were right about the king thing. He was king shit in these parts before TRS reopened the mill. He's been belly aching about it ever since."

* * * * *

That night, Otis received more names to call.

* * * * *

I called Morgan the next morning with Burl's reaction.

"I'm not too surprised," he said. "I hoped he'd mellowed some, but I don't guess people like him ever soften up. Thanks, Bishop. If you need any cheap lumber, you call."

He was safe on that account. As far as I was concerned, deferred maintenance had no statute of limitations.

"How're you doing with Otis?"

"Nothing more from him. Scooter says he's exclusively on white men. Somebody gives him names."

"Any more trouble at the mill? Log piles on fire?"

"No, Sir. All's quiet on the western front," he said. "We're shittin' and gittin' around here, making payroll, keeping our note current. I'm waiting to see what this day will bring."

We agreed to keep in touch.

I drove into town to pick up my mail. A letter from an out of state bank asked if I wanted to collect a bunch of charged off consumer accounts and delinquent student loans. I'd rather sell fish bait out of my jeep on the highway in front of Wal-Mart. I declined the opportunity.

With nothing better to do, I sprayed myself with mosquito repellant and paddled across the creek to explore the woods behind the beaver pond, to enjoy the peaceful calm of the sounds of nature. I poked my snake stick, a gnarled hickory limb, along the trail ahead of my boots to attract the attention of any moccasins that might be in the sun. I stopped for a handful of sweet berries at a blackberry bush. When I turned to move on, a briar snagged my pants' leg.

I cursed. They were practically new. That's when I had one of those intuitive flashes people sometime get. The judge's vest had a tear in it and a pink stain. Missy said the vest was new. So, how'd it get snagged? Where had the pink stain come from? Blood? The judges? Who else's!

I returned to the cabin to call the chief. "What'd the judge's autopsy show?" I asked.

"I'm reading the damn thing right now. Why, Bone? About to make a mountain out of a mole hill?" he asked.

Right on cue, I thought. "I don't know. Can I get a copy?"

"Just tell me what's on your mind, damn it to hell!"

I told him about the tear in the judge's vest, and the possible bloodstain.

"Cause of death was drowning, Bone," he said. "Most likely fell out of the boat. He was old and feeble. Here's something. Says there was a cut place on his shoulder. I'd say it bled, most likely caused the stain."

"Odd, don't you think? To die right after he told me he might have found a loophole?"

"You think everything is odd, Bone. You need more work. I'll ask the mayor to find you a job with Parks and Recreation. How does mosquito abatement strike you? Lots of job satisfaction. Lots of killings."

I let it pass. "So, how do you think his brand new vest got snagged? Had to be sharp enough to cut into his skin."

"Maybe a splinter or nail on the boat. Maybe snagged himself casting. His skill level wasn't what it had been you know."

"You mind if I go out there and have a look around?"

"If it'll get you off the phone, I'll pay for your gas."

It neared five when I walked onto the pier to inspect the boat. I found no splinters or exposed nails. I took the boat out to where I found the judge's body and checked for underwater snags, just in case. None. Hell, the lake was shallow enough for him to stand as far as I could see. As I rowed back, my eyes panned along the shore to the right of the pier. What caught my eye was a patch of flattened weeds in a gap between the trees. Right at the water line. It looked like somebody had stood there. In line with where I'd found the judge's body.

The chief would say, "So what? When somebody fishes in a spot, they mash down weeds. How do you know the judge didn't make a few casts from there?"

Nevertheless, it went into my subconscious, already busy with why anybody would want the auction files Rose gave me.

* * * * *

Chief Jenkins' personal car was beside the cabin as I returned, but no chief. I figured he'd be at the creek. He was, casting back and forth. The creek flowed with a gentle ease and sent a layer of cool onto the sandy bank. The sun had set behind the trees to send a blanket of gray from the woods to cover the creek in early twilight.

"Catch anything?" I shouted down.

"They're hitting! Come on down!"

I didn't want to fish, but I did want to talk about what I'd found.

"You been out to the judge's lake?" he asked.

"Yeah."

"Find anything sinister?" he asked.

I told him about the weeds being mashed down. "Obviously somebody had to be standing there to do that."

"Somebody. Yeah." He shrugged without turning.

"You guys find anything about the cut on the judge's shoulder?"

"I brought you a picture." He pointed toward a manila folder under a pinecone behind him.

I pulled it out. It wasn't just one cut, it was two, like a claw had dug into his skin.

"Any idea as to what made them?" I asked.

His attention was focused at the end of his line.

"We figured you'd have one. Me and Milty," he said. His body jerked as he yanked on his tackle. From the bend in his rod, he'd hooked a big one. After a couple of minutes of man-sized grunts, he dragged a big trout onto the sandy bank.

"Look at that, Bone. Now that's a fish. I bet you never pulled one out that big. Plenty of meat on them bones." He could butcher the King's English with the best when relaxed. He slid the fish into a bucket of water, smiled at his catch and watched it swish about. He twisted the cap off his second beer and looked over my shoulder at the photo of the cuts on the judge's shoulder.

"So, what do you think made the marks?" he asked.

"Looks to me like he was scratched by a two-toed cat."

"How about the ganged hooks of a fishing lure?" he asked.

"Yeah, that'd do it. He have any?"

"Several. He even had one at the end of the casting rod on the picnic table. It matched the cuts. And, guess what, it had a couple of khaki threads on it. Mystery solved, Bone. The judge snagged himself casting from where you found the weeds mashed down. He yanked it loose, left the damned rod on the table and went out in the boat with his fly rod where he got dizzy and fell in. Probably from the shock of snagging himself."

I had one of those adrenaline surges lawyers sometime get in a courtroom clash. "That's one theory. How about this one? What if somebody who knew how to handle a casting rod was already out there when Missy let the judge out? What if somebody took the rod from the table, hooked the judge and jerked him into the water? That's consistent with the angle of the cuts. The killer drags him around until he drowns, unhooks the lure, flips the judge over and shoves him back into the lake. Leaves the rod on the table for you to reach the conclusion you did, accidental death."

"Good God, Bone! Why'd anybody want to kill Judge Chancellor? The man was without enemies. Shit! I don't know why I even talk to you, Bone," he said. "What makes you think one 'what if,' piled on top of another 'what if' makes a theory credible?"

"Just trying to help, Chief."

"Help, hell! I don't like Maalox."

"Think about it. The judge said he called bidders and anybody else with a part in the auction. Everybody knew he fished on Monday afternoons. Suppose he scared somebody. The same somebody who stole my auction files. He told me he had concerns about a loophole he wanted to bounce off me."

"I'm going home, Bone." He picked up his bucket and trudged up the slope to his car.

He did not seem to put any credence into what I said, but I knew he'd go away and think about it. He always did.

Chapter 11

Billable work sent me to inspect a couple of restaurants on the Coast whose patrons had thinned since Casino buffets opened. They were going to advertise more and wait it out. Good enough for me. They had the staying power, as in money, to do it. Afterwards, I dropped my twenty. It took fifteen minutes, a victory. Usually, they closed me down in ten. I wished Kathy were with me. We could take in a show, see an over-the-hill star relive glory days with old hits. Who cared about a wrinkled face, or added pounds? The audience was in the same shape.

When I got back to Lawton, I detoured past the chief's office. I'd swear he got up to close his door when I asked Irene if he was in. She showed me in anyway. "Chief," I said. "Anything new happening?"

"You mean did we find the judge's killer?"

"Have you progressed that far?"

"Hell, no! You didn't bring donuts, why else would you be here?"

"You've become prescient in your old age."

"I talked it over with Milty. He says, given your track record of stumbling onto shit, we better do a follow up. The angle of the cuts bothered him a little, like the lure hit him from behind. Not conclusive, but enough to make him think. Yeah, I gave you credit. Anyway, I sent a detective back to take impressions where those weeds had been mashed down. Didn't get much. Impressions we did manage were most likely yours. I may arrest you. At least you wouldn't cause me any more trouble.

"Also, we asked anybody who's ever said a harsh word about the judge what they did that afternoon."

"What did you find out?" I asked.

"You see anybody in jail?"

"I haven't looked."

"Well, don't. We haven't arrested anybody."

"So, you didn't find anything?"

Irene's gospel music filled the silence.

"I'm going back to work, Bone. I hope you have someplace to go. I don't like people watch me work."

"I wouldn't think that'd be a problem."

He gave me a sour look.

I asked, "Why not ask his housekeeper if the judge told her anything pertinent?"

His next look was one of those I'm-going-to-kill somebody looks. I left.

* * * * *

Kathy told me of a restaurant out in the country everyone talked about, Cowboy Jim's. It had a deck that sprawled over a river on one side and a lake on the other. Goats, rabbits, ducks and chickens meandered at will outside; flowers everywhere, hummingbirds darting about. A dog lived on the second floor and roamed the roof to greet patrons with loud barks.

We went Saturday night. It lived up to its reputation and then some. An entertainer with a microphone sat in back of the barn-like building to strum a guitar and croon country ballads. We feasted on rib eye steaks and watched fish and ducks catch their dinners in the river.

Since Mrs. Sullivan's sitter had a prior engagement, I said goodnight at the door. As I drove away, I heard the wail of sirens. An ambulance roared past me in the direction of Morgan's mill. Another fire? An injury? I followed. A truck braked to a halt in front of the office. Morgan jumped out of his truck and ran toward a light held by an ambulance attendant at the log pile. I wasn't far behind.

Someone was pinned under the logs. Only an arm was visible. Policemen and firemen shifted the logs to reveal the body of Skinny Dearman.

A beefy man knelt beside his inert form and touched his fingers to Dearman's neck.

"Anything?" his partner asked.

"Dead as a door nail," he said.

"I'm Morgan Reynolds," Morgan told a policeman. "This is my mill. Skinny worked here."

"He work at night?" the policemen asked.

"Not this late, but it could have happened earlier. He comes in when he has time."

First the judge, and now Skinny Dearman. My files taken? All had a common link, the auction. What the hell had I missed?

* * * * *

The chief came by the cabin the next morning.

"Thought I'd come by for a cup of coffee," he said. "I just saw Claire Dearman. She's all broke up. It's a damn shame."

"Another accident?" I asked. "Lots of 'em, huh?"

"Yeah, but where's the proof? Two deaths, both men had something to do with the auction. Has to be a sinister connection in there someplace. Right?"

"Add in the theft of my files."

"Yeah, I have to say it looks damned suspicious. The brace holding the log pile broke and spilled logs on top of Skinny. Reynolds says he left the mill after six. He passed Skinny on the street so he knew he was there. Says he didn't come back till he got a call. Scooter confirms it."

"Why would anybody want to kill Skinny Dearman?"

"Same question Milty asked about Judge Chancellor," he said.

"Same question I asked about my files. Why would anybody want a bunch of files that had nothing in them, as far as I could tell?"

"So, we have lots of grief and questions, but no proof of a damn thing."

"How about the cut on the judge's shoulder and the impressions beside the lake?" I asked.

"Enough to make any defense lawyer jump for joy," he said. "Missy, his housekeeper said he had stewed about the bid procedure since the day of the auction. The spectacle you made of yourself set him to thinking. It challenged him to see if he and Rose missed anything."

"Apparently he found something."

He shrugged. "Missy said, after Osstrum stirred everybody up, he reexamined each step of the process, then got excited about something. I guess he wanted a second opinion, so he called you."

"He say anything to Rose?"

"Only that he wanted to be certain there was nothing they missed. Gotta go. If I learn anything, I'll let you know."

"By the way," I said. "Could Dearman have been killed before the logs fell on him? To make it look like an accident."

"Yeah. No way to tell really. Those logs are damned heavy."

I sat on the back porch and stared down at the creek. I needed the stolen files. If the judge found something, I could too. Maybe that was why they were taken. Not so much for what they contained as for what they could tell me had I been as meticulous as the judge.

* * * * *

I called Osstrum at the office number he gave me.

"You said the liquidation committee sent TRS a copy of the bid packages for the tracts sold at auction," I said. "What happened to them?"

"I think our lawyer still has them."

"How about the final accounting and other documents from the auction? Stuff you copied from my files. Can you get copies? I'd like to take another look."

"I'll call our lawyer, and let you know."

I reported on assigned bank loans, then caught up on filing. I didn't mind doing the reports. The facts were in my head and I was paid for each one, but I hated to file. A decision had to be made about where to put each piece of paper.

That afternoon, I drove to Morgan's mill.

"Mr. Bone," he greeted me. "What brings you out?"

"Skinny Dearman, I'm searching for a reason. A way to get out of the house, frankly. I got tired of filing."

Scooter came to the door. "Dad, new load of logs. You want to look at 'em?" There was not a dry spot on his clothes. Sawdust covered every inch, like yellow sprinkles on a sheet cake.

"Dump 'em on the ground," Morgan told him. "I'll check 'em later."

"I'll get out, " I said.

"No, it's okay. You were asking about Skinny Dearman?"

"More curious than anything serious."

"My insurance agent is sure Skinny's wife'll sue me. That's what I know."

"Have you heard from a lawyer?"

"Not yet, but my agent has. And my rates will go up."

"On a threat of a lawsuit?"

"There was an accident. Skinny died. I may have to hire a full time night watchman just to keep my insurance, which I need under the loan. Every little squeeze hurts my bottom line, and Burl's offering my main customer a sweet deal if they'll switch."

"Will they?"

"I don't know. The buyer's a brother, but his boss isn't, and he also has a bottom line to watch. By the way," he added, "Prozini came by. Said he might have a buyer for the mill."

"What'd you tell him?"

"I told him I wasn't interested. Some people spend their lives in search of what makes 'em happy. I've found mine! I was born to run this mill, Bishop."

He stared out the window to where Scooter supervised the delivery of logs. "You said you were curious about Skinny? You know, Skinny didn't have to be where he was. The logs he was scaling were in a pile behind the office here. I can't see why he wandered off like he did. If he'd stayed in the scaling area, he'd still be alive."

"An interesting bit of information, Morgan."

"My opinion, nothing more. Could'a been walking by when the brace broke. Who knows? Anyway, that's what I wondered."

"More info than I had this morning. Thanks. Any more out of Otis?"

"A model of efficiency, Bishop. Works harder than any hand in the mill. Stays late, pitches in if anything goes wrong. Couldn't ask for a better employee, but Scooter says he's gonna get in trouble accusing people about his sister's death."

I added Morgan's question about where Skinny's body was found to the rest of my suspicions. Was it happenstance? I doubted it.

* * * * *

I risked an upset to the judge's housekeeper and drove to his apartment.

Missy came to the door, red eyed. I introduced myself and expressed condolences. Her last name was Hodge.

"You … you may have … oh, how I wish you'd never got involved! I don't mean to hurt your feelings, Mr. Bone, but I just know he got careless thinking about that horrid auction."

"I'm sorry," I said. "I'd like to see if there is anything more to his death than mere accident."

Her mouth dropped open. "What do you mean?"

I told her what I found at the lake and my thought about the vest. "Somebody stole my auction files, and on top of that, Skinny Dearman had a fatal accident. I—"

"Mr. Rose said that I wasn't to talk to anybody. There might be a lawsuit over all this, and the less I say the better." She made a move to shut the door.

"Before I leave, answer one question, please, to help me sleep better. Did the judge make notes while he reexamined the bid procedure?"

"Yes, sir. He said he was looking at their file like it was a big case. Wrote down everything on a pad of paper."

"Can I take a look at his notes."

"It's not here. He left it at the office. I suppose Mr. Rose has it."

I thanked her.

The newspaper awaited me, my only good news since morning coffee. I was on the verge of a depression. I didn't like being the cause of anybody's misfortune, in particular a death. And yet, Missy Hodge, and I imagine, Rose felt it was all my fault.

* * * * *

The next morning I got out of bed raring to see the judge's notes. If Rose refused, I considered going public with it.

The front porch doorbell rang as I dressed. I looked out front to see who in hell was out at that time of day. Son of a bitch! Half a dozen people. Some with cameras. There was a paneled truck with a TV station logo on the side and a satellite up link dish on top.

I opened the door to a barrage of questions.

"What do you say to the charge that your questions about the auction contributed to Judge Chancellor's death?"

Before I could answer, another asked, "Judge Chancellor's housekeeper said that he was so distracted by your challenge that he wasn't himself and that caused his death. Is that true?"

"She told you that?"

"His partner, Daniel Rose, quoted her."

The spiteful bastard wouldn't let it go. He wouldn't sue, so he came at me through the press, which in the long run could cost me more than a lawsuit. My bank clients would not like it.

"I recommend that all of you listen to the recording made of the auction. There was no challenge. Some of you were there. Did I challenge him in any way? All I did was to ask for a copy of the files."

"Mr. Rose said the judge took that as an implied challenge," a woman said.

"I am not responsible for how people take things, but I may have stimulated his thinking. Did Rose tell you the judge called me the day he died?"

No one answered.

"I'll tell you what he said. He said there might have been a loophole in the bid procedures. Now, since Mr. Rose put those procedures together, a loophole would be his responsibility. If the judge was distracted, it was as much Mr. Rose's responsibility as mine, maybe more."

The cameras whirred and the media representatives made notes.

I said, "I'm not surprised Mr. Rose would like for you to look at me as a culprit since his name is up for appointment to the Supreme Court. He doesn't want anyone to look at his negligence. Excuse me, now." I closed the door. I hoped the last bit would make the news.

They retreated.

Kathy called to commiserate when she saw the clip on the evening news. She knew how little I relished the public eye, especially a black eye. I could always count on her to understand.

That night I went to the Pub to get out, still pissed that Rose pointed a finger at me. "So nobody'd point one at him," I said to myself. The bastard! I wasn't optimistic my rebuttal to the press whipped down the notion that I was responsible. I could shout loophole till my face turned blue, but where was it? Until I found out, I'd be on Rose's hook. The judge had only raised the possibility of a loophole, a big leap from that to the real thing.

To hell with it! The Pub was filled with the sounds of country western. Patrons laughed and talked over dinner. It's why I came, the distraction. I ordered a mug at the Pub's copper-covered bar and took a long swallow. Damn good! Thankfully no one I knew was there. I wasn't in a mood to talk.

Jimmy Pitts and Caleb Washington strolled in. They choose to sit at a table in the bar area and ordered drinks from a bouncy waitress. Jimmy reached out to grab her hand. She laughed, said something and pulled away. I slid off the stool with my mug and walked to their table. It was worth the aggravation to find out if they knew anything.

"Gentlemen," I said, and flashed a smile I didn't feel. "Mind if I join you?"

They were startled, especially Caleb. We knew each other from the auction, but had not formally met. Jimmy matched my smile and gestured at a chair. Their waitress came back with two beers, flashed her big-tip smile and asked if I wanted a refill. I didn't. I wasn't there to get drunk. However, with the day I had, the thought was there.

Jimmy and Caleb competed for extra attention from the waitress. She'd get a good tip. As she switched away, a black woman in a white cook's uniform stuck her head through the kitchen doors and scanned the crowd. She dabbed her face with an apron then disappeared back to the kitchen.

Jimmy said. "You had anymore to do with Reynolds?"

"I dropped by after Skinny Dearman was killed. How will you cope with the loss, Mr. Washington?" I asked.

He fiddled with his beer. "Caleb," he said. "I'm not important enough to be a mister anything."

"Ask his wife," Jimmy said as he slapped Caleb's back. Caleb gave him a dirty look.

"It's hectic," he said. "Have to work my ass off to keep up. That's the God's truth if I ever told it. That boy could handle a lot of work. Gonna be 'effn hard to fill his shoes."

"Did you know he moonlighted at Reynolds' mill?"

"I didn't pay much attention to what he did after we finished for the day. You know what I mean? He may have said." He raised his hand with a finger gesture at his head. "Went in one ear and out the other." He shifted in his chair and reduced the beer in his glass by a long swallow. "How'd you know Skinny worked for me?"

"Jimmy told me."

His eyes shifted toward Jimmy. From the look on his face, I'd say he was still pissed at Jimmy's dig about his wife.

I decided to poke around a bit. "What did you tell Judge Chancellor?" I asked.

"What?" Caleb's eyes widened.

"What did you tell Judge Chancellor? You talked." If he denied it, I'd be no worse off.

"When?"

"Right before he died, after he took another look at the bid process you guys used for the auction."

Washington took a loud swallow then said, "Of course. What did we talk about? He mostly asked if I'd heard any, you know, talk? He was chasing some notion that the bidders may have rigged the bids, something that Osstrum guy spread around. That's about it."

"What'd you tell him?"

"I told him I hadn't heard a thing. Nothing to hear. Not a damn thing wrong with the auction. What's to hear?"

"What about you, Jimmy? What did he ask you?" I asked.

"He didn't tell you?" he asked.

"Some. I'm looking for details. His memory, you know." I touched my forehead.

"I don't remember a hell of a lot. Had work backed up at the kilns the day he called. Mostly he wanted to talk about how we selected the tract we put our bid on. He might have mentioned a bid rigging idea, now that I think about it. He didn't seem very concerned about it though."

I pushed the truth a bit and said, "He told me he'd discovered how the bids were rigged."

Caleb ran the back of his hand over his mouth as people do when they drink beer. "No shit! He said that? How about that? Hard to believe. How?"

I wished I knew. "We didn't get that far."

Jimmy added, "Wonder what he meant? Do you see anyway bids could have been rigged, Caleb?"

"Hell, no! Asinine to think they were! I reviewed the damned appraisals from start to finish with Daniel before the auction date. Not a damn thing wrong with them. Judge Chancellor and Daniel checked the documents. No way in hell were any bids rigged. The judge was getting up there." He raised his eyebrows with facial gesture.

"Senile. You think he was senile?"

"I can't say for sure, but, hell, you know, you just said so yourself, he wasn't as sharp as he once was. Hell, you hit eighty you slow down some. Confused, more like."

"Did you keep copies of the bid packages or the full appraisals? In case you ever have to do it again?" I asked Caleb.

He shook his head no. "Daniel said that black guy from Chicago, Prozini, wanted all copies of everything we had."

An equivocal answer. What somebody wants and what they get are not always the same. I drained the remains of my mug and left. I drove by the library. Kathy might be working late. She did now and then. The lights were on inside. A maintenance man said all the staff had gone home. The route home took me back past the Pub.

What the hell! A scuffle on the sidewalk! Caleb, Jimmy and Otis Patterson! Up side of Otis' rippling muscles, Caleb and Jimmy looked overmatched. Otis shoved Caleb in the chest with his palms. Caleb shoved back and Jimmy raised his fists. Otis grabbed his shirtfront and threw him against Caleb's van. Caleb caught Otis in a chokehold and yanked him backward. Jimmy came off the van and hit Otis in the stomach.

I stopped the jeep and yelled out the door, "What's going on?"

Caleb released his chokehold. "Nothing," he replied. "Some asshole can't see in the dark."

Otis rubbed his neck and gasped for breath. He motioned with his fists, but another car on the street stopped him. He staggered away. Jimmy stepped forward like he might give chase, but shouted instead. "Bastard." He flexed his hand to see if any bones were broken.

I drove on. It hit me as I pulled off the blacktop onto my driveway. Otis probably accused Caleb or Jimmy or both, of involvement with his sister. Ah, another light came on. The black cook who peered at the crowd. She scouted for Otis. That's how he knew to show up. I'd pass that on to the chief.

Chapter 12

Rose sent a demand letter for me to make a public apology for my "slanderous" remarks about him to the media. As far as I knew, hell hadn't frozen over so my return letter demanded the same from him. One bastard to another. Score, zero to zero.

However, I knew that kind of confrontational back and forth name-calling would end up in litigation unless I made a move, so a couple of days later, I girded up my loins and drove to his office for a friendly sit-down. Thirty minutes of discussion beat the hell out of a year's worth of litigation. I learned that the first year out of law school. The receptionist relayed the message that I was there to see Mr. Rose. Rose's picture with the governor on the wall behind the receptionist jumped out at me. His high water mark?

She asked me to take a seat. "It may be a minute," she said.

I was half a page into an old National Geographic when Mrs. Lee, the prim lady who helped Rose at the auction appeared. "Mr. Bone," she said. "Mr. Rose asked me to talk to you. Would you come into the conference room?" She gestured toward a room on the left.

Damn! Plush chairs around a polished table atop an expensive Oriental rug. Inlaid wood ceiling with bookcases to match. High tax bracket room. In a space on one wall were three original oils of Louisiana swamp scenes a collector would envy. Who would have thought it of Rose?

A window in the front wall plus recessed overhead lights lit the room.

"Nice," I said with a hand gesture at the paintings.

"One of Chance's clients gave those to him for a case he handled. Before he became judge."

I was relieved. For a time there, I thought Rose had taste.

We sat down.

"Now, what did you want to see Mr. Rose about?"

"I want to put an end to our public squabble. I didn't cause Judge Chancellor's death any more than he did. Lets face it, at the judge's age and condition, he shouldn't be in a boat alone, but it made him happy." I left out my suspicions. "Personally, I'd rather go out happy than in a hospital bed ringing for my final shot of pain killer."

"I see. Let me see if Mr. Rose can squeeze out a few minutes." She left.

Rose appeared, forced a smile, and stuck out his hand. He was still a mean-faced man in a black suit and tie, but I was there to negotiate, not criticize. He looked me in the eyes and said, "Dora said you'd like to make peace." He sat down and made an open palm gesture to invite me to make my case. Arrogant asshole, I thought, but let it go.

"I don't think I had anymore to do with the judge's death than, say, a New York Times crossword puzzle. Missy Dodge says that he often got lost solving one problem or another."

He opened his mouth to speak but closed it.

"When you get right down do it, I'm not sure distraction is what caused your partner's death."

His mouth opened again. "What? What do you mean?"

"Let me ask you a question first. What did the judge say to you the day he died? You do know he asked me to meet him at the lake."

"Missy told me he had. And, you want to know what he said to me?"

I did.

He did a nervous finger roll on the tabletop and stared at the ceiling as he considered my question.

Decision made, he said, "Okay. He had been in an agitated state since the auction. Osstrum called him. As I reflect on it now, Osstrum's call might have pushed him over. You … well, in the interest of peace, I'll say that while the objections you raised at the auction provoked him, without Osstrum, he might have let it go."

Progress, but not there yet. He hadn't actually answered my question. I tried again. "He told me he found a loophole in your procedures." Actually the judge said he "may have found one," but why equivocate?

"He told you that?" Rose pushed back from the table with a frown. "Hmm, he never said anything that specific to me. Nothing." He shook his head. "Just said he'd been double checking our procedures. Turning over possibilities."

"You were his partner and you put together the plans for the auction. I would have thought he—"

"Are you saying I'm holding back?" He came out of his chair.

"No, indeed, Mr. Rose, far from it." I did think it was a possibility. However, I was there to make peace, not war. "We need to keep sensitivities out of this meeting. Not fit for a future member of the Mississippi Supreme Court to display sensitivities, wouldn't you say?" I knew I shouldn't have said it the second it left my mouth. The devil made me do it, that and the fact that every time I looked at Rose's face I wanted to knock the shit out of him.

His face flushed red. He leaned over the table to respond, but I beat him to it.

"I'm sorry," I said. "I apologize if that came out wrong. No disrespect intended. Let me put it another way."

He eased back into his chair.

I continued. "Missy Hodge said the judge made notes as he reexamined the bid process. I know he talked to Caleb Washington and the bidders so he was well into an analysis. It's possible the notes he made during the reexamination might tell us something."

He said, "Missy told me you asked about them. I know he was making notes, but his notepad isn't in this building. Missy searched the apartment. I can only assume that the cleaning crew threw it away. He may have left them in here where he was working. The janitor might have thought it was trash."

"You checked the trash?"

"Of course."

"You were telling me what he'd said, the day he died," I repeated. The man was like a hostile witness. Have to drag answers out of him.

"Not much. I was in court when he left for lunch. He told Dora that he wanted to talk to me 'in the morning.' Didn't say why. I'm not even sure if it had anything to do with the auction. We have other cases we're working together."

I had hoped for a break. Didn't get it. Back to do-it-myself. "How about the bid packages and your procedures? Did you keep a copy of what you gave John Prozini?"

"Of course we kept a copy of our procedures, but John took the extra bid packages and all the auction information, including the detailed appraisals."

"Even the tract maps you displayed?"

"The ones Caleb put together?"

"Yeah."

"Chance had them at one time, I think. I suppose to take a second look, if he felt the need. I don't know where they are at this moment. They'll probably turn up. I don't recall if John got them or not. They were of no use to us."

I said, "I often kept documents from complex transactions in case similar deals came up in the future. Oddly enough, they did."

He said, "I've done that too. And sure, I was tempted to bootleg a copy of everything, as a kind of template should we ever do another auction, or maybe for a bar association seminar, but John insisted on getting everything, so I didn't."

"Did you find that odd?"

"Not at all. Osstrum's bunch wants to sue for mismanagement. John wants to destroy anything that could be distorted by their attorney, should it come to that. Why do you bring that up? What does it have to do with Chance's death?"

"What if the judge was killed because of his investigation."

"Killed! Good God man! You think Chance was murdered? Ridiculous!" He raised out of his chair again. I thought to bolt to his office, but he eased back down.

"Look at the facts. Skinny Dearman and the judge are dead. Both were knee-deep in the auction. The judge said he'd found a loophole. Not hard for me to think both were killed to cover up something." I didn't mention the cut on the judge's shoulder. As far as I knew the chief hadn't made it public.

He shook his head and said, "With all due respects, Bone, I don't believe it. You may be trying to absolve yourself from guilt. Don't be offended. I know the feeling. I've lost cases I felt I should have won. Chance's death was accidental. Dearman's too. Talk to Chief Jenkins." He sneaked a look at his watch.

"You probably have work to do," I said. "I'll leave. Do you mind if I talk to Mrs. Hodge?"

"Waste of time, but go ahead. Don't upset her, please."

That gave rise to the ultimate question, the one I came there to get answered. "By the way, anything further on the lawsuit by the bidders Osstrum harassed? Maybe called is a better way to describe it."

"Are we finished with public innuendoes?" he asked.

"As far as I'm concerned."

"I'll advise against it," he said.

I detoured by the library to ask Kathy to share a pepper-beef sandwich at the Pub. One was too big to eat alone. I wanted to see her. I needed her smile to pick me up.

We grabbed a table along the wall and caught up on each other's news.

"Are you serious?" she asked after I'd recited my back and forth with Rose in particular my suggestion that the Judge and Skinny were murdered. "You think they were murdered? That's hard to believe, Bishop."

"That was Rose's reaction too," I said. "I don't know if the judge knew the bids were rigged or not, but I believe he found a way to rig them and wanted to bounce it off me. His investigation may have spooked somebody who didn't want the scrutiny."

"Somebody who really knows how to use a casting rod, right?"

"Yeah, I know. It sounds off the wall, but it'd be no problem to a good fisherman. And if it hadn't worked, the killer probably had a back-up plan."

"How do you tie Skinny Dearman's death to the judge's?"

"He was part of the auction. Maybe something the judge said made him suspicious. Could be he mentioned it to the wrong person. He knew everybody involved in the auction, all the bidders. Sure must have known the timber they auctioned."

"What are you going to do next?"

See the judge's housekeeper.

* * * * *

A white apron covered Missy Hodge's blue wraparound, her gray hair neatly arranged.

"Mr. Bone. Come in. Dora said you might call. I just made a fresh pot of coffee."

"I'd love a cup."

She brought me a cup. We talked in the apartment's sparsely furnished living area.

"I've looked all over for any notes Chance brought home. I can't find anything. Most likely left them at the office."

"Could he have taken them to the lake with him? That day?"

I could see by the look on her face that she hadn't considered that. "I don't know, Mr. Bone. I just don't know. I didn't see them if he did, but to tell the truth, I wasn't looking."

"Well, he must have discussed what he was doing with you. What he was thinking."

"He liked to ramble, Chance did. Always thinking about this and that. He was such a fine man." She lowered her face to brush the tears from her eyes.

"Good coffee," I said.

"Thank you," she said. "Where was I?"

"The judge liked to talk."

"Yes. I remember. He did. I couldn't always tell if he was talking to himself or me. Lots of things had to do with the law. Most of it was beyond me. He went on about that auction. It was on his mind from the first day, after that ruckus y'all, uh, had in the courtroom and after that man, Mr. Osstrum, called."

I didn't offer a rebuttal. Some feelings died hard.

"Can you remember anything, any phrase, any comment? Did he ever mention Skinny Dearman."

"He talked to Mr. Dearman on the phone, a couple of times. And all the appraisers and the bidders after that Mr. Osstrum claimed something had to be wrong with the auction. He claimed they'd lost a lot of money. Chance got concerned."

"Did he say why?"

"He was worried that he'd overlooked something. 'But how could that be, Missy? Too many people looking over our shoulders,' was the way he put it."

"Anything else?"

"One thing. How'd he put it? 'The appraisals were on the low side. Prozini said appraise low to get the bidders out. Not a surprise to anybody that the bids came in low. Human nature. Doesn't make it a conspiracy. I would have bid low.'"

"When he called me from the lake, he said he found a loophole. Did he tell you that?"

"Hmm, no, he never said anything about a loophole. Last thing he said to me was, 'Murphy's law, Missy, Murphy's Law. Just like Bone said.

I can't say for a fact, but it looks to me like there was a way. I should have been on my toes. That's what comes from getting old, Missy.' He wasn't old, Mr. Bone."

She bowed her head, took a sip of coffee and wiped away another tear with the edge of her apron.

I thanked her. The judge had found a loophole! I figured he had. Now, all I had to do was find it.

The humidity was high, and the heat damn near unbearable. The canvas top of my jeep let it all through and the air conditioning did little more than make noise. I needed a new one, but it'd have to wait for my billable time to build up.

The azaleas in my front yard looked wilted as I charged up my steps. It was one of those days when, budget notwithstanding, I turned on the air conditioning and enjoyed the merciful cool. I called Mrs. Lee to ask if she'd run me a copy of their auction procedures. She'd ask Mr. Rose. She didn't call back. My thoughts drifted to Skinny Dearman. What did he have to do with it? I knew he'd appraised some of the parcels being auctioned. I knew the judge had called him. Could be that Skinny told his wife something. I introduced myself on the phone and told her that I'd met Skinny at the Pitts' mill and how sorry I was to hear what happened.

"I miss him, Mr. Bone. A lot."

I wondered if I could drop by one afternoon. "Just to say hello. See if there's anything I can do."

"I doubt there is. Everybody's been helping out, but you can come by if you want to. Any time's okay. I'm not working right now. I'm going to Mama's this afternoon. The preacher will be there. Could you make it tomorrow afternoon?"

I called Dora Lee to again ask for a copy of the procedures used at the auction.

She said, "Mr. Rose is concerned about violating a continuing duty to TRS. He's called Mr. Prozini for authorization. We don't know if they'd help you anyway. It's just a series of steps and sub-steps telling what each member of the liquidation team was supposed to do."

I still wanted to see it. I wanted to see everything that had anything to do with the auction. I missed whatever the judge, and quite possibly Skinny, had spotted.

She'd call back as soon as they heard from Prozini.

I wasn't optimistic. Prozini could be anyplace in the country, glad-handing fresh investors at cocktail parties.

"By the way," I said, "Mr. Rose said the large tract maps used at the auction to give a visual of the tracts were around the office someplace." I had thought they were too general to be of any use, but that was before the Judge died. Maybe he saw something I didn't.

"Mr. Washington put those together."

"Right. Do you know where they are? I talked with Mr. Rose about them. I want to look at them."

"I've seen them but not recently. I'll see if I can locate them. Are you sure Mr. Prozini didn't take them?" she asked. "He wanted everything."

"No, but Mr. Rose wasn't sure," I said.

She'd look around and call me if she found anything.

I was thinking on the back porch, searching my thoughts for that damned elusive "loophole" when the chief drove up. Like Kathy, he parked at the back, less distance to walk to the creek. He got out, fishing tackle in hand. He looked up where I stood in the opened screen door.

"Let's catch a few," he said.

"Not for me. Got too many things on my mind."

"You gonna pass up that?" He pointed with his tackle at the creek and beyond. It was a sight to see. The creek ran clear, the sun danced off its currents and the beavers pushed sticks into their damn. Resident ducks paddled about the pond and dove for minnows. Each time something silver came out of the creek's rippling creek waters, the chief edged closer to the trail down.

"Go on," I told him. "I'll watch you pull them in. By the way, anything on the scuffle between Otis and Caleb Washington and Jimmy Pitts?"

"They're striking right now, Bishop." He exhaled. "Okay. I'll make it quick. Caleb claims Otis showed up, cursed and accused them of carrying on with his sister. They denied it, but who knows? No real harm done, so we'll leave it where it is, his word against theirs."

He'd also cautioned Hattie Brown, one of the cooks at the Pub not to stir up trouble. "You keep me busy, Bishop." A smile took the edge off his complaint.

"Hattie said the talk in the kitchen was that Chandra rode with somebody on a motorcycle. When a waitress said that Jimmy Pitts drove up on a motorcycle, Hattie called Otis. I told her she might be the cause of somebody getting hurt real bad if she kept it up. She couldn't describe who Chandra rode with. Just a motorcycle. Lots of men around town have motorcycles."

Yeah, but do they drink at the Pub?

He wandered on down to the creek's edge and began casting. A few minutes later, I gave up and joined him.

* * * * *

When I called Osstrum to see if he'd had gotten copies of the bid documents, he sounded down in the dumps, maybe drunk. Possibly both.

"No," he said. "Our lawyer got a temporary injunction to stop Prozini from throwing anything away, but he'll contest it. In any case, he most likely tossed the documents before they made it to his office. We're a day late and a dollar short."

"Doesn't he need it for tax returns? Reports to the investors?"

"The bookkeeper said he told her to use the final liquidation report to show sales prices. The inventory was worth so much on our books and brought in so much at the auction. Anything left, after taxes, will be distributed to investors, pro rata. I doubt there'll be a hell of a lot. Most of what I get will go to the banks to cover my loans."

"How about the stuff you copied the day you were here?"

"I got that and some other files from Chicago, the summary appraisals. Not the detailed ones that you had. Not a hell of a lot in the summary appraisals. You want a copy?"

"If it wouldn't be too much trouble."

He'd bring what he had over the weekend.

Technically, Osstrum was a suspect. His wife died and he lost a lot of money. It wasn't too much of a stretch to suppose that he held the judge responsible, possibly Dearman as well. He didn't strike me that way, but the jails were full of people who looked innocent. One problem with that. Why would he come back to steal my files? He had copied what he wanted. Unless it was to divert suspicion away from himself. And, was he a fisherman? Could he cast well enough to snag the Judge's shoulder?

Chapter 13

Claire Dearman said 'mid-afternoon' so I arrived at two thirty, and parked under tall pines at the front of the house. They swayed in the breeze and moved patches of shade back and forth over the ground. Drifts of green lay in the yard, evidence of a fresh cut. Fragrance from pink, red and blue blossoms arose from flowerbeds at the porch steps. The beds had just been weeded.

Skinny Dearman's young widow opened the door to my knock. Her face was somber; her dark eyes bloodshot. Her lustrous dark hair brushed the shoulders of a plain dress. I introduced myself.

"Come in. The house's a mess I'm afraid. I haven't been able to think straight. People have been so good. The church has been over every day, bringing food and just being so kind." She forced a smile. The room didn't look all that bad. A blanket and book lay on the sofa, along with a pillow. Vacuum cleaner prominent. A couple of boxes partially filled with papers.

She looked out the window into the front yard and said they'd cut the grass and weeded that morning. I bragged on the yard. It looked good. She cleared the sofa so I could sit.

"Mr. and Mrs. Washington sent a fruit basket." It was on the floor by the door into the kitchen. "Caleb drops by when he can. He's been a dear. He says he doesn't know what he'll do without Skinny." She paused for a sigh.

I handed her the sympathy card and Wal-Mart gift certificate I'd brought. My ex-wife taught me well. She thanked me and lay both on the fireplace mantle. A picture of Skinny and Claire hung over it. A couple more, smaller ones, of people I didn't know stood on top of the mantle.

"Can I get you a glass of sweet tea?" she asked. "I'm having one."

Hers was on the coffee table in front of the sofa.

"Sounds good."

When she returned with the tea, she said, "The Pitts sent a plant. Jimmy called to say how sorry they all were. It was so nice of him to call. Mr. Reynolds called too. He offered me a part time job in the office. I don't think I'll take it though. Skinny said they were hardly covering their overhead. Besides, somebody from Mr. Rose's office came to see me about filing a law suit." She sat in a soft chair facing me. Sofa and chair matched, a floral pattern.

Damn it! That's all Morgan needed.

"I don't want to sue Mr. Reynolds. Skinny said he was good people. Caleb thinks I should sue. What do you think, Mr. Bone? You're a lawyer."

"I can't give you any advice, Mrs. Dearman. I don't represent Mr. Reynolds, but I do know him. I wouldn't feel right to advise you one way or the other."

"Mr. Rose said it'd be the insurance company paying."

"That's right to a certain extent. His insurance company would pay any settlement. And that would depend on what, if anything, Reynolds did wrong. I can't say because I don't know enough about mill safety requirements."

She said she'd think on it. "Skinny had a little life insurance. That'll help. As soon as I'm able, I'm going to look for work. I don't want to mope around here all day."

"Best to keep busy," I said.

"That's what Mama says."

"Did Skinny ever talk about his work?"

She gave me a blank look. "Sure. Everyday. What do you mean?"

It was clear I'd have to ask a direct question. "You see, I think it odd that Skinny and Judge Chancellor had accidents so close together."

She frowned. "Skinny was always talking about his job. I never understood half of it though. Cruising a tract of timber. Goodness me, I thought that was what me and Skinny used to do on his old motorcycle on Saturday nights when he was at JC. Come to find out, it had to do with timber." She gave a nervous kind of laugh.

A motorcycle? Hattie told the chief that Chandra had been riding with somebody on a motorcycle! I bet she was hitching a ride with Skinny to class. Was there more than that? I didn't dare ask Claire, but I'd mention it to the chief.

I smiled and asked my next question. "Was he mad at anybody?"
She shook her head no.

I tried a different approach. "Was anybody mad at him?"

"He never had an enemy in the world! Everybody says the brace broke and the logs fell on him. It was an accident. Wasn't it?"

"As far as I know."

"Why are you asking?"

"I'm sorry. I didn't mean to upset you."

"It seems like you think maybe it wasn't an accident."

I gave one of those "who knows" gestures with my hands, but didn't answer. "Did he talk about the auction?"

"He thought he should be paid more. He worked hard. He said everybody made big money but him." At that point, she sat the glass of tea on the coffee table, but instead of letting it go, just held on and stared at it. After a couple of seconds, she straightened up, looked at me and said, "You know … he did say something one day."

I leaned forward to encourage her to continue.

"It was the day Caleb was here. Skinny was talking about that guy who'd called. I can't remember his name."

"Osstrum?"

"Sounds like it. Anyway, he said the guy complained about how much money they'd lost. Skinny said he'd pretty near accused him of making a mistake on his appraisals … came close to saying Skinny had done something wrong. And the judge called too. Skinny said he put him through the wringer. It upset Skinny a lot to be talked to like that. He said he had to think about it."

She went on to say that Skinny never said anything else about it, and never said what, if anything, he meant to do about it. Then, the logs fell on him. Too damn much of a coincidence to suit me.

I thanked her for the tea and for talking to me. I knew it must have been hard.

She swabbed at her nose with a tissue. "Thanks for coming, Mr. Bone. I'm fixing to get up and clean this place. That's what Skinny would want me to do. He was counting on going out on his own one day. He told me …" She choked up and closed the door. I heard her crying as I walked away still mulling over all she'd said.

＊ ＊ ＊ ＊ ＊

A story in the paper about a Jackson art exhibition of Mississippi impressionists caught Kathy's eye. One of the artists lived in Lawton. That was the motivating force behind the trip, that and just a reason to spend time together. We drove up on Sunday. It was one of those summery days in Mississippi where there was enough breeze to keep the heat at bay. Kathy's snug summery outfit, gathered at the waist, turned heads as we strolled through the viewing rooms.

"Beautiful," she said of a collection of watercolors done by the Lawton artist. "She caught the sun sparkling on the waves. See the sea gulls hovering over breaking waves. There," she pointed, "waves washing onto the sand. So peaceful and relaxing."

I couldn't see a damn thing but shades of blue and white with splashes of yellow. She put her arm around my waist and pulled me close. "When you look at art, Mr. Bone," she said, "you don't look for anything specific. If you do, you will look right past the impression the artist captured, the soul of the scene."

"Uh, as in, don't focus on details but on its impact when you see it."

"That's it," she said. "Let the image run through your mind until it finds a resting place. When it does, it'll tell you the impression it's made. That's a mood."

"Not me trying to tell it?"

She gave me a squeeze. What did that tell me?

We ate at a place in the shadow of the Capitol building. It was the Lawton equivalent of the Blue Plate Café. It had a rickety, wide front porch, and a squeaky front door. When we walked inside, a mouthwatering aroma of fried chicken, breaded pork chops and fried catfish met our noses. There was also a spread of fresh collard greens, field peas and hot cornbread right out of the oven.

Our impression? We thought it had been too long since we'd last eaten. We proceeded to load our plates, somewhat indiscriminately. Collards were said to have been brought over by African slaves. Good idea, I thought. The ones we ate that day were some of the best I'd ever had. I'm ashamed to say we ate in complete silence for awhile. Who needed talk when there were so many tastes to be experienced? When we slowed down, Kathy smiled and said, "I can see what you think of the food. What did you think of the exhibition?"

"I don't know if I'll ever understand impressionism."

"You don't have any problem getting an impression from a bunch of facts." She wagged a finger at me. "It's your impression that the TRS auction had something to do with Judge Chancellor's death, Skinny Dearman's too. Everybody else sees both as accidents."

"Could be that their impressions are better than mine."

"You don't believe that for a minute, do you?"

No.

For dessert, we chose the lemony "icebox pie," a southern favorite.

Late the next Monday, the files Osstrum retrieved from Chicago, plus those he copied of mine, were delivered. I read through each for anything odd, much as I had with the files Rose gave me after the auction. Tracts of timber were described, road locations and estimated quantities of timber, and estimated values given for the timber and land. I preferred the detailed appraisals that Rose kept in the conference room for prospective bidders—the ones somebody stole—but Osstrum never had those and Prozini most likely disposed of the ones he got with the rest of what he picked up in Lawton. I finished none the wiser. I was beginning to doubt there was anything wrong with the auction even if the judge felt he'd found a loophole.

A bank asked me to visit a shop in Oxford, the home of Ole Miss University. The owners did not make loan payments and would not take the bank's calls. The shop had done well, then the payments stopped. When I arrived, a sign on the front door said, "closed." I banged on the door until the owners let me in. I got the story. They returned from a month long vacation to find the shop closed and their daughter in tears, alone with their grandson. Their son-in-law was gone and their bank account was empty. Drugs, they said. I urged them to refinance their home, take the excess equity out to catch up the loan payments, and to buy new inventory. They agreed and vowed never to go on vacation again.

It made no sense to go home since I had to meet a florist near Memphis the next morning. So, I drove to Memphis, checked into the old Peabody Hotel, ducks and all, and had a night of "blues" and great barbecue ribs on Beale Street. I wished Kathy were with me.

I slept reasonably well that night. Maybe it was a mistake.

* * * * *

Otis shoved the phone to his ear.

"This be Otis Patterson?" a man's voice asked.

"What you want!" Otis replied.

"I hear you looking for the white dude who knocked up yo' sister, Chandra."

"So what?"

"I know who done it."

"I'm short right now. Have to catch me payday."

"I'll get it later, man. Dude's name's Bishop Bone. Lives out in the country."

"How you know it was him? First I heard his name."

"I done heard him talking to his buddies, some tall dude with gray hair and some other one, about the fun he had with her. The things he made her do. He was bragging big time, Bro."

"I'll take care of that bastard! Where does he live?"

The caller gave directions.

"If she was my sister, I'd feel the same way as you."

"Much obliged, Bro," Otis said.

Click.

Bro? Otis frowned. Who gives a fuck? I got me a name. Bishop Bone did it to Chandra.

* * * * *

When I got home from Memphis that night, my plan was to call Kathy and get something cold from the fridge when a black shadow waving a baseball bat flew at me from behind the porch steps. The meat end was aimed at my head. I used my briefcase to block the blow. Even so, it drove me backwards. I hit the ground, stunned. The briefcase was dead. I threw the bent briefcase at the guy and jumped to my feet. That's when I saw his face. Otis Patterson!

"Hold it, Otis! What the hell are you doing?" I shouted.

"I'm gonna kill you, you mother fucker!"

"Hold on! You're making a mistake."

"Ain't no mistake! You made the mistake, fucking Chandra and leaving her to die. Now you gonna die!" He parried the baseball bat and closed in. I sidestepped toward the rear of the cabin.

"Wait a damn minute! Think, man! I've never met your sister. Never! Somebody's feeding you a pile of shit!"

"Ain't no shit! You done it! You been bragging! I heard!" He whipped the bat at me. I ducked and stumbled backwards.

Just when I thought I wouldn't need my automatic, I did. I backed down the slope toward the creek where I could dive in and swim to safety.

A noise came from the driveway, but I didn't stop to look. I had to duck and back away from Otis' bat. When he saw the creek behind me, my escape, he charged. I turned to run, but fell flat on my face. I rolled over to see Otis' raised bat about to smash my head.

I stuck out my hands. "You're making a—"

Crack! Something black snaked around the big end of the bat and yanked it backwards. It was a whip, a damn pretty sight. I couldn't see who was on the other end, but I was damned glad. As Otis jerked to free the bat, I jumped up and hurried toward the cabin, specifically, to get my twenty-two automatic.

Otis cursed me and jerked at the bat again.

A voice said, "Turn it loose, Otis. Right now or I'll whip you good, boy!" A black man I'd never seen before stepped into the light, gasping to catch his breath. "You put that bat down." He wore an old felt hat and work clothes, wet through.

Otis turned toward the old man.

"Grandpa?"

"Turn it loose."

Otis lowered the bat. The anger in his face drained away. I edged closer to the porch steps.

The black man, who came from nowhere to save my butt, grabbed the bat and threw it into the brush. "I ought to whip yo' black ass till you can't shit! Ain't got no cause to put me and your granny through this again!"

"He's the one who killed Chandra," Otis said, pointing at me.

"That's what they got the law for," the old man said. "You don't know he done anything."

"A … bro told me."

"That don't make it so. Last week it was some other one. Week before was somebody else. Getting them names. Paying hard-earned money for a bunch of no good names. That woman ain't seen nothin' but talkin'. You ain't got spit to go with it and now you ain't got no money either."

I had one foot on the steps. "Listen, for whatever it's worth," I said. "Whoever told you I had anything to do with your sister was lying."

"You hear that, boy! That man says he didn't do it! Look at that man! Look now!"

Otis turned his face.

"Chandra wouldn't look twice at the likes of him no how," the old man said. "She went for them flaaashy types, them no good kind with the easy money up front but warn't to be found when she got on to needing help. This here man ain't one of them. He's a working man."

Damned if he didn't have me pegged.

Otis stared hard at me, assessing what his grandpa said. I was half way up the steps. No matter how their debate turned out, I felt safer.

The old man turned to me and said, "Mr. Bone. Yes, Sir, I knows who you are. I seen you on the television many a time. I'm begging you to let this here crazy boy go. I'm sorry I was late getting here. Elsa told me soon as I come through the door what this boy was up to. I'm this crazy boy's grandpa, Willie Patterson." He lifted his hat and rubbed his arm over his face to soak up the sweat rolling down. The old man's white eyebrows and head showed brightly in my security lights.

"I drove fast as I could, but my old truck give out of gas about half a mile down the road. I run the rest of the way." He'd caught his breath by that time.

"I thank you for that," I said. It was most likely the understatement of my life. I reached for the screen door.

"Did you hear me, Mr. Bone? Don't go in there and call the law. I'm begging you to let this pass. This boy's got some good in him. I know he does. He's a good boy at heart. Elsa and me raised him after his mama done run off. He works hard at the mill. You ask Mr. Morgan Reynolds."

"Mr. Patterson, I'd be doing the same thing in your place, but I don't think you're the one who should be." I gestured at Otis. I opened the screen door and went inside. It felt good to get something between Otis and me.

"Yes, Sir, I reckons you right. Otis, you get down on your knees and beg this man to let this pass! You hear me! As God is my witness, I'll beat you till you can't stand up." He unrolled his whip.

Otis looked at him, then at me. He dropped to the earth, on his knees. I had a hunch forcing a boy that headstrong to beg wasn't the thing to do.

"Tell you what, Mr. Patterson," I said. "You look like you could use a drink of water." I had in mind something stronger for me.

"Let's talk about this inside, out of the way of the mosquitoes." I slapped enough on the steps to qualify for a blood transfusion. The first thing on my agenda was my automatic. Otis looked calm enough just then, but who could say how long it might last.

"Let's see if we can sort this out," I said. They came through the screen door as I slid the automatic into my pocket. I gave the old gentleman a glass of ice water. He turned it up and finished it without pause. I gave him another. Otis didn't want anything. I would get something after they went. We sat down at my worktable.

"Otis," I said, "you just tried to kill me and would have if your grandpa hadn't shown up when he did. They wouldn't just tell you to leave town, like the last time."

"I didn't break into no car," he said about the crime he'd been accused of before.

"I don't know anything about that, but I know you tried to kill me."

He lowered his eyes. "Yes, sir, I ain't denying it. I'm sorry. I ain't mad at you no more. Grandpa's most likely right. Ain't no way Chandra'd look at the likes of you twice. Somebody done fooled with my head. When I find out—" His grandpa stopped him with a sharp look.

I appreciate brutal frankness. I would have appreciated it even more fifteen minutes earlier.

"You may not be mad right now, but how do I know you won't get another phone call and get mad all over again?"

"He won't," his grandpa said. "He ain't never broke his word to me and his grandma. Has you, boy?"

"No, sir. I ain't gonna bother you no more. I swear it to the Lord."

"Amen," the old man muttered.

"The next phone call might not be about me."

He looked at his grandpa and said, "I ain't gonna bother nobody no more, Grandpa. I'm gonna let it pass."

Willie Patterson patted the boy's shoulder.

"Suppose I do this. I'll make a report to Chief Jenkins but ask him to hold it. No charges, but if anything happens to me in the future, or to anybody else who knew Chandra for that matter, he'll know where to start looking."

Mr. Patterson said he'd rather I didn't make a report but didn't argue about it. Otis simply shook his head and stared down at the table.

"Before I do that," I said, "I want to know something from you."

He raised his face.

"Who called you?"

He shook his head. "Don't know. Said he was a brother. Didn't sound like a brother, now I think on it. More like some white dude trying to sound like a brother."

"What were you thinking, Boy?" Mr. Patterson asked. "Letting somebody stampede you like that!"

"Man be messing with my head, I expect. I was thinking more on what the dude said. I'm sorry, Grandpa."

"Uh huh."

"Who else have you been calling?" I asked.

He handed me a folded piece of paper from his back pocket. Over twenty handwritten names were scrawled on it.

"Hattie give 'em to me. Ain't called all of 'em yet."

I scanned the list. I knew some. Washington, Dearman, Rose, both Pitts, Ray Cooper, one of Kathy's old suitors, no surprise there, he was a chaser. The others I'd never heard of.

At one time or the other, all could have been at a table being serviced by Chandra. That didn't prove that any of them had a relationship with the young woman. Rose might have been in the Pub with Jimmy Pitts or Burl too, but I imagine a woman would get more action out of a dead man. Dearman was likely a classmate at JC and may have picked her up for class, but I doubted it went any further than that. Though I'd only seen him briefly, Dearman didn't strike me as the type to dabble about. But, who knows when a man will reach the limits of his moral resolve. I left it as a possibility, albeit a remote one.

Except for me, Otis said he'd only confronted Washington and Pitts face to face. That was the night they scuffled outside the Pub. The ones he called didn't admit anything, he said.

"Did you know Skinny Dearman?"

"I seen him at the mill."

"What'd he say when you asked him about Chandra?"

"Never did ask. Was going to, never got the chance. Them logs fell on him."

I couldn't tell if he was lying or not.

"What about Judge Chancellor. You didn't like him." The chief intimated as much when he told me about Otis' prior run in with the law.

"That old man made me say I'd did something I hadn't. I ain't never broke into no car. Hadn't been for him, I'd been here when Chandra needed me."

"Did you talk to him?"

He shook his head. "I knew Chandra wouldn't have nothing to do with him. Old man like that."

"Didn't you want to pay him back for what he did to you?"

"My mind was set on finding who run off after they put that baby in Chandra's belly."

"You keep on with this vendetta and sure as hell, you're going to end up in jail or worse. Folks don't like being accused of something they didn't do."

"Yes, sir. I told you I wasn't gonna do nothing else. It's the law's job. Like Grandpa says."

Just then he thought that. What about when he got another call?

"Got yourself a good job now," Willie said. "Working for a good man. Best you think on that Otis Patterson. Jesus done said that vengeance was his, not yours."

"Yes, sir. I will. I swear."

I took the gallon of lawnmower gas from the shed and drove to the old man's truck. He said he had more at home. After a couple of tries, the engine fired. By then, Otis retrieved his car from down the road where he'd left it and pulled up. They drove away in tandem.

My shotgun stayed by my bed that night. It most likely slept better than I did.

Chapter 14

I handed my report of the attack to the chief the next morning and explained what happened.

He looked me over, searching for bruises, then turned his attention to the first paragraph of the report. From there, he flipped to Hattie Brown's list of names, and read through it slowly. He glanced up a couple of times to frown or shake his head to show his surprise at one name or another.

"Your old buddy, Ray Cooper's on the list." He ribbed me. "I'm not surprised, stud like that."

Kathy and Ray were tennis partners at one time. I had a knock-down-drag-out with him in the Pub one night after he asked Kathy to marry him. He backed off. A wise decision as far as I was concerned.

"His new wife's left him already," he said.

That'd meant he would be on the prowl again.

"I just had an idea, Chief," I said.

"Yeah," he said.

"Chandra had a car, didn't she?" I asked.

She did. Just bought it, he told me. A few weeks before she died.

"Why not check to see where she bought it?"

"Come on, Bone. Cooper?"

"Did she use cash as a down payment? Did she even have a down payment?"

"You keep forgetting there was no crime. I can't go out there"

"Yeah. You know what else bothers me?"

"I hate to think."

"You said her front door was open. Would you leave your front door open if you were going to do what she did? You'd at least close the damn door."

"Could'a blown open or something. House is old and rundown. People get in a panic when they're faced with that kind of shit. But, I see what you're driving at."

"Suppose the guy comes in, sees she's dead or dying, grabs anything incriminating and hauls ass, forgets to close the door," I said.

"Hmm, doesn't take the money 'cause it was in the car. I'll give you credit for creativity, Bone. And you think your good buddy Cooper could be involved."

"Well, it wouldn't hurt my feelings. By the way, what happened to the car."

"Otis drove into town with a junker, like yours. He took over Chandra's payments. Willie and Elsa let him do it."

"She have anything valuable, besides the five hundred dollars you found? Big bank account or anything? Is anybody probating her estate?"

"The Pattersons owned the house where she lived. They're letting Otis live there. The car was about the only thing she owned. A few clothes and books. We gave the money to the Pattersons. Help with the funeral. You're not wanting to do her probate, are you?" He smiled.

"No, I've already done my probate for this decade." I probated Jennifer Winston's estate. By the time I'd finished looking for her assets, I damn near got finished myself.

"Yeah, and insulted half the town's upright citizens in the process," he said. "Anyway, Willie asked Rose for an opinion about probate. One of the junior members of the firm has it."

I shrugged. Not my problem.

"I'll see if anything falls out when I shake Cooper's tree. By the way, I've never liked the guy either." He winked. "I think I'll have a look at her phone records."

Jenkins shouted to Irene for a cup of coffee and asked if I wanted one. "Fresh made," he assured me.

I said yes. Black, no gospel, I thought. Her radio flavored everything on the floor with messages of grace. He returned his attention to the rest of the report. When he finished, he looked at me over his coffee cup and said, "I don't know how you do it, Bone! You're the only man I know who could piss Jesus Christ off on Christmas."

I opened my mouth to respond but he waved me off.

"I'm not saying you haven't stumbled into something." He tapped the two sheets of paper on his desk. "Somebody sicced Otis on you for damn sure. What the hell have you been doing?"

"Nothing. I thought what I said at the auction was innocuous. Osstrum's calls to the bidders were attributed to me. Payback for that, maybe. I don't know. You saw the television thing. I mentioned the 'loophole' Judge Chancellor said he found. That might have made somebody nervous. I haven't pissed anybody off lately. I've been tactful."

"Ha. You don't know what the word means, Bone."

"Skinny Dearman was upset that both had called him. He told Claire he was thinking about it. Then he gets crushed under a pile of logs in a place he did not need to be. Two people worried about the auction. Both now dead. Coincidences?" I asked with raised eyebrows. "Not to my way of thinking."

"Man can get upset when he's found out, Bone. Who's to say he wasn't upset that the judge was onto him? Might have made him careless. Stood where he shouldn't have."

I scoffed at that. "And you accuse me of some wild theories! I don't think so, Chief. I think he was killed."

"Thinking's cheap when you're not responsible for enforcement, Bone. You want me to go to the grand jury with that! Who do we name? What do you recommend we do? Give lie detector tests to every person who bid at the auction?"

"I wish to hell I knew. So far, I haven't found a damn thing that'd suggest any wrong doing at the auction. Hell, it looks like it was on the up and up."

"Where's that damn loophole you said the judge had found? Wouldn't it be nice if you had one hard fact to back up your suspicions? Worrying the hell out of me with all this … bull shit."

"Yeah, yeah, rub it in. To be exact, the judge only said he may have found one. I think he did, but I can't find it and he didn't say anybody used it."

"Had to be pretty damn big loophole, worth big bucks, if somebody was willing to kill for it … two times if you're right. Which, I have to say, don't look too promising."

If not bucks, maybe worth something very important, say a Supreme Court appointment, I thought, but kept it to myself. "Well, Chief, keep your eye out for an angler skilled with a rod and reel."

"Yeah, that'd be half the men in the county." He shrugged and waved my report about. "You sure you don't want to file charges? No telling what that boy might do next. I should let Milty know."

"I'd appreciate it if you'd just put it in your drawer for now. I promised the old man I'd let it go."

"Willie Patterson is a damn fine man. Elsa, too. I've known them for years."

"Yeah."

"Uh, by the way." He fussed with his desk drawer. "I'll tell you something, but you have to absolutely swear to keep it to yourself. It's part of our investigation."

"Fire away."

"Otis was at the mill the night Skinny Dearman died." He twisted his head to emphasize the point. "We can't place him in the log yard or even pinpoint the time, but he was there. And, Dearman's on this list."

"You talk to Otis?"

"I did. His grandpa, too. Said he and the old man were working on the house, Chandra's house. He drove to the mill to pick up some scrap lumber Reynolds said he could have. We verified that. Mr. Patterson backs him up. However, Otis had time to hit Dearman over the head—he had that baseball bat—and break the brace to let the logs fall on him. You sure you don't want to change your mind about this report?"

"It gives me something to think about. For sure, the boy is headstrong, but I'll put my trust in Mr. Patterson."

"One more thing for you to think about. The fact that Otis didn't succeed doesn't mean you're out of it."

I knew. I packed my automatic again. I had a permit.

I walked to the library to have a cup of coffee with Kathy. Her coffee was so much better than Irene's.

"I've come from City Hall," I told her. "Had to see the chief. Otis got the notion that I knew his sister and came by last night to settle accounts. His grandfather saved my butt." I added the details.

"And you're going to let it go!"

I shrugged. "I think the old man can handle him. Morgan says he's a hard worker. I'm willing to risk it."

She shook her head. "You'll be careful?"

I planned to.

"Tennis Saturday morning?" I asked.

"Early," she agreed. "Eight o'clock." It was too hot to play any other time.

The rest of the morning I filed and made reports. That afternoon, I jogged to the waterfall like I usually did, then read the paper on the back porch.

I was on somebody's list. That was clear, and I didn't like it. It was most likely the same list the judge and Skinny Dearman had been on and look what happened to them. I had to find out who had it, before they had another crack at me.

* * * * *

Dora Lee called with bad news. "As long as Mr. Rose has the bid procedures, they will be part of his work product and not discoverable by Mr. Osstrum's group. If you get them, they will be. Mr. Prozini said to tell you that he's sorry, but as far as he's concerned you should no longer be involved in anything related to the auction.

"Damn it!" Popped out.

"Sorry. Also, we have not been able to locate the auction maps or Chance's notes. Mr. Rose assumes they were inadvertently thrown into the trash, possibly by Chance. There is the possibility that Mr. Prozini took them. He doesn't recall and he's destroyed most of what he picked up."

Yeah, I bet, I thought. No way would the judge have thrown anything away if he'd discovered a possible loophole.

"I can tell you this," she said, "Chance and Mr. Rose reexamined the bid procedures and all relevant documents when Mr. Prozini said that TRS had retained you to observe. Also, Mr. Washington re-certified his work. As bids came in, I removed the mailing envelopes and put the sealed bid envelopes into portfolio boxes which I locked up at night."

"Who else had keys?" I asked.

"Daniel had one. Chance also. No others that I know of. The office is always locked at night."

I saw that all bid envelopes were sealed when Dora Lee handed them to Rose, but had they been opened earlier and resealed? Was it even possible? Even if they had been, what would it prove?

"The judge told me he found a loophole." I said.

"In our bid procedures?"

"He didn't say, but if he found a loophole anywhere it could mean the bids were rigged."

"I doubt that, Mr. Bone. Mr. Rose is a meticulous man. So was Chance. I think Chance was mistaken."

Well, I'd spun my wheels a lot and supposed a lot, but I'd discovered nothing. I could see only one ravel I hadn't pulled. I called Morgan Reynolds to get the name of the attorney who asked him to be a straw buyer. I didn't know if it was relevant, but I knew it'd bother me until I found out.

I heard Morgan scratch around in his desk. "Ah. Found it! Julian Swegman. Haven't heard from him since."

"Do you mind if I call?"

"I guess not. How can it hurt anything?" He gave me the phone number.

* * * * *

Swegman was cordial. He acknowledged that he'd hired "Mr. Reynolds" to bid on behalf of a client who wished to remain anonymous. He didn't know the judge or Mr. Rose, except for their names.

"The client is a shell corporation with one asset, the timberland it bought at the auction. I formed it to acquire, hold, and sell timberland. Holdcorp's its name," he said. "I'm the only officer."

"Somebody had to ask you to do it." I said.

"You know I can't tell you that."

"I hear it's a listed company," I said.

"Can't tell you, Mr. Bone. Sorry."

Damn it to hell! He was right, of course.

"Does your client look to buy a mill in the area?"

Same answer. End of conversation.

I picked up Kathy for our Saturday morning tennis match. We split a couple of sets and played to a draw in a third when the heat stopped us.

"How are you coming along in your search for clues?" she asked. "I can tell you are distracted."

"I don't think so."

"Well, you lost count of the score three times."

"I'm like a cat with a ball of twine, scratching around to find the damn loose end."

"If I can't find a book title, I search the author. Maybe you can approach it from a different perspective," she suggested.

Maybe there was another approach. Might it be useful to know if the properties had changed hands since the auction? Co-conspirators would sure as hell want to divide the property? Why hadn't I thought of that already?

* * * * *

The auction dogged my thoughts the rest of the day. A buyer had the right to transfer title to anybody for any reason, but under the current circumstances, two deaths, a transfer soon after the auction would get my attention. And, Swegman's Holdcorp tract. That damn thing was stuck in my craw. More because of what I didn't know. Probably not relevant to a damn thing however? It still stuck though.

At six o'clock I picked Kathy up for margaritas, chips and dip and something good off the menu at a Mexican restaurant south of town. Television sets rang with south of the border favorites, soccer, variety shows and dramas, all in Spanish. We were early enough for two-for-one margaritas. The waiter brought chips and salsa right away

I said, "I hear that Ray is loose again."

"I know," she said with a smile. "He's checked out three books in the past three weeks."

I mumbled, "I didn't know he could read. Even with all the alimony he has to pay, I suppose he's a good catch."

"Mother doesn't like him," she said, juggling a chip and salsa.

"Your mother is very astute."

"I don't like him, either." She smiled her devastating smile.

"Intelligence and good taste run in your family."

We had a spicy entrée, but I didn't pay much attention to it. My entrée was Kathy, a very astute lady.

* * * * *

Birds in territorial disputes woke me early Monday. The sun was up in a cloudy sky. Outside it felt like a sauna. I spent a few minutes on the porch with coffee and a muffin that passed for breakfast. I had other things on my mind. Bank reports I began on Sunday needed to be finished and mailed. Then, I planned to do a title search of the three timber tracts in Lawton County. A challenge.

It rained for five minutes. On the way to town, twisted mists of white curled up from the hot asphalt and wrapped around my jeep as the sun reclaimed what the clouds dropped. To drive in hot fog with the smell of asphalt was eerie.

I mailed the reports, then walked across the street to the Chancery Clerk's office in the old Courthouse. Fans hung from high ceilings to stir the air. I told an older lady at the counter that I wanted to look at conveyances from the TRS auction.

"They're all of record," she said and led me to a vaulted room where land records were kept. "Ever done a title search?"

I hadn't. She gave me a quick overview and said that I might find it a little slow at the start, but I'd get better as I went along. After two hours, I wasn't any better. A young attorney watched my struggles with the huge books and asked, "Having trouble?"

Ah. We negotiated a price for him to do the search. I wanted copies of all documents that transferred TRS tracts, with any mortgages or any other documents recorded against them. Like agreements to divide proceeds in the event of a sale. I knew I'd never find that, just wishful thinking.

With the Lawton search underway, I drove to the Sampson County Chancery Clerk's office. Sampson County held only one tract of timberland sold at the auction, but it was a big one. Having learned from my prior "search" experience in Lawton County, I hired help right away. Like the lady said, I got better as I went along.

TRS auctioned off tracts of timber and land in Mississippi, Alabama and Louisiana, but none were as large as the four in Lawton and Sampson Counties. There was enough money in those tracts to motivate corruption, and murder to cover it up. What I did in the other counties and states would depend on what the searches in Lawton and Sampson Counties showed up.

On the way back from Sampson County, I saw Jenkins on the sidewalk outside City Hall steps and tapped my horn. He smiled automatically and waved, but the smile vanished when he saw my jeep.

I pulled up and asked, "How's it coming?"

"Which assignment do you need a report on, Bishop?"

"I thought you'd be prepared to give a report on all of 'em, Chief."

He opened the door and sat one leg in and one leg out.

"Chandra wrote a check for a down payment on her car. She did buy it from Cooper. And, she'd just deposited cash into her checking account."

"Tips?" I asked.

"Six hundred dollars?"

"Not tips."

He agreed. "We looked for her phone records. None in her name. Her coworkers said she had a cell phone. Something with a rainbow on it. We couldn't find one in her house or car and no local provider had her down as having one of theirs."

"You think she used somebody else's?"

"Yeah. Whose? And, where is it?"

"Anything else?"

"Scraps. She and Skinny Dearman went to JC together for awhile. We confirmed that. He picked her up on his motorcycle now and then. Drove to class, dropped her off at the Pub. Most likely what the Pub people heard, the motorcycle noise. That was before she bought the car. Nothing serious between them that we could find. I can't say how Otis saw it."

Otis said he had never talked to Skinny, but what would he say? No one could prove otherwise. From my lawyering days, as a matter of convenience, I tended to make conclusions early on about people, so I decided to believe him. I always watched for reasons to change my mind, however. Something else from when I lawyered.

"When you boil it all down, Bishop, nothing clearly points to murder. Hints and possibilities, even motives, but no evidence. Otis and that guy Osstrum are on our watch list. Otis had a grudge against the judge and may have thought Skinny was involved with Chandra. Osstrum was pissed at the judge because of a notion that a rigged-bid conspiracy lost him money."

"There was a hell of a lot of money on the table, Chief. Big money begets big temptations. Add that to what the judge told me about a loophole."

He gave me one of those looks that would have said, "bull shit" if looks could talk. "Theories and gut feelings are fine for creek talk, Bishop, I need some real proof. Listen, I know some of the people who bid, the ones from around here for sure, and I'm damned certain they wouldn't rig a bid and they sure as hell wouldn't commit murder. They're tough, but not stupid."

"Whoever killed the judge and Skinny wasn't stupid."

"If anybody did. If."

"I'm past if. I'm at who and why." I didn't mention Rose. Would he kill to protect his pending appointment?

"Milty had someone call every damn one of the bidders, in and out of state. Yeah, Bishop, we do our jobs. He said most of the bidders have dealt in timber all their lives and are hardheaded businesspeople … solid citizens."

"We've missed something, Chief."

"I agree. Too many coincidences to suit me, but that's all we have. Coincidences."

I decided to nudge him a little. "Maybe we're looking too far afield."

"You mean insiders, Rose and that bunch. Yeah, I hear your wheels clicking. They're doing okay money wise, but they don't have the money to play in a game with stakes that high."

"So, with both ends covered," I said, "no bid rigging."

"Yep. No insiders and no outsiders. As a theory, it has merit, but when you get down to the practical side, the money and straw buyers to make it work, it gets weak. Hell, the auction looks legitimate to me."

"Yeah. Might have to rework my theory," I said.

"You said it, not me," he said. "Theorizing might not be your strong suit."

I wasn't ready to toss in my cards. I was certain he knew that from the way he grinned as I drove away.

* * * * *

Morgan called. "Bishop," he said. "I've been served."

Rose and Associates served him with a complaint for Skinny Dearman's wrongful death. His insurance agent told him the company might terminate coverage. "Officially, I won't be in default under my loan agreement until it's cancelled. I told my agent to find a backup carrier."

"Carriers like premiums, not claims," I said. "You may get lucky and find another carrier."

Neither of us believed that.

I was sorry that Mrs. Dearman sued and wasn't certain she had a case. On the other hand, it was her right to have a jury decide. With a sympathetic one, she would likely receive a good award. It looked like a case that should be settled out of court and probably would be. In the meantime though, Morgan might be up the smelly creek without a paddle.

Osstrum called. He said, with the exception of what Prozini kept to file a tax return, everything from the auction was shredded before Prozini was served with an injunction not to destroy any of the papers.

"So, you have as much information on the auction as anybody," he said.

"What did Skinny Dearman tell you? I assume you talked to him after the auction," I said.

"I did talk to him. He swore his appraisals were on the money. And everything about the auction, as far as he was knew, was on the up and up. My son said he'd been accidentally killed," he said.

"Your son?"

"He read about it."

"In the Chicago papers?"

"He was in Mississippi at the time."

"He has clients down here?"

"His firm does," he said.

"Must be big. Does it specialize?"

"Tell you the truth, I don't know," he said.

That was the second oblique reference he'd made about his son.

"Dearman told me he was told to appraise low to encourage bidding. Prozini's orders. He did the cruises in Lawton and Sampson counties. He said he didn't know anything about rigged bids. 'Never heard of such a thing' was the way he put it."

"How about other appraisers?" I asked. "What'd they say."

"They said pretty much the same thing. Appraise low to encourage bidding. Their only interest in the auction was to get paid."

"Caleb Washington as well?"

"Uh huh. Except to say he was a member of the liquidation committee. He said his job was to coordinate the work of the other appraisers. To maintain an objective perspective, was the way he put it. He acknowledged Prozini's orders to appraise on the low side of value. He thought it was a good idea."

"I don't know how objective he could have been if he asked Skinny to appraise properties. Skinny worked for him," I said.

"I agree, but don't know if it gets me anyplace."

Well, Osstrum didn't sound like a killer. Not to say he wasn't, just he didn't sound like one. His son seemed to know what was going on in Lawton at just the right time. It struck me as odd that an accounting firm in Chicago would represent clients in Mississippi. Something was missing.

Chapter 15

"I talked to Bishop Bone a few minutes ago," Osstrum phoned Fitzgerald. "I let it slip that you knew about Skinny Dearman's accident. He might suspect you're in town or have been in town. I hope it doesn't cause you any trouble."

"It'll be okay."

"Have you found out anything more about the auction?"

"No. The buzz has died down. When are you coming to Lawton again?" Fitzgerald asked.

"I drove up last weekend, but you were out. I didn't leave a note."

"Edna and I went to the Coast with her parents. If you'll let me know when you're coming, I'll introduce you. I'd like for you to meet Edna and her parents. Maybe we can have dinner together."

"I feel funny knowing you'd just as soon not have anybody know we're related."

"That was only a concern while the auction was news, Dad. Now that it's over, I don't think it matters."

* * * * *

"Thought you might be interested," a clerk said into the phone. "Guy by the name of Bishop Bone ordered title searches on some of that timberland sold at auction awhile back. Ordered copies of the recorded documents."

"Appreciate it. Maybe he's wants to buy land for a client or something."

"That's what I thought, too."

Bone. What is he up to?

* * * * *

Copies of the recorded documents for tracts in Lawton County and Sampson County arrived in the mail. I poured a glass of zinfandel and sat down to study my way through them. It wasn't a beer kind of job.

Alice Kitchens from Atlanta, Georgia, was the successful bidder on two tracts in Lawton County and was still the record owner. Her bids were within dollars of four million for both and about fifty thousand dollars above competing bids.

Mortgages totaling two and a quarter million in favor of a local bank were recorded against the parcels. I rummaged through a stack of papers Osstrum brought to find Skinny's summary appraisals for them and did a quick addition.

He'd appraised the parcels at three point seven million. Since Skinny had appraised low, per Prozini's instructions, I figured her bids of four million were probably not too far off the parcels' real value. No wrong I could see. But, why did somebody from Atlanta want to bid on timberland in Mississippi? I tracked down her number and called.

After identifying myself as the TRS observer, I said "I'm doing a follow up survey on the auction and have a couple of questions for you, if you don't mind."

"Go ahead," she said.

"How'd you learn about the auction?"

"It was advertised in our newspaper," she said. Why hadn't I thought of that?

"We wondered if the ads were effective. I guess they were." I lied. "Okay, my next question is why would someone from Atlanta bid on property in Mississippi? Do you have contacts in the area?"

She replied, "My family has speculated in timber for as long as I can remember, all over the South. I saw timber around there and liked it. I asked someone knowledgeable to check the tracts for signs of beetle infestation, burning, that sort of thing and got a good report, so I put in a bid on the two parcels. I liked the fact that they were next to each other."

"You financed the land."

"Yes. I got mortgages through a local bank my family has dealt with before."

She sounded in her thirties, young for a speculator? But, things have changed. There is no "too young" anymore.

She said, "I'll sell the older timber from time to time, and re-seed. However, I'd sell it all for the right price. I've had a couple of calls."

"How'd you arrive at your bid?" I asked.

"I heard buyers would bid on the low side of the appraisal, so I elected to go on the high side to make sure I got it. It's good timberland and I bought it right. I expect to make a good profit."

"Who did you say checked the land for you?" I asked.

"I didn't. A land man we use sometimes. Is that all?"

I wanted a name, but didn't get one. That was "private" information. I thanked her and moved on to the tract Morgan bid on for Holdcorp.

Morgan's straw bid was four million, one hundred thousand dollars. The Pitts' bid was a few thousand over four million. The other bids were closer to Skinny's appraised value of three million, six hundred thousand dollars.

No mortgages were recorded against Morgan's tract. That meant the "listed company" had access to a good line of credit or had one hell of a lot of surplus cash.

Barbara Gibbs of Montgomery, Alabama, was the successful bidder on the single tract of land and timber in Sampson County. Her bid was four million, two hundred thousand dollars. The property had a mortgage of two and a half million from the bank that mortgaged the Kitchens' tracts. I'll be damned!

Her story was the same as Mrs. Kitchens'. Her family, with a history of speculating on timberland, encouraged her to bid.

"They helped me with the money," she said.

I asked if she knew Mrs. Kitchens. She didn't.

"She got her mortgages from the same bank that you did," I said.

"That bank does a lot of land loans," she said.

"Did you walk the land yourself before you bid?" I asked.

"No," she said. "I hired someone." She hadn't actually talked to anyone. Somebody a business associate knew, someone local, that the "associate" contacted for a recommendation.

"Who?" I asked.

She said that she didn't recall. I suspected that she did, but, like the Kitchens' lady, didn't want me messing around in her private affairs.

Nothing else jumped out at me. I poured another glass of wine and tried to make sense out the mess of stuff on my worktable. The chief called me from the back yard.

"Got a new fly," he said. "Come on down."

"I'm trying to organize the crap I've accumulated since the auction," I said.

"Better you than me. I never got the hang of reading metes and bounds legal descriptions. You need maps and then you need to go out with a surveyor and put down stakes. Even then you still don't know a hell of a lot."

"Anything happening around town?" I asked.

"Not a thing," he said. "I'm the program chairman for Rotary this month, been scraping around for speakers. I thought of you, but didn't want to risk a killing."

"Good. You know I try to stay out of the limelight."

"Yeah. I had this young guy, Bob Fitzgerald, give us the latest IRS changes. He gave a good speech."

"I know him."

"He's doing alright. An Ole Miss graduate. Going to marry the daughter of one of the firm's partners. Came here from Chicago."

What? Wait a minute! Osstrum's son was from Chicago!

"Jonas Osstrum has a son in Chicago," I told him.

"No shit! Small world. See you later," he said and moved on toward the creek's edge.

He shouted up when he left, but I was so engrossed, I took little note.

It took me an hour of trial and error to connect the timber tracts carried on TRS' books with the tracts sold at auction. I compared TRS' book values with the successful bids on corresponding tracts.

More than two thirds of the auctioned tracts went for close to book value, low, but close. In light of the "distress" aspects of the liquidation auction, and the fact that TRS had likely logged some of the tracts, investors didn't lose a hell of a lot on those tracts. Especially in a down market. I did not know how much had been logged, but TRS had to get timber from someplace. Nothing suspicious in any of that.

Only on the four tracts I studied was there a clear loss, approximately three million dollars, more than would have been expected based on what the other parcels went for. I saw why Osstrum was upset. I called him to see if he wanted to look at what I'd done. He drove up in the late afternoon. I met him at the front door. He stopped half way up the steps, looked around and said, "Beautiful place. Makes me wish I had a place just like it." His face was grim, but I couldn't recall it with a smile. He wore a suit.

"Thanks."

I showed him the organized piles of papers on my worktable, topped by a summary sheet.

"Need these," he said and put on his glasses. He dragged out a chair, and like an IRS auditor, began a review.

I watched beavers on the back porch and nursed a beer.

An hour or so later he came to the door and said, "Good job of putting it together. Let me show you something."

I came inside.

"I knew we lost money, but to see it laid out like this brings it home. Why in hell did we overpay on these parcels?" He ran his finger along entries for the four parcels in Lawton and Sampson Counties.

"Maybe book values weren't adjusted for logging," I said, "or forest fires." Or for liquidation adjustments, but I knew he understood that.

"Umm. I know we logged our own timber—we got regular reports—I just can't remember a report on the tracts around here. We were supposed to inspect for infestation, but who knows what Prozini did to cut costs."

"I can ask Morgan. He might know," I said.

He said. "I'd appreciate it. Look." He put his finger on an entry for a parcel in another county. "Look at the date on this piece. We bought it at the same time as the others and yet it sold for what you might consider in a liquidation sale. And we definitely logged it. I remember the report."

Next he poked his finger at the parcels in Lawton and Sampson counties and said, "These are the ones that don't make any sense. This is where our big losses show up."

"Maybe Prozini sold off some of the timber. Forgot to tell anybody," I said.

"I wouldn't put it past the bastard," Osstrum said. "Hell, he probably sold timber and pocketed the money."

"That'd be a risky move."

"He's an arrogant son of a bitch! I wouldn't put anything past him!"

"Sounds more like they were overvalued when you bought them? Bought high, sold low," I said.

Osstrum said, "Hmm. Unfortunately, that has a ring of truth." He put his finger on another parcel. "Here, look at this parcel. Another one we logged and it sold for what I'd consider a reasonable amount. Compare it to the four parcels around here. We did no logging that I know about and we lost our shirts. Bought 'em all at the same time. Doesn't make sense. Wait a minute! I'll be right back." He bolted out to his car, and returned with a bound booklet.

"This is from the audit we paid for," he said. "Somebody by the name of Tommy Newsome appraised the parcels we lost big on, the four around here."

I said, "I don't recall seeing Newsome's name on any of the auction appraisals."

"Wonder why?" he asked. "His incompetence catch up with him?"

I pulled out a phone book. Newsome wasn't listed as a timber appraiser. In fact, he wasn't listed at all.

"Hell, one damn dead end after another," he said.

I said, "I wish I had a map of these parcels, the four around here. I need a damn picture to help me visualize this mess. It's complicated enough as it is."

"What happened to the maps they used at the auction?" he asked.

"Nobody knows. Prozini may have ended up with them. Besides, they didn't have the detail I'm looking for."

"If Prozini did, we won't ever see them."

He turned to me and said, "I'll be going. I don't suppose I'll see you again. I appreciate your interest." He picked up the audit booklet.

I thanked him and asked, "Are you going to see your son?"

He laughed. "So, you doped it out?"

"Stumbled onto it."

He said that Fitzgerald was his stepson. "Bob didn't want his link to TRS to be known while it liquidated. He thought it might hurt his efforts to get new accounts."

"It's possible."

"I'm to have dinner tonight with him and his fiancée and her parents. That's why this suit on a Saturday. They sound like nice people. I need to practice my smile. Nobody likes a grump." He laughed

After he'd gone, I dialed Morgan's number and told him about Osstrum's visit.

"Do you recall anything about the four large tracts of timberland in Lawton and Sampson Counties, including the one you bid on for

Holdcorp. Logging, fires or infestation? Timber sales. It looks like TRS lost about three million on those parcels."

"Whew! Three million! I had no idea. Let me see. We logged some forty-year old veneer trees right after TRS bought the land, a special order Prozini asked me to fill. A couple hundred thousand dollars worth of lumber, as I recall. We thinned as well, to give the rest of the trees room to grow. Should have added value since then, not lost."

"Osstrum didn't recall a report of logging around here."

"Prozini took care of the reports. Could be he buried that order in mill operations someplace. I don't know. Have to ask him."

"How about fires? Beetle infestation?"

"No fires to speak of. We paid some outfit to inspect periodically for infestation in our timberlands. If there was infestation, it never got back to me."

"Maybe the earlier appraisals were too high."

"Could be. Can't say they weren't. Foresters are human."

"On the order of three million?"

"Rarely, but it can happen. Those were big chunks of land, several thousand acres. If somebody picks the wrong cruise area for an appraisal, it can hurt you."

"Anything on the parcels in your files?" I asked. "Old appraisals would help."

"Not a thing. Prozini took every file I had for the liquidation."

I'd have been suspicious of Prozini in general but for the fact that he wasn't in Lawton, as far as anyone knew, when the judge or Skinny had died—murdered according to me—and the fact that I'd bet he didn't know one end of a casting rod from another. Not only that, how could he have rigged bids from Chicago? I hated to admit that I still didn't know how anybody could have or that they were, but that didn't stop me from being suspicious.

I left Osstrum a message. "Reynolds told me nothing worthwhile."

* * * * *

On my way to the post office Monday, a sign caught my eye.

"Timber Appraisals. We buy, sell and cruise." I'd probably passed it dozens of times, but I'd never been interested until then. I stopped.

It was a single room, no receptionist. A middle-aged man with thin hair and thick glasses sat bent over a drafting table; his eyes fixed on handwritten notes spread out before him. He looked up and gave me his best "new customer" smile.

"Making sure I haven't missed anything from my last cruise. I like to review my survey notes before I sign the appraisal." He touched the papers with his fingers. "What can I do for you?"

I introduced myself and asked, "I saw your sign and wonder if you know a timber appraiser by the name of Tommy Newsome."

"I did know him. He's dead now, has been for, I don't know, some years. He and Caleb Washington shared office space. Caleb took over the business after Tommy died."

"Newsome did some appraisal work for that outfit out of Chicago, TRS, that just liquidated their holdings."

"Uh huh. At one time he did most of the appraisals around here, the big ones, but as he got older he couldn't get around as much so his values weren't always up to snuff, if you know what I mean."

"How was Skinny Dearman? As an appraiser?"

"Skinny was alright. Very careful. I'd say his work was as good as any around."

"He appraised the TRS properties around here. For the auction."

"Yeah. Caleb put together a panel of appraisers and assigned them tracts, but if one of us got busy someplace else, one or the other of us would step in. He didn't want there to be any holdup in the auction."

"Who signed off?"

"Whoever was assigned the tract. We trusted each other. It didn't matter much, we all got fixed fees."

"What's Caleb going to do now that Skinny is gone?"

"We may combine offices. There're three of us in the county. If one gets busy, somebody else can take the call. That way, we're less likely to turn away business."

He told me where I could find an engineer to order maps of the four parcels in Lawton and Sampson counties.

* * * * *

That evening, I partnered with Seth at the Club to beat a couple of local guys in two sets of tennis, both tiebreakers. Losers bought afterwards. After the losers left, Seth and I sat beside the pool to talk and listen to the vibrations of pine needles driven by the breeze. It was like an eerie concert. No tune, but nevertheless fascinating. Like Morgan said, pines grew like weeds in the Pine Belt.

I talked about my finds since the auction. "It looks like TRS bought high and sold low, three million dollars low. Osstrum was upset, but resigned."

"That'd hurt," Seth said. "I'd guess they've logged the parcels over the years. He has to take the money they made from that into account."

"Apparently there's been no major logging."

"Who appraised it?" he asked.

"Tommy Newsome, but he's dead and I don't have his appraisals."

"Newsome was a fine forester," Seth said. "Even when his arthritis slowed him down—some of the country around here is pretty hilly—you'd never find an error in his calculations. When he couldn't walk a tract of timber he'd study what he could from the road and use the map to come up with a value. Could be, on the tracts you're talking about, it was the timber he couldn't see that caused the error. Hold on!" His face lit up like faces do when someone's just had a brilliant idea. "You know what, I just might have an idea that'd help you!"

"Anything," I said.

"You said the summary appraisals Jonas Osstrum gave you showed the quantity and species breakdowns for the timber?"

"Yeah."

"How about acreage?"

"No acreage, just estimated values for the timber, but I've ordered maps of the tracts using the deed descriptions. The engineer can calculate the acres in each tract."

"I know a couple of guys at the Mississippi State Forestry Department. I bet they have timber and land prices for the time the parcels were first sold to TRS. That should tell you, roughly, how accurate Newsome's appraisals were."

"I hate to put you to that much trouble, Seth, but it might help put the matter to bed."

"No trouble. I have a soft spot for timber. It's in my blood. I'll enjoy the look back."

"I'll drop the packages by your office after I pick up the maps from the surveyor. Thanks for offering," I said. The dates TRS bought the parcels were on Osstrum's audit.

"You sure there was no logging after TRS bought the land," he said.

"No. Morgan told me they logged some veneer timber, but not enough to impact value. Plenty enough time has passed for the timber to recover from that."

"How about land sales? That'd affect value. Or fires, that sort of thing."

"No sales, no fires and no infestations that he's heard of."

Chapter 16

The phone rang the next morning. It was Morgan. From the tone of his voice, he was damn near in tears.

"Bishop," he said. "I'm dead."

"What happened?"

"When Scooter started the mill this morning, there was a god awful noise. Like the whole damn place'd come apart. A log jammed as it went into the canter saws and swung around like a giant baseball bat. It knocked out everything."

He said his main saw assembly and equipment around it were completely destroyed. One motor was totally demolished. A section of the conveyor belt broke loose. Pieces of it took out part of the edger saw assembly and ripped the other motor off its base. The saw broke up and flew around like shrapnel. One of the blades ripped through the side of the building and landed at Morgan's feet.

"It's a wonder nobody got killed. Thank God for that!" I said.

"I'm ruined. I don't have the heart to tell Rooster."

"What about insurance? Have they cancelled you yet?"

"No, not yet. I'm still insured."

"Won't they take care of the damage?"

"Lord, no! It's a market policy. Cheap. All I'll get's what this stuff would be worth if I went out and tried to sell it. Hell, it wasn't worth much when Scooter and his friends came in here and got it working."

"Will it be enough to get the mill running?"

"The insurance company will likely offer me twenty percent of what I need, even tracking around for second hand stuff. Where the hell am I going to get the rest? You got any?"

"I could come up with five hundred dollars if pressed."

"I'm in the same boat."

"How about friends?"

"You know how that goes, you don't have friends when you need money. You have folks who'll get back to you. I'll beat the bushes though. You can count on that."

"How about contracts? Could you assign your receivables to the bank for what you need?"

"They aren't that high. I live close to the vest. With the lumber in the kiln and what's ready for the planer mill, I'll be able to make this week's shipment. That'll cover payroll and my next note payment. After that, I don't have a clue."

"Mind if I come out and take a look?"

He'd appreciate any advice I had.

I was there in fifteen minutes.

Scooter and Otis stood beside the steps at the middle section of the mill, hands shoved into their pockets. Morgan sat on the steps, chin cupped in his hands. Not a happy bunch. He stood up as I parked. "Bishop. Come on."

I followed him inside with Scooter and Otis behind. It was quiet, except for a piece of tin that flapped in the wind. The gouge ripped in the side of the building by a piece of metal was almost a foot wide. We came to what had been the saw assembly. Half a log stuck out from one of the giant motors like it was driven in by a pile driver. The huge covers for the band saw assemblies were gone as were the saws. What was left of the linked conveyor belt wrapped itself around the other motor and twisted it inward. A piece of one of the saws lay along the protective railing. Other triangular pieces stuck out of the walls here and there like tips of daggers. The control booth window was an obscure pattern of spider webs. The edger saw assembly looked as if it had been ripped open with an axe.

"Damnation! What the hell happened?" That was the best I could come up with. I'd never seen such destruction.

"We tried to look inside the motor." Morgan pointed at the smashed up motor with the log it in. The log stuck out like a giant toothpick. "Couldn't. The best we can figure is that one of the saws or motors bound up and pulled the log into it. Once that happened, the other saw fouled and broke up, ripping up the conveyor chain."

"It happened so fast, Mr. Bone, we didn't have time to shut off the power," Scooter said.

"I called the insurance agent," Morgan said. "He wasn't happy. Can you tell Rooster for me? I want to wait to see what replacements will cost, if I can find anything. What am I talking about? There's no way I can come up with what I need. No way!" Tears formed in his eyes. He turned away.

I left them staring at the twisted metal with their hands stuffed in their pockets, their heads lowered. Rooster had to be told and it wasn't the kind of news I wanted to relay by phone.

"At best," I told him. "He'll have at least a month's downtime. I expect he'll lose customers. It doesn't look good."

"How about the worst?"

"The mill won't reopen at all."

There was a long pause. Finally, Rooster said, "Usually when we make a shaky loan like his, we don't expect the worst. Honestly, I don't know what we can do! We stretched to make the loan, gave maximum weight to his management skills. I'll call a special board meeting."

"Why not wait until he gets a report from his insurance company and an estimate of replacement costs. You'd have a better idea about what he needs."

"Good point. I have to tell you, Bishop, it's not likely the bank will advance him anywhere near what he needs. Most likely nothing. The numbers just aren't there. I'll put the loan on our watch list for now."

"I'll let him know," I said.

I called Morgan on the way home. He took the news in stride. "I've got the phone in my hand, Bishop. I know lots of people. They gonna have to turn me down personally."

"Maybe you'll get lucky. You did last time."

"I did." He didn't sound convinced.

By mid-afternoon, everybody in town knew what had happened.

"Does he know what caused it?" Chief Jenkins asked when he called me.

"No, and he doesn't want to do anything until the insurance people have their say. They may offer him fair market value, cancel his policy and call it a day. That'd put him out of business."

"I hate to see it close. The payroll helps the town. Most of all, I hate to see a man lose everything like that."

"Me, too."

"My daddy worked in that mill when I was young. I ever tell you that? Seth's dad owned it then."

He hadn't.

"One year the mill closed for some reason and we drove to the Delta to chop cotton to make ends meet. In those days times were tough. I'll tell you a story. One day we were in the field chopping cotton, hot as hell, steamy. Young as I was, I lagged behind the others."

"Never knew you for a farmer," I said.

"I wasn't. Just helping out. Anyway, here comes the water boys, water bucket bouncing off their legs, holding onto a dipper. A step or two before they got to me, they stopped. One of 'em stuck his hand into the bucket, swished it around, then shoved something in his pocket. He saw me looking at him and said, with a shit eating grin, 'had to catch my frog.' I passed on the water," he said.

I laughed. I told him I'd call if I got anything new.

I stared across the creek at the beavers. Nothing ever fazed them. If a storm knocked out a section of their dam, they got up the next morning and replaced it; just another day's work to them, probably happy to have something to do.

SBA loans occupied my time for awhile, one a bookstore, the other a transmission shop. I visited, said hello, looked around, took pictures, and picked up current financial statements. Easy fees. Business at the bookstore was good. They advertised once a week book signings for the next five weeks. That always brought in people who liked to chat with authors. Could be a future best seller. Who knew? The transmission shop was busy, employees all around, radios blaring, people in the waiting room. Cars were in every bay and the phone rang off the hook while I was there.

There was a phone message from Morgan when I returned.

"Bishop," he said, "the insurance people were in here. Bottom line, the damaged equipment is a total loss. I'll get market value for it. The edger can be repaired. I've asked the manufacturer to have a look. We freed the log while they were here and found a screwdriver stuck inside the motor. Can you believe it? It was the one Otis kept in a clamp on the wall. No way it accidentally fell in."

"You don't think Otis–"

"No. He was way too shook up about it. The adjusters called it deliberate. They want an opinion from their attorneys before they do anything. From the look they gave me, I think they suspect insurance fraud."

"Fraud happens when you have something to gain," I said.

"Without trying to sound defensive, I suggested as much."

"What's your next move?" I asked.

"I don't know. Nobody I called has any money. I might as well pack my bags and look for work. Maybe somebody needs an assistant mill manager. Chief Jenkins said he'll send somebody out to have a look."

* * * * *

I drove to the mill the next morning. It was quiet and gloomy, a dead thing. An overcast sky didn't help. The hint of cut pine hung in the air. Morgan's truck and a car were by the building where the disaster took place. I heard the screech of metal on metal from the inside where Otis, Scooter and Morgan worked to clear more of the wreckage. From the look of their sweat-stained clothes, they'd been at it for awhile.

"Bishop," Morgan said with a wave. Scooter and Otis acknowledged me with quick glances. Afterwards, they stared at what was left of the job. It was considerable.

"Looks better than it did," I said.

"We're making progress," Morgan said. "The chief and a couple of detectives were out first thing. He didn't seem optimistic they'd find out who did it."

"Hmm. Any luck with replacements?"

He shook his head. "Still looking. We shipped the last of the lumber we had under the shed yesterday. We can make a loan payment. I've about run out of people to call. John Prozini says he doesn't have any money."

"Never does, does he?"

"Not for me. He did say he might be able to find a buyer for the mill, as is, if the loan is assumable. He knows Rooster got me a good rate."

"He made a similar offer before, didn't he?"

"Yeah."

"What'd you tell him?"

"I told him, thanks. What else could I say? My house is pledged as security. I want the bank to release it, but you and I know that won't happen. A buyer won't give a damn. Things get coldhearted things when you're down. The world wears spiked boots."

"Any other prospects?" I asked.

"Not really. Lots of people will 'call back.' We'll clean up as much of this mess as we can, but after that, to quote our preacher, 'It's in the Lord's hands. He'll show us the way.' Didn't say when though. Never do."

"Yeah. You may not be able to wait that long."

"Even if I take what the insurance company offers, I'll be way short. I've got to go out and start all over. Damn. I can't think about it right now."

A thought occurred to me. "This may be one of those cases we were told about in law school."

"What's that?"

"When the facts are against you and the law is against you, shout 'public policy.' In other words, this ain't right! Sometimes it works."

Otis and Scooter stopped what they were doing to listen.

"Let's call a press conference. Let the mayor know. Your message will be about the injustice of it all, loss of jobs, loss of benefits to the city and county, that sort of thing. Lay it on heavy. You notify the NAACP, local congressmen, every damned public official around and every newspaper and television station. And, don't stop there, call CNN and the networks."

"Hell, Bishop, I don't need pity, I need money."

"You won't ask for anything. You're the guy who took a chance, the guy who gave the community a payroll. You'll let your preacher make the appeal for help."

"Sounds good, Bishop, but it's way over my head. I'm not much more than a glorified mill hand, sure as hell not a politician or marketing type. I'd be a fish out of water."

"More than a mill hand, Morgan. People around here appreciate what you've done. They'll back you."

"Wouldn't it look self-serving? Folks, I've called this press conference because I need your help. I need your money." He stopped what he was saying and stared at me. "But, … you … you could do it, Bishop! I've seen you do it, when you helped the chicken growers."

He was right. It would be better for him to be a victim. Well, as someone said, if you walk behind the horses in the parade, you'll likely get covered in it. Looks like I had just volunteered to walk behind the horses in Morgan's parade. Is there something in the Bible about to whom much is given, much is expected? I wonder if it says anything about to whom little is given, much is expected. I'd just have to make do.

I made the big calls, the media, public officials, Rooster and

NAACP. Morgan primed his preacher to talk about the mill's impact on the community. When the time came, I'd put in a good word for Morgan. Somebody had to ask for donations. I had figured the preacher for the job and called to ask. As it turned out, he was way ahead of me.

"The Lord gave that job to me, Mr. Bone. Brother Reynolds is an example to us all. If I had any money to give, I'd give to him. I want to ask good folks everywhere to reach deep into their pockets to help our brother in his time of need."

I told CNN and the networks that highly ranked public officials would be present along with the families hurt by the closing. Public officials could always be counted on to show up for TV exposure. Morgan would get his timber owners out. They had an interest to protect. Only open mills bought timber.

"What if nobody shows up?" Morgan asked.

"I'll look pretty damn stupid," I said.

That's on all fours with what the chief said when I told him. Kathy was more charitable. "That's noble, Bishop. I'm proud of you." She kissed me on the cheek.

After my last day of calls, I got out of bed with a head that felt like I'd been on an all night binge. The adrenaline was all gone and I wondered if I had taken leave of my senses. Had I overstepped my abilities? It nagged at me that I had, but things looked better after a pot of coffee on the back porch with the birds and the creek. I used the rest of the day to outline what I wanted to say. By the time I picked up Kathy for our Saturday out, I felt like I'd been in a long trial, totally exhausted. And, the case hadn't gone to the jury yet.

We picked the restaurant on the river for dinner. With its roughhewn timbers, wood floors and old concert posters on the walls, once inside, we felt instant relaxation. I brought a bottle of wine with their blessings. A cheerful waitress brought wineglasses and a complimentary pot of fresh turnip greens and a basket of spicy, just fried hush puppies. We devoured the turnips and hush puppies and vowed we'd never tasted better. The theme for the night was western so the staff wore skirts complete with six shooters, cowboy hats and boots. It was good for us to put Morgan's problems with the mill behind us, even if for only an hour or so. Young children fed the ducks from the deck over the river with pieces of bread. Ducks squawked over the scraps.

We ordered blackened catfish from a menu of delicious entrees. The catfish was our favorite since we first tried it; spicy with great tasting

Cajun seasoning.

"What's your goal?" she asked about our plan to go public with Morgan's plight.

"I want a public outpouring of support and money! That's the short answer, money. For example, suppose a representative of NAACP stands in front of the cameras and asks people to send in at least a dollar. The preacher will ask for contributions. I'll make sure the sign with the mill's address is prominently displayed."

"That kind of pressure might encourage the bank to be a little flexible. The insurance company too," she said.

"I'm counting on it. A lot depends on how people react to Morgan's sincerity—he'll say a few words—and how people see the hurt to the mill workers and their families. I'll ask the Pattersons to be there. The old man makes a good impression."

* * * * *

Sunday afternoon, Morgan, his preacher and I met at the mill for a rehearsal.

As much of the damaged equipment as possible was removed from the mill and placed under a tented shed in the yard for inspection by the media. The heavy stuff, primarily what was left of the motors wasn't moved, but tin wall panels were taken down to let the media see that equipment. The saw assembly area looked like a car with its hood torn off, its motor reduced to scraps.

We were ready.

Morgan told me, "It's in the Lord's hands, Bishop. You did your best." I hoped the Lord heard.

Only bar exams in California and Mississippi had left me as tired.

* * * * *

The engineer called to say that two copies of the maps I ordered were ready. I picked them up at noon, then left a set at Seth's with the backup information Osstrum gave me on timber quantities, estimated land values and dates of acquisition.

One map showed that the Holdcorp property Morgan bid on contained a little over eighteen hundred acres. TRS lost over seven hundred thousand dollars on the property. The next map described the Gibbs' parcel in Sampson County. It contained just over two thousand acres. TRS's lost over a million dollars on that one. The two Kitchens' parcels were contiguous and totaled just under nineteen hundred acres. TRS lost nearly a million dollars on her two parcels.

That TRS had bought high and sold low was obvious. Nothing inherently wrong about that. Investors take risks. Some make money, some don't. Could be I was wrong about the auction being rigged somehow. The deaths of Chance and Skinny might not have been related to the auction at all. Likewise, my burglary could be passed off as a simple theft. But, I didn't really believe that and hoped Seth could find something that I'd missed.

* * * * *

Scooter escorted a media group around the yard, joking and carrying on. He was good at it. They filmed the damaged equipment assembled in the shed. What was left of the screwdriver was secured to a board and attached to a post. Like a bizarre work of art, the half-chewed up log that caused the destruction was on display in the shed as well. I leaned against the front of my jeep to watch. Half a dozen politicians moved from one media cluster to another. They issued prepared comments with hope that their faces would make the evening news. Morgan chatted with reporters on the catwalk inside the mill as they walked along the path of the conveyor belt through the mill. A camera crew trailed along.

Morgan's mill hands and their families stood here and there in the yard. They dressed for the occasion in work clothes. A "shutdown" mill stood between them and their next meal. A reporter talked to them on camera about what it meant to be without work. They'd make the news. Otis and his grandparents, the Pattersons, arrived, as did the City entourage led by the mayor. I moved toward the steps and the platform at the mill door where the speakers gathered.

Rooster and I exchanged greetings. Impeccably dressed in a dark gray suit and green tie, he always gave the impression of being a fastidiously dressed toy poodle that bristled with nervous energy. The silver rimmed glasses he wore matched his platinum hair. His nickname stemmed from high school days when, even though he was only five and a half feet tall, he'd take on all comers.

When Seth first heard about the plan, he called me and volunteered to speak. "That mill is part of my heritage, Bishop. I don't want it to close. Dad ran it for the longest. It's where I learned to work. That was before the days of computers. We did everything by hand." He promised to bring a U.S. Senator and did, the highest ranking official there, icing on the cake for the media. He didn't disappoint anybody.

After Seth and the Senator arrived, I grabbed the mic and said, "Ladies and gentlemen …" After that it went pretty much as planned.

Seth recalled how his father built the mill and shipped lumber all over the country, how he spent his summers sweating inside the old tin buildings, rough cutting lumber, how he was determined to help Morgan reopen it. At the end, he presented Morgan a check for ten thousand dollars. Morgan accepted it with tears in his eyes. The Senator followed Seth and pledged his support to get the mill reopened. He didn't back the pledge with a check. However, by the time he finished, no one there doubted that his friendship with Morgan dated from birth.

The preacher gave a stirring, heartfelt plea for help, complete with "amens" and "praises" to the Lord. All the speakers did a good job, I thought. All mentioned the need for money several times. It made the evening news. The chief was present, a face in the crowd.

"Looks like you ended up on the cutting room floor," he told me afterward. I had intended to say a few words, but with so many others standing in line to speak, I didn't have to. I wasn't disappointed. It wasn't about me and I wanted it to stay that way.

"Nobody said much about the screwdriver either," he added

"I know, but when you boil it down, whether it was deliberate or accidental, the need is the same. I thought it went well. Damn good crowd. From the comments, I'd say everyone was genuinely sympathetic."

"Me too. There were no prints on the screwdriver. No reports of anybody lurking around the mill that night either," he said.

The story aired the next day on network news. CNN Headline news repeated the substance of it half a dozen times. The expanded coverage came from follow up interviews with dignitaries and the mill hands and their families. Rooster was asked on camera what the bank planned to do. "We've pledged to do everything we can. As far as the bank is concerned, this mill, and the people who depend on it for their livelihood are part of our responsibility to the community. Morgan Reynolds is a fine man."

Two days later, I called Morgan. No army had shown up to help and only Seth and his company had given money so far. The insurance company did not retract its termination letter. The mill was still a dead thing, forced to lie fallow.

"What do you think?" Kathy asked me.

"It's like one of those old movies. The patient is in intensive care. If he makes it through the night, maybe he has a chance. I'd say the mill needs to make it through the night."

Chapter 17

The irresistible aroma from my automatic coffee maker pulled me out of bed near six in the morning. The sun was a bright orange ball at the top of the trees. I filled a cup and drifted onto the porch to ease into the day. Across the creek in the pond, three young beavers chewed at a clump of bushes and two white cranes stood motionless to watch for hapless minnows and crawfish. The creek was alive. Fish struck at unlucky bugs. A bird swooped down for a drink and turtles climbed out of the water to sun on a half-submerged log.

Morgan's moribund mill came into my thoughts, much as I'd tried to shut it out. I read something from a book a long time ago where an old trapper liked to say that he "hoped for the best but expected the worst." Well, as far as the mill was concerned, the worst had happened. I could only hope that the best waited around the next bend. I had bank assignments so I distracted myself with those. I knew Morgan would call when he had news. There was nothing I could do but wait. Morgan did call.

* * * * *

"I damn near couldn't believe it, Bishop."

When he told me, I wasn't sure I could either.

He said that the sun had just poked its golden rim over the tree line when a flat bed truck rumbled through the gates of the mill. The truck doors bore the sign Pitts Lumber Mill. Burl Pitts sat in the passenger seat, an arm rested in the window, his head covered with a cap. His face was grim, jaw firmly set. Three men in overalls sat in the truck bed, two black, one white. When the truck entered the gate, they stood to stare over the cab. Morgan and Scooter were midway between the office and the mill when they saw the truck.

It shuddered to a halt. Dust mushroomed out for a few feet. The three men in back hopped off and walked toward the front. Burl rolled out and slammed the door behind him. He adjusted the hat on his head, hitched at his belt and headed toward them. His boots thudded against the dirt and sent up puffs. The other men fell in behind him. Their faces showed no expression.

Though the sun's rays filled the day with light, the night's moisture hung in scattered patches around the mill. Birds flitted about in the morning calm. An old dog poked his head around a stack of logs in the log yard, saw the men approach and vanished.

Morgan said that when he saw "that big white man" get out of that truck, he began to look for a place to hide. Scooter said he felt the same way.

A stride or so away, Burl stopped and pointed in the general direction of Morgan. "Reynolds," he said. His deep voice pierced the morning quiet. "I won't lie to you. I never liked you. Well, I guess that ain't exactly right. For sure, I never liked this damn mill here. You know as well as I do that it's downright stupid!"

Morgan said he stepped back and opened his mouth, but Burl cut him off. "And, I ain't likin' to be here neither! I just want to make that clear!"

Morgan said he thought the same thing. He didn't like that Burl was there anymore than Burl did. Five to two odds and there wasn't a brick in sight.

"Sunday, the preacher said the Lord commands us all to open our hands to a neighbor in need. Jesus said that whatever we do for those in need, we do for Him."

One of the men behind him said, "Amen."

"I believe in the Lord, Reynolds, and I want to see my mama in heaven one day so, we've come to help."

Morgan said he praised the Lord to himself, but said to Burl, "I appreciate any help you can give. The Lord knows we need it."

Burl looked at the damaged equipment in the shed. "That it?"

"Yes, sir." Morgan acknowledged. "That's what we could get out of the mill. The heavy stuff, motors mostly, are still on line inside." He gestured toward the open mill wall behind him.

"Get the tools, Boys," Burl said and went to the shed. "Let's see what we got."

* * * * *

So, for the next two and a half days, Burl Pitts and his maintenance crew slaved over the damaged equipment under the shed and inside the mill. They used a forklift and winch to muscle the rest of the damaged equipment from the mill to the shed where it was easier to work on.

The sun's rays beat down on the metal roof and at times the temperature exceeded one hundred degrees underneath. The men cursed, sometimes at each other, sometimes at the twisted mess of wires and metal they tried to make sense of and they drank lots of water. Now and then, one or the other would leave in the truck to return with a box of parts or a new tool. Morgan stayed out of their way as much as he could, but checked their progress every day.

On a Saturday morning, Burl told him, "Damndest mess I've ever seen in my life. How in the hell did you let this happen? Don't you have safety rules, man?"

"Yes, sir, we do, but somehow a big screwdriver got from a wall clamp a yard away and fell into that motor there." Morgan pointed to the motor the log had turned into scrap metal.

Burl frowned, wiped the sweat from his face and said, "You mean to tell me somebody did this?"

Morgan said somebody had, only he didn't know who. Hell, he thought the Pitts did it, or at the very least had it done. In fact, when he saw Burl get out of that truck, he figured that they'd come to finish the job.

"Whoever did it ought to be shot! Nobody ought to treat equipment like that. Damn crying shame!" His head shook back and forth.

One of Burl's crew stood and, pointed at the motor that was yanked loose by the conveyor belt and said, "Burl, this one's ready to be put back on line."

Burl said, "Reynolds, we salvaged that motor and some of the peripheral equipment. That'll save you some. We've brought some old band saws you can use. We upgraded to a curve sawing gang awhile back and don't need them.

"The scanner couldn't be repaired. You'll have to get a new one. Used, I reckon. They're around. Floor console was smashed too."

Morgan said they did a hell of a lot better than he imagined possible.

"We've repaired most of the damage to the edger. Should be able to pick up what you need to do the rest for next to nothing. Might need adjusting now and again. It's far from perfect, but it's better than nothing."

"I'll start looking for a used motor for the other side and the rest of what I need," Morgan said. "Have to wait till I settle up with the insurance company before I can do much."

"Yeah. They'll cancel you if you're a day late, but make you wait forever when you put in a claim. Never liked 'em. Too much like banks. Some of the incidental pieces of equipment'll have to be replaced. 'Made you a list of what you're gonna need. Not going to be cheap."

He handed him a clipboard and pointed to a pile of parts and pieces of housings lying to one side of the shed. "Can throw that stuff out. I'd like to get my hands on the son of bitch who did this!"

"Yes, sir. I would too," Morgan said.

"We'll come back Monday and put what we've been able to salvage back on line. I reckon you can see to the rest."

The obligation imposed on Burl Pitts by Jesus according to Matthew was duly satisfied. He would see his mother again.

Burl and his crew left. He didn't smile the entire time he was there, but then, no one could recall ever having seen him smile anyway. He didn't offer his hand to Morgan and Morgan didn't risk extending his. Aside from all that, Burl was clear in his mind. He'd done the Lord's will.

After the dust from Burl's truck drifted away, Morgan said he went over to the equipment the men repaired and touched each piece. The war against lost hope wasn't over by any means, but thanks to the Lord and Burl Pitts, he had won a battle.

After Morgan told me about Burl's visit and what he'd done, he said, "You should have seen that big old man hunched over that motor in that killing, hundred degree heat. I'd never have believed it. It was as close to a miracle as I've ever seen."

Damned if I didn't agree.

"More good news, Bishop. The postman brought us a pile of mail this morning, a big pile, all with money inside. I'm not ashamed to say, Bishop, it choked me up."

He didn't yet have enough to save him, but it was a start and I was certain there'd be more.

"You remember that lawyer who asked me to be a straw bidder? The one from New Orleans?" he asked.

"Yes."

"He called again. Guess what he wants this time?"

I didn't have a clue.

"He says he has a buyer for the mill. His client will take the mill as is, assume the loan, and negotiate with the bank to get my house released. I'd have to agree not to open another mill in the state or any contiguous state."

"What'd you tell him?"

"I wanted to tell him to stick it, but I know, as it now stands, even if I get more cash in the mail, I might be short of what I need. So, I told him I'd think about it."

"Anything on your insurance claim?" I asked.

"The agent called, says they're going to throw in their reserve as a gesture of good will."

In some cases I'd heard about, an insurance company might hold some in reserve in case Morgan hired a lawyer and sued. In that event, they put the reserve amount on the table in a settlement offer, most of which would go to the lawyer. I didn't know if that was the case with Morgan's, but I was cynical.

"The publicity helped me out there," he said. "They're still not going to renew my policy. My agent is beating the bushes for a new carrier, but so far no luck.

"Technically I'm in default, but Rooster said the bank won't do anything for awhile. I think I can make my next payment with what I have and maybe the one after. Rooster's talking about waiving interest for a couple of months and re-amortizing the loan. That'll help if I can get the mill running again."

"What about replacement equipment? Any luck finding it?"

"Dealers all around the country called to see what I need. They offered discounts." His face broke into a smile.

"I guess they watch CNN."

"That's what they say. I've faxed out the list Burl left me. I won't have the money to pay for everything until I get a check from the insurance company, probably not even then. But, thanks to you, Bishop, things look better than last week."

I followed his progress for the next few days in newspaper and television news reports. He continued to receive donations, but when the mail dwindled to nothing, he was still short of what he needed to become fully operational even with the insurance money. CNN sent a crew from Atlanta to tape his "Thanks to all those who cared" message.

* * * * *

Two trucks trailed by a portable saw mill rolled through Morgan's mill gate. A man from Alabama saw Morgan's story on the news and would rent the portable mill to him for a few months. A slump in demand had all but put him out of business.

"Only charge you what it'll cost me for insurance," he said. "It's top of the line, this mill. Got all the bells and whistles. Even so, it can't cut nearly as much lumber as your mill does … did anyway, and it requires a lot more manual support, but if you work two shifts, you might be able to get by for awhile."

Morgan looked hard at the portable mill. He'd worked them before. He doubted seriously if it would be profitable, but at least he could satisfy some of his contractual commitments. To stay alive two more months, seemed a better alternative than to close up or sell out.

"I can run three shifts if that's what it takes," Morgan said. "Let's get it set up."

Morgan and Scooter helped the man unload the portable mill and set it up in the log yard. They'd have to haul the cut lumber to the kiln and the planer mill, more labor, two shifts instead of one, but they could ship lumber.

"I appreciate your offer," Morgan said. "Thank you."

"Glad to help out," the man said. "If you want, I'll help run the mill, one shift anyway, for an hourly wage. That'll get you started."

"Crank it up!" Morgan said. "I've got lumber to cut, orders to fill! Damn!"

Scooter got on the phone and ordered logs. "We're in business!" he shouted. The mill hands were put on notice. They'd show up ready for work after supper. The mill would run a second shift that night.

* * * * *

"Hello," the man said, picking up the phone.

"Did you hear what happened?"

"I saw it on the news if that's what you mean. Pissed me off. I thought the son of a bitch would have to tuck tail and leave town."

"Not that. Hell, I'm talking about the portable mill. One of those fancy dual band saw things. Morgan'll be able to ship lumber!"

"Son of a bitch! Damn it to hell, how the hell does he manage? By rights, the damned mill should be closed by now. My luck's not running good."

"Let's hope it doesn't get worse."

"You mean Bone?"

"Exactly. He ordered some survey maps. I guess he thinks if he stares at 'em long enough, he'll see the loophole the judge told him about." He laughed.

"He's like a damn leech. Once he gets hold, he won't let go."

"Yeah. Could be a problem."

* * * * *

I met with a bank's special asset committee in Jackson. They were responsible for the bank's problem loans and wanted to meet me. I answered questions for thirty minutes and left with a promise of more loan assignments. When I returned home the chief had both boots planted in mud at the creek's edge, floppy hat and all. He fished with crickets and from the pleased look, was doing okay.

"Chief," I shouted from the back steps.

He turned and waved. "I'm thirsty. Have you no consideration for hard working public officials?"

"I've never seen one. I thought they only worked to get elected."

"Yeah, yeah. Well, I wasn't elected."

I changed into a pair of shorts and a shirt, my "invisible clothes" as I called them. In them, I was virtually invisible to responsibilities. My pajamas, in the evenings, also satisfied my requirements to disappear. Let me relax.

He already had half a dozen good-sized bream in his bucket when I got there.

"Striking as fast as the crickets hit the water," he said.

I handed him a beer.

"Thought you'd never get here," he said. "I brought a six pack, but they weren't cold. I'll leave 'em for next time."

I flipped a red and yellow fly up stream. He stayed with crickets in his lucky brush pile down stream. We fished for the next ten minutes without a single strike. I swapped flies and tried again. Still no luck.

"Damn," he said and feigned a grimace. "I was doing alright till you showed up."

"You just caught 'em all."

"No, you spooked 'em. Might as well quit." He reeled in. He had enough fish in his bucket for a good meal.

"You been suffering withdrawal pains?" he asked. "Hell, you haven't been in the news for, what, a week or so? How can you stand it?"

I laughed.

"By the way," he said, "Otis was at the mill that night before that screwdriver ended up in that saw motor … picking up more scrap lumber. I don't think he did it, but he was there."

"Not with his own screwdriver."

"Guess who else was there that night?" he asked.

"Who?"

"That Fitzgerald boy."

"Be damned. Osstrum's son?"

"Yeah. He saw Otis come and go and then, he says, he left. He was working on an interim tax report. Morgan backs him up as far as the interim tax report."

"You think he'd know enough about mill equipment to sabotage it?"

"I don't, but on the other hand, how much would anybody have to know? If you stick a piece of metal into something that moves, it's sure gonna play hell with it."

"You talk to him?"

"Yep. He said he went home. His neighbor heard him, but who says he didn't make a five minute detour through the mill first."

The chief took his catch home. I sat on the back porch with my last beer and the newspaper. When the beer was gone, I thawed something ordinary from the freezer, watched the evening news and finished a book about a Russian murder mystery before I fell asleep.

The search for the judge's "loophole" had gone stale. I was ready to think it didn't exist. My subconscious hadn't helped a damn bit.

In the morning, I elected to return the book to the library for another one. Mostly I wanted a cup of coffee with Kathy, but she was not in her office. I left a note and got a cup at a charming little café downtown with autographed pictures of musical groups on the walls. I caught a few words of a conversation at the next table. It sounded like Burl Pitts was in the hospital or, was it Jimmy? I shifted to get more of the story, but the conversation changed. You can't let a story like that go without getting the details, so I walked to City Hall. The chief sat at his desk looking into space. Irene was not at hers. In fact, the radio was off and her desk was clean.

"Bishop, come in!" he said. "Irene's out today, but I made coffee. Help yourself to a cup."

I declined on the grounds that I'd just had one, but I'd smelled it at the main entrance. Had something crawled into the coffeepot and died?

"What brings you into town?" he asked. His smile did little to offset the gloom that hit me every time I walked into his office. The windows were so clouded that very little light made it through from the outside and the water-stained bead board ceiling seemed to absorb what little that did. That, plus all the old yellow photos that decorated his walls, gave the place a look of decay. It never seemed to bother him.

"Nothing much. Did you hear about one of the Pitts being in the hospital?" I asked.

"In fact, I did hear," he said.

"Well, you gonna tell me or what?"

As soon as I stopped talking.

Burl, he said, was in the Lawton hospital with a fractured skull inflicted by Jimmy. Jimmy was in the Sampson hospital for a cracked jaw and numerous cuts and bruises, including broken ribs and jaw. He was not in serious condition. Burl, on the other hand, was still unconscious. The fight started to brew in the morning. When the office staff showed up, Jimmy and Burl were in Burl's office at each other.

"It was not one of those friendly arguments either. Jimmy stomped off and went to that air conditioned shack by the kilns where he works."

"What was the argument about?"

"Apparently Burl was pissed because Jimmy hadn't done something and Jimmy wanted his money or something to that effect. They always argued. That was not unusual, the vehemence of it was. They've never gotten along. That's why Jimmy works out of a shack by the kilns."

"Looks like they would have inherited the mill equally," I said.

"They each own fifty percent of the stock, but according to some kind of document, Burl has the final say in a disagreement. He runs the mill and Jimmy has to take it."

"I can see how that would lead to arguments."

He shrugged. "About eleven, Jimmy storms back into Burl's office. This time Jimmy's calling him names, you know, 'dumb bastard,' that sort of thing. When Burl charged around his desk, Jimmy left again, fast. Nobody did much work in the office. It was like a circus, one lady said."

"I can imagine. You can sell tickets to that kind of ruckus."

According to the Sampson County Sheriff, the chief's source for the story, Jimmy came back from lunch about two, not drunk, but looped enough to be arrogant. He went inside the building, about midway to Burl's office and shouted. 'You were born a bastard. You know that?' Then he hauled ass. Burl tore out after him, but Jimmy escaped.

"Burl didn't say shit to anybody the rest of the day, the sheriff said, and nobody said shit to him."

"So, what happened? Jimmy sneak up behind him?"

"I'm getting' to it! When Burl got to his car to go home, Jimmy rolled by on his motorcycle, decked out in his leather jacket and pants. Well, as he passed Burl, instead of just going on like anybody with an ounce of common sense would have, he did one of those wheely things where the back wheel swings around, and showered Burl with dirt."

"That was probably the last straw," I said.

"Yeah. Old Burl grabbed Jimmy by his black leather collar, jerked his ass off the motorcycle and threw him down. Jimmy jumped up and charged Burl like a mad dog, hit him with every thing he had. They said ole Burl never moved, never blinked, just reached back and hit Jimmy with a right fist that knocked him backwards."

"Like a gnat after a bumble bee," I said.

"Just about. Jimmy wasn't done though. He wiped blood off his face and came at him again. Burl knocked him back on his ass, but Jimmy kept coming back."

"Had to be pissed out of his mind to take that kind of punishment."

"Sheriff said he tried head butting, kicking, kneeing and as many lefts and rights as he could deliver but Burl kept knocking him down with pile driver rights. Barely used his left. Burl's face showed some wear, busted lips and a black eye, but he never backed up, just stood there like a stone wall and waited for Jimmy's charges."

"They'll talk about that fight in Sampson County for the next twenty years. Didn't somebody try to stop it?"

"The night watchman showed up and tried, but they ignored him. He told the sheriff he didn't feel comfortable standing up to Burl."

"Can't blame him for that," I said.

"The only thing that saved Jimmy from a worse beating than he got was the fact that Burl got tired and arm weary. Burl just beat the shit out of that boy."

"Burl ended up with a cracked head. How'd that happen?"

"I'm getting there. Caleb rolls up in his van. Tries to break it up. Can't. Finally grabs Burl's arm and twists him sideways. Without thinking, Burl plastered him good, knocked him flat on his back. Jimmy saw his chance and took it. He picked up a piece of two by four and hit Burl up side the head."

"That how he got a concussion?"

"Yeah. Jimmy took one step and fell flat on his face, dead to the world."

"Doesn't sound like Jimmy will be doing much womanizing in the near future."

"Sheriff says his face is a mess, bumps and cuts, both eyes black. They say he can't take a deep breath because of broken ribs."

"Jimmy has more guts than I gave him credit for or he's crazy as hell. Burl is scary when he's not pissed. I'd hate to be around when he's pissed. Jimmy must have really pissed him off and vise versa."

"Their children are coming to town … check on their daddies," he said. "They're all married, live out of state. I hope it doesn't become a civil war but if does, I'm relieved it's not in my jurisdiction."

Chapter 18

Seth left a message on my answering machine that he had a preliminary report from the Forestry Department at Mississippi State. "They adjusted the auction info we sent for growth and inflation and concluded that Newsome's earlier appraisals were at or above market when made. Skinny's auction appraisals were below current market values."

A detailed report was in the mail to him and he'd call me when it came in.

"Hope this helps," he said.

It shed light, no doubt about that.

Skinny was instructed to appraise low, but what was low? Three million dollars low? I wished I could talk to both men, Skinny and Newsome, but they were dead, and unless I could come up with something, so was my investigation. Based on the report, TRS bought high and sold low. Bad judgment, but no crime. I'd worry about it later. Kathy was on her way out with a bottle of Chianti and I had to clean up the place.

She bounded up the front steps in a golden brown blouse, tight where it needed to be, with matching shorts. I greeted her with a hug and kiss. I almost forgot why she came. Actually did for a time.

Later, we put steaks on the grill and ate by candlelight on the porch. The security lights filled the woods around the cabin and enveloped us in a silvery, comfortable glow and turned the creek into sparkling ribbons. Beethoven's Moonlight Sonata played through the speakers. A herd of deer, led by a big buck, drank at the creek's edge, then scampered into the darkness of the woods.

Like everybody else in both counties, she knew about the fight between the Pitts and listened with great interest to the details I learned from the chief.

The next day, I undertook to put my TRS papers into a box and forget about it. I'd done as much as I could and hadn't come up with the judge's "loophole." I picked up the Gibbs' mortgage to throw onto my stack. More by chance than design, I glanced at the legal description and began to read it against the metes and bounds notes on the surveyor's map, the same one the Forestry Department had used. I'd read so many legal descriptions by then, metes and bounds didn't seem so arcane. I meted along, bound to bound, until I came to a ten degree turn. Instead of following the map boundary, the mortgage description turned and lopped off nearly five hundred acres.

"What the hell is that all about?"

I did the same with Kitchens' mortgage. Her mortgage descriptions "lopped off" about two hundred acres off each of her parcels. A sinister thought sprang into my mind. What if the legal descriptions were "cooked?"

"Use one set of legal descriptions for the auction and bank loans but switch to a second set when the deeds were recorded?" Was that the judge's loophole? The Holdcorp property was not mortgaged so I couldn't tell if a switch had been made there or not. Could be one of those crazy mistakes people make. A clerk grabs one set of legals for the auction appraisals but uses another for the deeds. I couldn't begin to come up with a reason how that could happen. Besides, one mistake I could buy, but three? That'd strain even Murphy's Law.

It looked like Skinny's appraisals matched the acres mortgaged to the bank, but not the acres Gibbs and Kitchens actually got. That would explain why Skinny's appraisals were lower than Newsome's.

"Hell, he just didn't appraise as much land as Newsome did," I thought. "Somebody switched legals on him. His appraisals were likely accurate for the acres he appraised." I couldn't avoid the thought —was he in on it or did he discover it? And, if he was a part of it, he should have been paid. Claire said they didn't have a lot. Hmm, unless he hadn't been paid and complained. I called Claire for Skinny's back up files.

"I don't think Skinny had anything left, Mr. Bone. That Mr. Prozini wanted everything he had, including his appraisal notes. Let me look."

After a few minutes, she returned to the phone and said, "All of his files are gone, Mr. Bone."

I expected that. "How are you getting along?" I asked.

"Pretty good, I guess. I'm looking for work. Skinny's insurance'll pay our bills for awhile but it won't last forever. Caleb bought Skinny's motorcycle. Said he might use it now and then. Made me a good price for it. It was in pretty good shape."

* * * * *

I bundled up the maps and papers for the properties I'd studied and drove to the mill.

Morgan and two others fed logs into one end on the portable sawmill. Scooter and a helper stacked the lumber that emerged onto the flat bed of a trailer for transport to the kiln and planer. Otis hauled logs in and lumber out on a tractor. Big umbrellas that covered the portable mill offered scant protection from the sun's rays.

Morgan saw me and called for everybody to take a break. Scooter and the others found a shady spot, plopped down and drank water from a yellow cooler on the ground.

"I wanted to see how you were," I told him.

"It's damned hard. Harder during the day when it's hot. I'm staying alive, but only just. Let's stand over here." He pointed to one of the few shade trees in the log yard.

"To put it bluntly," he said, "I'm up to my asshole in alligators. The insurance company terminated my coverage. I'm using the insurance of the portable mill owner, the guy I rent it from. That won't last.

"I'm supposed to get an insurance settlement in a couple of weeks. I'm afraid it won't be enough to get the mill up and running even with Burl's help. When this is over—" He made a head gesture at the portable mill. "I'll be faced with some hard choices."

"Sell out?" I asked. We plopped down and leaned against the tree's trunk.

"That may be my only choice. I could rent another portable mill, but they aren't made for high production. Killing work."

"Anything from the bank?"

"Rooster called. As long as I'm not in default, they won't do anything. The loan's on their watch list, on the brink of default."

"The other day I asked you about four parcels of timberland. Three in Lawton County and one in Sampson."

"I remember. Several thousand acres. We did a little logging, but no infestation or forest fires that I could recall."

"It's the acreage I want to nail down. The legal descriptions. Do you know where I could pick up the appraisals TRS relied on when it bought the parcels?"

"You think somebody's been playing games?" he asked.

"It's possible. Might have something to do with the deaths of the judge and Skinny Dearman. Maybe a cover up. At this point, I'm still trying to get a handle on it."

He grimaced as people do when they try to remember something that happened a long time ago. "Prozini bought for the partnership. My job was to manage the mill. He consulted me for sure, but he made the decisions. I walked the land, some of it, before he bought it and reviewed the appraisals, but I only cared about the timber. For details, you'd have to ask him. He's the only one who'd know that."

"You must have records. You were ultimately responsible for logging it," I said.

"Sure. I had records, surveys, appraisals, quantity takeoffs, thinning schedules, the works, but as I told you, Prozini came by and took every file I had. We were scheduled to log the Holdcorp land this year."

Damn it to hell! More blanks. I needed someway to corroborate my suspicion.

Morgan glanced at his watch and motioned at Otis and Scooter and the others. The break was over.

"A cloudy sky wouldn't hurt," he said. "Cool things down. By the way, I called the paper to tell them what Burl Pitts did for us. They said they'd run a story on it."

The sun was hot, but an order had to be filled. I was confident they'd fill it and was damned glad it wasn't me. My cell phone rang as I drove toward town. It was Chief Jenkins.

"Just called to see if you were still alive," he said.

"So far so good. By the way, I have an idea how the bids might have been rigged. What I need is proof and a good suspect." I recited my "cooked legals" theory.

"I didn't figure you'd stop until you found something," he said. "Tell you what. Meet me in Milty's office in an hour. We might as well let him hear it first hand. Bring your maps."

With an hour to kill, I detoured by the library so see Kathy. She was at her computer. I knocked on her office wall.

She looked up and smiled. "Bishop. What are you doing in town?"

"I came in to see Morgan," I said.

"Everybody in town is pulling for him," she said.

"He's down to skin and bones. Works in the sun all day and then half the night. He may be forced to sell if he doesn't get a lucky break."

"That's too bad. I know what that mill means to him," she said.

"It's his life, but he may not have a choice."

"I hope he does."

"Me too." I said. "How about dinner on the river Saturday night?"

The smile left her face. She shook her head.

"Can't, I'm afraid," she said. "I'm going to Sante Fe for a few days to see my children."

That wasn't a total surprise. She usually used some vacation time to visit her two children who co-owned a gift shop on the square.

"I'll miss you. Your mother going?"

"No, she doesn't feel up to the trip. And, wants to finish a painting she's doing. Why don't you come?" she asked.

"Ah, I wish I could. Unfortunately, I have a couple of bank assignments next week. I'll take you to the airport though."

"I, uh, I already have a ride," she said.

Oh? "Just tell them I'll take you. 'Give us a little time together."

"Well, it's … Ray. Ray's going to Sante Fe on business. He offered to drive me to the airport."

"What!" That son of a bitch! I'm sure my jaw dropped. "You're going to Sante Fe with Cooper!"

"A coincidence. He overheard me talking about it and said he was going too."

"I don't like it."

"I didn't think you would, but there's nothing more to it."

"Hell, I can't stand the thought of you next to him for three hours going and coming."

She shrugged. "Not much I can do about it."

"What happened to the intelligence that runs in your family?"

She laughed without conviction.

"You know why his wife left him don't you?" I shouldn't have said that.

Her eyes widened.

If I was any kind of decent human being, I'd keep my mouth shut, but I wasn't, so I didn't. "It's been said that he had some involvement with Chandra Patterson."

"Come on, Bishop! That's ridiculous. You're just saying that!"

"That's what I heard."

"I don't believe it!" Her face took on a frown. "I have to get back to work." She turned to her computer.

"Have a good trip," I said.

She gave me a sideways look without a reply.

Hell, I probably shot myself in the foot with the Chandra thing, but it was the truth, well … sort of, and I didn't like that son of a bitch, Ray Cooper. Going to Sante Fe with Kathy. Coincidence my ass!

* * * * *

Milty and the chief sat at the end of Milty's conference room table. In contrast with Rose's, the room was like most I'd been in over the years, a worn table long enough to seat several attorneys, comfortable chairs and law books in shelves should they be needed. Dust showed where I could see, most likely where I couldn't. Obviously they hadn't been needed in awhile.

"Come in, Bishop," both said.

The district attorney, in his middle years, was a tall, plain-faced, plainspoken man with narrow shoulders. He wore glasses and a dark suit. When he was deep in thought, his face sometimes carried a thin, cruel smile, as if he'd like to kill someone. Except for that, his public face looked like a kindly old uncle. Lots of defense attorneys found out the hard way that he was not so kindly in the courtroom.

"Chief. Milty." I dropped my maps and papers on the conference room table. The DA and I exchanged handshake hellos. It'd been awhile since I'd seen him.

"The chief says you have a new theory," Milty said, speaking in his familiar drawl. "Fresh coffee back there if you want it." He gestured toward the back of the room where a small table held a pot. I declined. Late in the day for me.

"I was going to let it incubate overnight, but the chief asked me to show you, so here I am."

"Let's hear it," he said.

I spread maps of the Gibbs' and Kitchens' parcels on the conference room table. I omitted the Holdcorp map because without a recorded mortgage it didn't show a discrepancy.

"TRS investors lost almost three million dollars on four tracts of timberland. Two parcels bought by a Mrs. Kitchens out of Atlanta and one bought by Mrs. Gibbs from Montgomery." I tapped a finger on the three parcels bought by the women. "I'm not showing the fourth parcel, the one Morgan was a straw bidder on, because it doesn't have a mortgage."

I told them what the Forestry Department said about Newsome's and Skinny's appraisals on the same tracts. Newsome's was at or above market and Skinny's was below market.

"Most likely where the losses came from," Milty drawled and placed the summary sheet on the table. "Judgment error."

"Yeah. Skinny was told to appraise low," Chief Jenkins said.

"Hmm." The DA bobbed his head in agreement, stared at the maps and gestured for me to continue.

"That's how I saw it too."

"So, what's the problem?" Milty asked. "They should have expected losses."

I said. "Look what happens when I compare the mortgage descriptions of Gibbs and Kitchens with the legal descriptions of their recorded deeds."

I traced the boundary of the Gibbs mortgage along the boundary of the property she bought at the auction.

"Right here," I pointed. "The mortgage description turns. That leaves almost five hundred acres unencumbered. Free and clear. Same thing with the Kitchens' mortgages. Each mortgage lops off two hundred acres. She got almost four hundred acres free and clear." I had used a red ink pen to show the mortgaged property lines.

Milty and the chief bent over to look. "Be damned," Milty said. "How do you account for it?"

"I can make a case for using one set of legal descriptions for the bids and the mortgages and another for the final deeds."

"Is that your loophole?" Milty asked. "Switched legals?"

"That's where I was when the chief called me."

"I don't suppose checking the prior conveyances to TRS would help?" he asked.

I shrugged. "I considered it, but what could they show? More acres than they sold at auction? If I'm right."

"Uh, huh." Milty stared at the maps, and traced his finger along the red line I'd used to mark the Gibbs' mortgage. "Well, well. Interesting. Most intriguing. I suppose it'd stretch credibility to think a mistake occurred."

I agreed. "Not three times."

Milty said, "Losses on four parcels, you say, but the discrepancy only shows up on the parcels with the mortgages. Too much to ask for all four to have the same discrepancy?"

"It may have a discrepancy, I just haven't had time to find it. No mortgage like the other parcels. I haven't digested these yet."

"Intriguing. Yes sir, I like it … except for one little bitty thing. Suppose the ladies wanted to keep some of that property they bought free and clear for immediate resell. Suppose the bank said, okay, but you'll have to pledge additional security and they said 'no problem.' What then?"

"Then, my theory wouldn't be worth a damn," I said. "You're right. That is a possibility, but what if that's not the case?"

"Looks like we'd have a nice case of fraud."

I said, "I think Judge Chancellor suspected a switch when he told me there might be a loophole. Skinny was killed when he found out."

"Lots of guesswork, Bishop," the chief said.

"Gotta 'nother flaw," Milty said, staring over his glasses. "What if the ladies weren't the high bidders? Same with that other piece, the one Morgan bid on. Somebody else would get the windfall? How do you cover that?"

"Somebody made damn sure they were the high bidders." I said.

"Make us a conspiracy then, wouldn't it?" He drummed the Gibbs' map with the ends of his fingers. "I assume you talked to the ladies."

"They said they regularly invested in timber land and had connections with the bank."

"Well now. That makes me think the discrepancies may be more from bank negotiations than mistake or fraud. That's what happens when you throw facts at a theory. The theory goes away," he said.

"Ask the bank," I said.

"I will. Yes, sir, I will. Sooner or later, if it comes to it. I don't want to ruffle feathers until I beat the bushes around here." He pushed his glasses up. "Problems, gentlemen, problems to solve." He tapped the maps with his fingertips. "Chief?"

"If it's fraud, everybody on the liquidation team is a suspect. Not to mention Mrs. Kitchens and Mrs. Gibbs," Jenkins said.

"Rose, Washington, Rose's assistant," Milty said.

"Dora Lee," I said.

"Right. Who else? Chance's dead. So's Dearman," Milty said.

"When you boil it down, Milty, only Rose and Dora Lee.

They prepared the documents. All Caleb Washington did was pass out appraisals," Chief Jenkins said.

"Somebody killed two people to cover it up," I pointed out.

"Have to be careful there, Bishop. There's no evidence that Chance and Dearman were murdered. Suspicions, but no evidence," Milty said.

"Add the break in. And somebody sicced Otis on me." I didn't know how Morgan's sabotaged mill played into it, but suspected a link someplace. I kept it to myself.

"You are not without enemies, Bishop," the chief pointed out. "It's happened before."

Just then, I could be convinced that Ray Cooper did it. Logic be damned. I just preferred it.

"The investors lost four million dollars and two people are dead. Murdered, my conclusion, to cover up fraud. Lots of coincidences even without the break in and Otis. Don't you think?" I asked.

"Yep, too damn many," Milty said. "Fact is though, we don't have one scintilla of hard evidence. What do you think, Chief?"

The chief said, "You want to accuse a future Supreme Court Justice of possible fraud? Daniel would be our number one suspect. He ran the liquidation."

"You can see what he says," I said.

"Hell, Bishop, if Rose was part of anything, he'd be savvy enough to have a story ready," the chief said.

Milty turned and asked, "Even so, Chief, lets put it to old Daniel. What do you think? A little due diligence on our part might be warranted."

The chief shrugged. From the way he looked at me, I'd be careful driving through town for a few weeks.

"He could tell us how much access Caleb Washington or Skinny Dearman had to the legal descriptions. Maybe others we don't know about. That Prozini guy might have said something suspicious to him. Does he know the two ladies? I think we can talk about it without pissing off His future Honor," Milty said with a grin. "And, what if we don't?"

"Most likely tell us we're full of shit, tactfully, of course," the chief replied.

"I'd be surprised if he didn't," Milty said. "Let's do it anyway. I haven't talked with Daniel for awhile. Might be the last time I'll be able to before he becomes God almighty."

"Has the Bar Association sent in its recommendation?" I asked.

"I'm told it's a slam dunk," Milty said.

"I suppose you'll call Prozini?" I asked.

"He was definitely in the loop," Milty said. A smile creased his face. "This case may end up as Daniel's first appeal after he's appointed."

"Can we borrow your maps?" the chief asked. "Be easier to explain to Rose."

"Take 'em."

Milty asked me, "Any wild ideas or theories about the Holdcorp piece. Without a mortgage, it doesn't smell like Kitchens or Gibbs."

"Looks like TRS bought high and sold low. It could be a legitimate loss."

"They all could be. That's the problem here." Milty looked hard at me and said, "We'll take it from here, Bishop. You've given us enough to suggest fraud. That makes it the chief's business … and mine." He looked at me as if to say, understand?

I got the message. I was to back off. I had thought to follow up on the Holdcorp parcel, but I'd let them do what they thought needed to be done. As he said, it was their investigation now.

Chapter 19

I sat on the back porch and stared across the creek at the beavers. Kathy on a plane to Sante Fe with Ray Cooper! I couldn't believe it. Nothing ever upset the damn beavers. They never make a faux pas, just do what nature tells them. I made 'em all the damn time. The look on Kathy's face when I told her about Cooper and Chandra said it all. Hell, it's over. Why didn't I keep my mouth shut?

It was a four-beer evening. I paid for it with a terrible headache the next morning that started around three. That's when I got out of bed and turned on the coffee. I sat at the kitchen table and resolved to put it behind me. I hated defeat, especially by Cooper. But, what the hell, if Kathy wanted to tie up with that low life son of a bitch, I call that poor judgment. I made a second pot.

A few minutes before seven, the sound of a lawnmower snapped me out of a stupor. Damn it was loud! I poked my head out the front door. What the hell! Willie Patterson and Otis were in the yard. Willie, his head covered by his old felt hat, hoed the beds like the devil was after him. Otis worked my rusty lawnmower like he was after the devil that was after his grandpa. His head was wrapped in a red headband. How could people work that hard so early? It was already hot enough to melt the flesh off a man's bones. I tried to make sense of it. Had I said something to them that I didn't remember? As overhung as I was, I did not understand.

I stumbled down the front steps and waved. Otis turned off the mower. Willie stopped his motion, smiled and said, "'Morning, Mr. Bishop. Me and Otis decided to do us a good deed this day and cut your grass. You did us one."

"That's not necessary, Mr. Patterson. It's hot out here. Besides, you don't owe me anything. Otis has a full day ahead of him at the mill. I know Morgan needs him."

"Oh, we got time. Won't take me and Otis long to do this piddling ole yard."

It didn't seem so piddling to me, but in one of those indecisive moments we all have, I acquiesced. I was certain it meant something to Mr. Patterson at least. Otis, well, I wasn't as certain about him. I brought out a round of ice water. They finished within the hour. It always took me longer. They promised to be back. I tried to dissuade them, but doubted success. What the hell, I decided not to feel guilty about it. Yard work is hard in the summer.

In the early afternoon, when my head was clear enough to process thoughts, I decided to visit Burl Pitts in the hospital. A nurse showed me to his room. A young man and woman sat on a sofa in his private room. An older woman sat in a chair beside Burl's bed. Flowers occupied the room's shelf space.

"Mr. Pitts," I said. "I heard you'd been hurt. Thought I'd come by and see how you were." He looked sleepy, but otherwise not all that bad. What did Jimmy look like, I wondered?

He looked at me, hesitated a second, but figured out who I was and muttered, "Bone. Uh, thanks for coming." He made a feeble gesture with his hand to the thin, gray haired woman on his right and said, "My wife, Melba. This is Bo—, Mr. Bone. I told you about him."

"I'm pleased to meet you, Mr. Bone," she said with little enthusiasm and looked away. I could only imagine what Burl had told her. "We'll be glad when Burl can come home."

"I'm ready now, by God! Can't stand this damn place," he said. "D'you meet my children?" He pointed toward the young man and woman. I hadn't appreciated that he had children. It turned out that the boy was a petroleum engineer working in Houston. His daughter taught school in Baton Rouge. Both were married.

"By the way," I said. "I think what you did to help Morgan Reynolds was tremendous. It takes a pretty big man to do that."

He mumbled, "… the Christian thing to do."

He didn't volunteer anything about the fight and I didn't ask. I stayed the customary fifteen minutes and left. I wondered if Jimmy's family rallied around his hospital bed. By then he was probably home already. A thought hit me. I bet Jimmy moved into the main office to run the mill in Burl's absence. Sitting in Burl's chair! Most likely the reason Burl wanted out of the hospital. I hoped Jimmy had the good sense to clear out before Burl was released.

Saturday was over. In the morning Kathy would fly to Sante Fe with that bastard Ray Cooper. Sunday promised to be a long day, and was.

* * * * *

On Monday, Milty and Jenkins asked to see "Mr. Rose." When the receptionist called back, they wandered into Rose's plush conference room. In the center of the polished table was a vase of red roses. Their fragrance filled the room.

Milty nudged the chief and smiled. "Red roses." Both knew red roses were Rose's trademark. Every day, someplace in his office was a vase of red roses. Milty spread Bone's maps of the Kitchens and Gibbs tracts on the table. The chief's eyes drifted to the swamp paintings on the wall.

"The judge loved those paintings," he said. "His wife too."

Rose appeared. "Gentlemen." He extended his hand. Milty and Jenkins reciprocated.

"What brings you here?" Rose asked. His eyes went to the maps. "Those look like … are they mine? I thought I'd given them to Prozini."

"No, we brought them," Jenkins said.

"Why?"

Milty answered, "It's this way, Daniel. By the way, congratulations on your appointment. I hear that you'll get the full backing of the Bar Association."

"Thank you," Rose said. "I'm humbled by the opportunity to serve the people of Mississippi. I pray I can live up to the standards of my predecessor."

"I'm sure you will. I'm sure you will," Milty said. "Anyway, back to these." He tapped the maps with the fingers of his right hand.

"The chief's wants to wind up his investigation of Chance's death, Dearman's as well. He thinks there might be a connection with the auction."

Rose said, "Come on Milty! What's to investigate? Chance fell out of his boat and drowned. Dearman died from negligent safety procedures at Reynolds' mill. We filed a suit on the widow's behalf."

"I know. I bet you'll get a good settlement out of it. However, back to the task at hand, we more or less agree that the deaths were accidents. Certainly could have been. Right, Chief?"

Jenkins nodded in agreement. However Milty wanted to play it.

"No connection whatsoever with the auction!" Rose gestured with his hand.

Milty glanced at him and said, "Nevertheless, the chief has a couple of questions he needs to put to bed. You know how he is." Milty smiled and patted Chief Jenkins on the back.

Jenkins said, "I am bothered by what the judge told Bishop Bone the day he died."

Rose stepped back a pace, his face flushed.

"That business about a loophole Bone's told anybody who'd listen? We only have Bone's word that Chance said anything!"

"Bone's not the only source," the chief said. "The judge also said it to his housekeeper. It might not mean much, but I thought I'd better turn it over and look underneath one more time before I close the file. It is a connection."

"Gentlemen, I had the utmost respect for Chance. He was like a father to me, a real friend, but as he aged, the more cantankerous he got. Bone set him off at the auction and he wouldn't let it go."

"We know about that," Milty said.

"Well then." Rose shrugged. "I think he worried himself to death, if you want to know what I think. There was no loophole. We reexamined those procedures in minute detail before the auction. Don't you think we would have found a loophole if one existed?"

"I understand how you might think that, Daniel, but Chance, you see, said he did find one. We can't ignore that now, can we? Here. Take a look at this." Milty bobbed his head toward the maps. "Look," he touched the map for the Gibbs' parcel and repeated what Bone had told them. "This line follows the legal description on her recorded deed. And, this one in red, follows the mortgage description." He did the same for the Kitchens' parcels and opened his mouth to speak, but Rose interrupted. "Did you pay for this?"

"Things cost money," the chief answered

"Waste of taxpayers' funds, as far as I'm concerned," Rose said. "With all due respects, gentlemen, I'd put this meeting in the same category."

"We have a duty to investigate suspicious deaths, Daniel. What if Chance was murdered?" Milty asked. His eyes narrowed. "Wouldn't you prefer to see his murderer brought to justice? With all due respects."

"Of course. You have anything else?" Rose checked his watch. "I have a court appearance at ten thirty."

Milty put his finger on the red line outlining Kitchens' mortgage and said, "An argument could be made that she bid on—"

"What? You want to say this Gibbs woman bid on fifteen hundred acres and ended up with two thousand? Come on!"

"Yes," Milty replied. "That could be the loophole the judge said he found. Use one legal description for the bid, another for the actual transfer of title. Pretty hefty windfall, wouldn't you say?

"Just curious, did your procedures cover that possibility?" He looked over his glasses at Rose. "Somebody switching legals like that?"

"We had safeguards in place, if that's your question. The documents were under lock and key at all times, except during the day when they were available for inspection, here. It's ludicrous to assume somebody made a switch then with as much traffic as we had. I'd say, yes, our procedures covered it!"

"I would think so too, Daniel, but look at it from the other end. Large parcels of timberland around here should bring at least twenty five hundred an acre, even lowball. The Gibbs bid, if spread over two thousand acres, would be closer to two thousand an acre. The same differential shows up on the Kitchens' parcels. Suspicious, don't you think, Daniel?"

"Fantasy, Milty! Not suspicion. Nobody switched any legal descriptions. To make that work, somebody needed access to the bids before they were opened. Otherwise, how could the winning bids be steered? The bids were sealed! Locked up! And Gibbs and Kitchens! I'd never heard of them until we opened the bids!"

"Right," Chief Jenkins said. "But what if somebody did do it, as remote a possibility as that seems to you? Any ideas?"

"Nobody around here! I can tell you that! We used legal descriptions from John Prozini. If anybody asked for a legal description to support a standby loan, Dora sent a copy or they made their own."

"Where were the legal descriptions kept?" Milty asked.

"The originals never left this conference room. Think about it! Not only did the legal descriptions have to be switched, the women had to know how much to bid to come in high. Come on Milty, this is—" His arms flew out from his sides. "I don't know what to call it."

"I reckon the investors'll call it unacceptable, Daniel. They stand to lose millions of dollars on the deal."

Rose opened his mouth, but Milty waved him down.

"There's that other piece of land too. The piece Morgan Reynolds bid on for some out of town outfit. You know the piece?"

"I heard about it."

"They lost a million on that one. That's right close to a three million dollar loss. I don't know about you, but a loss like that'd do serious injury to my bottom line." He shoved his glasses back onto the bridge of his nose.

Rose had begun to shake his head no by then, but Milty waved him off and continued. "It appears to me, this is just a first glance mind you, that we have a pattern here. Lots of money on the table in that auction. Lots of money. What do you think, Daniel? You've had a vast amount of experience. Do you think that much money could tempt somebody?"

"Don't bait me, Milty! I'm not some jack-leg just out of law school! Of course that much money might tempt somebody. But, temptations notwithstanding, it didn't happen! Not in this office!"

Milty smiled. "Don't get your bowels in an uproar, Daniel. Just doing my elected duty."

"Call it what you want, Milty. You're wasting taxpayer money! I didn't screw up that auction. And I didn't commit fraud. Or, murder. I resent your innuendo that I did. I gave you more credit for good sense than that." He glanced at his watch. "I have to be in court. Finish up what you came to say."

"Do you still have the legal descriptions Prozini sent you? I'd like a look, if you don't mind. If they read on the recorded deeds, I'll call the bank over there and ask how they arranged the loans. One step at a time, Daniel. The wheels of justice do grind."

"Prozini took all our files to Chicago. He said it was an abundance of caution. He didn't want anything dissident investors could use out of context."

"A bit unusual, don't you think?" the chief asked.

"No. He knew there'd be losses and consequently, investor complaints. The market had dropped. We kept some stuff, location maps and the like, but most everything got thrown out. We can't find anything and we've looked. Bone asked for it."

"Too bad," the chief said.

From the reception room, Caleb Washington was heard to say, "Here's the appraisal Daniel asked for."

"I'll see that he gets it," the receptionist said. "He's in conference right now."

Rose turned when he heard Washington's voice. "Caleb," he called out. "Do you have a minute?"

"Sure," Washington said and strolled in. "What's going on?" he asked. He greeted both visitors.

Rose told him, "They say that somebody switched legal descriptions after the auction. What do you think?"

"May have," Milty corrected.

Caleb scoffed and asked the chief, "Is this from Bone? He stampede y'all into this? He's—"

"We investigate when we feel it's proper," Milty said. "No one dictates what we do, Mr. Washington."

"Of course," Caleb said. "Of course, but he's been at it since the auction."

"Look here." Milty traced the mortgage descriptions of the Gibbs and Kitchens' parcels on the maps. "Some of that land they bought got left off. Looks a little odd. We just want to find out why."

Caleb said, "Yeah. Looking at it like that, you could jump to that conclusion. However, that doesn't show that anybody switched anything." He cleared his throat and said, "From my experience, I imagine the buyers wanted to have some of that land free to sell. That's why they only mortgaged part of it. Most likely pledged other collateral to get it released."

"That's what I was about to say," Rose said. "For sake of argument, I'll stipulate that Chance may have seen this as a possible loophole, but it's a big jump to go from possibility to reality. What do you say, Caleb?"

"I agree. We were on top of this auction all the way, especially after Prozini hired that Bone guy to look over our shoulders."

"How'd you get the legal descriptions?" Milty asked Rose.

"I thought I'd said. John Prozini sent us the legal descriptions for every piece of land TRS owned."

"The legal descriptions Prozini sent us were identical to the ones in the original appraisals, the ones he used when he bought the property," Caleb said. "I double checked every one."

"Does that answer your questions, Chief? Milty? We did what we were asked with appropriate safeguards. If you want to waste more time, I suggest that you talk to Prozini," Rose said, stealing another glance at his watch.

"I called his office," Milty said. "He's traveling."

"That's right. I forgot," Rose said. "He's on his way to New

Orleans. He said he might stop by Lawton coming back. Probably will. He wants to talk to Reynolds about the mill. He may have a buyer for it."

"He say when he'd be here?" Jenkins asked.

"This afternoon."

"Would you have him call us? I'd like a few minutes of his time," Milty said.

"Sure. If I hear from him."

"You need me for anything else?" Caleb asked.

"One more question," Milty said. "You know Mrs. Kitchens or a Mrs. Gibbs?"

"Never heard of them," Caleb said. "Not before the auction, anyway. I don't know 'em."

"Daniel, who else had contact with the legal descriptions you used for the deeds?" Milty asked. "How about Mrs. Lee?"

"Let's ask her." Rose asked Dora Lee to come into the conference room and repeated Milty's question.

"Don't look at me, sir," she told the district attorney. "I know a legal description when I see it but I'm certainly not skilled enough to alter one."

"But, you prepared the deeds after the auction?" the chief asked.

"I did. And I attached the legal descriptions that were here and sent them to Mr. Prozini to sign and mail."

"Unfortunate that Skinny Dearman had that … accident," Milty said. "He did the cruises on that land and had knowledge of the acres involved."

Rose shook his head with a frown.

* * * * *

"What'd you make of it, Chief?" Milty asked as they walked back to City Hall.

"They sounded convincing enough to me," the chief said.

"I'm curious to see what we get out of Prozini. If we don't come up with something that smells like evidence pretty soon, we might have to throw in our hand," Milty added. "I will call the bank. Might not get anything without a court order, but it's worth a try.

"You going to let Bishop know? When he gets his teeth into

something, he hates to let go," Milty said.

"When he does, he's usually right. I'll call or go out there. You ought to come with me sometimes. There's some good fishing in that creek of his."

"Maybe I will. I haven't been fishing in God knows how long," Milty said. "Let me know sometimes when you go out."

Chapter 20

I slid a bank report into an envelope and mailed it with my bill. The chief called before I left. It was almost eleven o'clock. "Milty's about ready to give it up, Bishop. Me too." He recited their meeting at Rose's office. "If he draws a blank at the bank, he may tell me to drop it. I don't think we need your maps for that. You want 'em back?"

"Yeah. I'll pick 'em up." There was a little more I could do on the Holdcorp piece, but by then, I was about as ready as the Chief and Milty to throw in the towel.

"Rose said Prozini'll be in town this afternoon."

"You mind if I speak to him?" That'd finish me up, I thought.

"Knock yourself out. We left word for him to call us. I have to tell you, Bishop, sooner or later you're going to piss people off. People do file lawsuits you know."

"I'll be tactful."

He laughed. "What do you expect Prozini to say, 'I did it.' Why would he consider such a scheme? Hell, he had a lawsuit on his back from the day they voted to liquidate. He knew they'd be watching. He even hired you to watch! And, how would he know those two women? Too many unanswered questions for that to make sense."

"I agree and I don't know the answers. But, the man's got balls," I said. "Could have seen it as a challenge. Three million dollars worth. By the way, you ever find out why Burl and Jimmy went at it?"

"Nobody's saying more than what I've already told you. Right now Jimmy's king shit over there with Burl out of action. Sitting in Burl's office, I hear. I imagine that'll end."

"Let's hope not in a fatal sense."

I called Morgan. A young woman put me on hold while she tracked him down.

"Yeah?" he said, slightly out of breath.

"Bishop," I said. "I hear that Prozini is coming to town."

"After lunch. One or one thirty. 'Says some broker has a buyer for the mill."

"Are you going to sell?" I asked,

"I don't know. I work my ass off daylight to dark, and I still lose money. I don't know that I have a choice. I have a line on some used equipment, a good buy, but even with the insurance check and the TV money, looks like I'll be a little short. I'd be a fool not to listen to what he has to say."

Just when Burl thought he might get rid of Morgan's mill in comes another buyer. I wondered if head-to-head bids would help Morgan—Burl versus Prozini's buyer. What would Burl pay to get rid of the mill once and for all?

"I'd like to sit in," I said.

"Would you? Hell, I'm a mill manager, not a negotiator. I'd appreciate any suggestions you can offer."

After a stop by the chief's office for my maps, I'd be there.

* * * * *

It was hot as hell when I drove into the mill yard. A jeep's worn canvas top provides no relief. The air conditioner was at the max and hardly made a dent. There wasn't a cloud in the sky. A hawk that floated on the currents above cried out. Probably a complaint about the heat.

Morgan and Scooter were at the portable mill, drenched in sweat. Yellow sawdust sprayed out on both sides to cover the ground as blades whined and chewed through a log. Otis got on a tractor in the log yard to pick up a load of logs. The smell of cut timber mingled with the smell of dust. I waved on my way up the steps to Morgan's office.

"I'll wait inside," I shouted. Where it was cool!

I cleared a table for the maps. I wanted Prozini's reaction to them.

Prozini parked and walked to where Morgan and Scooter worked. His white shirt was crisp, his pants freshly pressed. They swapped comments and gestures as a log ended its transformation from timber to lumber.

Morgan turned it over to Scooter and walked with Prozini to the trailer. Prozini's unblemished shirt turned gray before they reached the door. Morgan's clothes were already black with sweat.

"A man of your talent shouldn't slave in the hot sun like that, Morgan," Prozini said, as they entered the office. He shook at his shirt to free the heat. "We're free now." He smiled.

"Free, John," Morgan said, "but not lazy."

"Touché." Prozini pressed the thin mustache on his upper lip. When he saw me, he said, "Mr. Bone. I hardly expected to see you here."

I stood and shook his hand. "Thought I'd sit in if you don't mind."

"No indeed. If it makes Morgan feel better, be my guest. That must mean you're seriously considering my offer," he told Morgan. "Actually, it's not my offer, per se. I'm only the messenger. I don't have the authority to bind anybody, just want to see where you stand."

"Who do you represent?" I asked.

"I'm here to gather information, Mr. Bone, not represent."

"Maybe I should ask who sent you?"

"I can see that I'll have to be on my toes, Mr. Bone. A representative, whose name I shall not reveal, at his request, called and said he had a client with a real interest in 'our mill.'"

"It's not—" Morgan said.

"Indeed. It is no longer ours, but I said I'd see if Morgan wants to sell since I had to pass through Lawton. Have I made my position clear?"

"I'd say so, Mr. Prozini," I said.

"Call me John, and I'll call you Bishop. Our days of confrontation are behind us. Let us be friendly here."

"Fair enough." The caution flag went up. Anytime the guy on the other side of the table wants to be friends, at the beginning of a negotiation, I check my wallet.

"So, Morgan," Prozini said, "I'm told that the client is reputable and financially viable. This mill would be upgraded to state of the art mill technology.

"Log count could be increased by twenty percent. Yield increased by five or six percent. Not bad huh? Might make the mill profitable."

"I was okay till somebody put that screwdriver in the motor," Morgan said.

"Sure, you changed water into wine, so to speak, but be realistic, man. How long can you keep it up? Sweat to compensate for outdated equipment. You are week to week, payday to payday. One shift removed from a hospital bed. One breakdown away from having to close your doors."

"It's my mill, John. My chance to do what I want to do. If I sell out, I got nothing."

"I haven't heard an offer yet," I said.

"Ah, well then, let's move right along. The client will take over your loan. It's not like you have much leverage," he said.

I asked, "What about a contract for Morgan to stay as the mill manager?"

He gave a palms up gesture with a grimace. The answer was no.

"I walk away with nothing?" Morgan's shoulders dropped.

"If it were up to me, you'd stay. I've always seen you as the best damn manager around, Morgan. You know that. I hired you."

I said, "I don't like to negotiate with someone who has no authority. If Morgan agrees to terms and conditions, not to say he will, who's to say the client wouldn't use Morgan's best offer to start more negotiations? Why negotiate twice?"

"Dear me, Bishop. I suppose that could be true with a shady client."

"We don't know who the client is, do we?"

He shook his head. "That's true. Actually, I don't know the name of the client either, but I know the broker only deals with reputable people."

"Why isn't he here?" I asked.

"Convenience? Secrecy? Take your pick. If Morgan wants to sell, formal negotiations can be initiated. I haven't heard Morgan say he wants to sell. You said you hadn't heard a real offer, well, I haven't heard a real interest in selling."

"I don't want to sell," Morgan said, "but I'm backed into a corner. With all your contacts, John, I don't know why you can't find an investor for the mill. I'd give them stock. Bishop could help—"

"If I find investors, I want them for my ventures. This meeting is an accommodation to a business associate. I scratch his back today. He scratches mine tomorrow."

"I'm not willing to give the mill away," Morgan said. "Every dollar I have is in this mill."

"Maybe so, but what do you have to sell?" Prozini asked. "Some old equipment that doesn't work. Half a crew. Tell me what you can put on the table that's valuable. Businessmen are interested in profits, not charity!"

"What does Morgan have to sell? A business is more than its equipment," I said. "There's its place in a community, its relationship to suppliers and timber owners, customers, the people who work here. It's called good will. Morgan built it, and that's what he would sell with his old equipment, a lot of which still works, and, don't forget, the damned good location of the mill … square in the middle of the pine belt."

"Cela va sans dire, Bishop, that much goes without saying, but only viable concerns have good will. Morgan's is practically closed. How much can all that 'good will' be worth when the mill is closed?"

"It's a going concern. Look out there! That's lumber being shipped." I pointed out the window. "Morgan has a basket full of contracts. People who would rather buy from him than the Pitts, even in the face of Pitts' lower prices. That should tell you something about the good will Morgan has created."

"Okay. What's it worth?"

"I'd say Morgan could sell with a lifetime contract at a competitive salary plus stock options, plus … one million in cash or tradable equities."

"What!" He stifled a laugh. "Ridiculous! You can't be serious."

The activity in the trailer stopped. I could picture the two clerks, as they edged closer to the door. The conversation would be all over town by evening.

"Why is it ridiculous?" I asked. "Because it's one sided?"

"Exactly. Nobody makes a one sided offer and expects it to be negotiated. That kind of offer is a slap in the face. You don't respond to an offer like that, you walk."

"Well, maybe we agree on one thing," I said. "One sided offers are not offers at all."

"Right. I'm—"

"So, when you made your one sided offer earlier, it was a slap in the face."

"Okay, okay," he sighed. "I get your point. Can we say this? Morgan is interested in a good faith offer."

"Not a give away," Morgan added. "Bring me something that makes sense and we'll talk."

"Deal," Prozini said. "We've made progress."

"What about a time frame?" I asked. I looked at Morgan and said, "Don't forget that outfit in Louisiana."

Morgan glanced at me for an instant then bobbed his head. Yeah, that bunch?

"You have another buyer?" Prozini asked.

"An expression of interest," I said.

"Hmm, you're so full of bullshit, Bone, I don't know whether to take you seriously or not," Prozini said.

"We agreed to negotiate on a first name basis."

"You can take him serious, John," Morgan said without a blink.

"Okay, give me a week."

By then, I wasn't sure Prozini's reaction to my maps was worth getting—saving Morgan's mill just topped my new priority list—but I wanted it anyway.

"Before you leave, let me show you something." I pointed to the maps on Morgan's worktable and talked him through what I'd told Milty and the Chief including the possibility that somebody switched legal descriptions after the auction and killed the judge and Skinny Dearman to cover it up. He began telling me "no" with his facial expressions well before I'd finished.

"No way! You're wrong, Bishop. Totally. Listen, I know we lost money. The market went soft. Otherwise we would not have liquidated. I regret the hell out of it. It put me out of business, but let me educate you a little." He touched the Gibbs and Kitchens tracts outlined on the maps.

"The bank likely released land because the women pledged equivalent collateral. Standard practice. Just because the bank didn't encumber all the property doesn't mean somebody switched legal descriptions … or killed anybody."

I pointed out what the Forestry Department had said about Newsome's and Skinny's appraisals.

"That just means we got screwed. We bought high and sold low. Still doesn't prove legal descriptions were switched! I'd be damn sure of my facts, if I were you, before I accused people of fraud … or murder."

"I just wanted to point out the discrepancies, in case they come up. Say, during litigation."

He scoffed. "You point with a damn heavy finger, Bone. You're practically accusing the liquidation committee of fraud!" He shook his head.

"Or somebody close to the committee," I said. "Could be somebody in your office. Could be you."

"How? We had no access to the bids. How could we benefit from what you're talking about? We sent the judge legal descriptions. I signed the deeds from the auction and we mailed them according to Ms. Lee's instructions. The deeds were prepared by Rose's office."

"Did you crosscheck to make sure they were right?"

"Why would I? I relied on Rose and the judge. Besides, according to you, the recorded deeds were okay."

"I meant against the legal descriptions of the tracts TRS auctioned," I said.

"We gave Rose our files. Hell, do you think I had time to come down here and read every damn legal description on the auction list! Would you have?" he asked.

"Do you know Alice Kitchens or Barbara Gibbs?"

"I've never heard of 'em! And I wish to hell I'd never heard of you! Thanks for ruining my day."

"Glad to help," I said.

To Morgan he said, "I'll get back to you in a few days. If not me, a broker. Give me that much before you offer the mill to anybody else. I hadn't considered you seriously wanted to sell."

"I want to keep the mill. If I can't do that, I want to stay on as manager."

A twist of Prozini's head answered that. It wasn't a yes twist.

He and I left at the same time. His practiced smile vanished. We didn't speak on the way to our vehicles. He turned toward town and I turned toward home.

Morgan trudged back to the mill as we cleared the gate. Scooter needed a break. They'd work late into that night. The temperature was in the high nineties, but there was an order to fill.

* * * * *

Dora Lee escorted Prozini to Rose's office at the rear of the old building. He scoffed as he passed the picture of Rose and the Governor.

"John. Come in" Rose stood and said. "Take a seat." Framed photographs that attested to his many career accomplishments occupied the upper walls of his office, bookcases the lower.

Prozini eased onto the sofa. Rose walked around his desk to offer his hand. Prozini reciprocated, but without enthusiasm. Rose took a chair to face him. "I'm pleased you could stop by. Can I get you something to drink?" Dora waited for instructions.

"I'm not here to drink," Prozini said.

Rose waved her away.

"You sound disgruntled," Rose said. "What's the—"

"That's an understatement! You were the attorney on timberland we bought, what, five or six years ago, from the Pitts."

"So."

"We sold those parcels at auction, lost three million dollars. Bone claims the legal descriptions were altered somehow. He may be full of shit, but two bidders ended up with nearly a thousand acres of timberland, free and clear."

"I heard about it. The district attorney told me the same thing. It's fantasy as far as I'm concerned. Nothing to worry about."

"I'll tell you what's to worry about! You were the Pitts' attorney when we bought that damn property. How could you represent us? If that's not a conflict of interest, I don't know one! Osstrum and his bunch sure as hell will see it as one!"

"Wait a minute, John. Look at your file. I let Chance … Judge Chancellor, handle all deals that involved the Pitts. It wasn't that I had a conflict of interest so much as there was an appearance of a conflict."

"A lawyer's dodge as far as I'm concerned. The judge sat in the next office. You guys were partners. What one partner does, the other one stands behind! We got screwed! And it looks like I let it happen. That's what Osstrum's bunch will say!"

"You're misdirecting your anger, John. Did you find anything wrong with the legal documentation? No! Did you get clear title? Yes! There was nothing wrong."

"We paid the Pitts too damn much for that timberland if Bone is right. And, guess what? Pitts put in a low bid on one of the parcels they sold us at top dollar, one of the deals you handled."

"I told you that Chance—"

"Bullshit! They sold high to us—your deal— and bid low at the auction, also your deal. How many times were you going to let me get screwed? When Osstrum and his bunch of crybabies find out, it's going to be my butt they come after!"

"As I recall, you negotiated the price when you bought the land. All we—"

"We negotiated on appraisals you ordered! I called my office on the way over here. Newsome did every damn one of the appraisals. The letterhead on his bills listed Caleb Washington as an associate."

Rose made a so what gesture with his hands.

"Everybody knows that Washington appraises everything the Pitts buy. He's practically on the payroll. Washington was on both ends of our deals, high and low. How do you think that will sound in court? I can tell you. Mismanagement!"

"Appraisers are like attorneys, John."

Prozini scoffed. "Attorneys! Wow, that really gives me confidence!"

Rose ignored the interruption. "They're professional people. Anything Newsome appraised was independent of Washington. Dearman appraised the properties for the liquidation. Dearman is, was, a professional appraiser with his own reputation to protect."

"Yeah, and I can't help but notice that all of a sudden he's dead as hell."

"An accident."

"A convenient one, if it was," Prozini said.

"What do you mean? You sound like Bone."

"Yeah. Well, maybe he's right. Cutting through your legal bullshit, I'm saying TRS has been screwed to the tune of what, close to three million dollars and Osstrum's gonna blame me. You know who I'll blame?" He pointed a finger at Rose. "Call your carrier. You're going to need a defense!"

Rose's face turned crimson. He stood. "You'd waste your time and money. We submitted our liquidation plan to you for approval, including the appraisal committee and its chairman, Caleb Washington."

"The Pitts' man, I—"

"It would be impossible to find appraisers who hadn't appraised timber for some or all the bidders. Besides, appraisals were for information purposes only. You directed that they reflect the low end of value to encourage bids. That letter is in the file. It was your job to review the appraisals before the auction. Did you?"

Prozini didn't answer.

"I didn't either, but I'm an attorney. You're in the business. You knew, or should have known, the going rate for timber. It is not my responsibility to pass on the accuracy of an appraisal. Appraisals differ. It was your job to check! Not mine. You set the minimum bidding limits. So don't point a finger at me!"

"Maybe everything was on the up and up and maybe it wasn't, but if Osstrum's shit hits my fan, I'm going to make damn sure some of it hits yours. I paid you to protect me. You didn't. That's the bottom line."

"Say what you will, John, but think before you act. Look at your files, if you have any left. You'll see that everything was fully disclosed to you."

"I get it. You say I didn't read the fine print. I didn't think I needed to with you."

"I don't use small print," Rose replied.

Prozini slammed Rose's office door behind him.

Rose asked Dora to bring him their files. Minutes later, he called Caleb. "Prozini was just in here, ranting and raving about the Lawton and Sampson county parcels TRS bought some years back. I handled the sale. You and Tommy appraised 'em. Prozini claims we screwed him."

"Ha," Caleb said. "Nobody screwed anybody. Newsome signed the appraisals and he's dead. Skinny signed the liquidation appraisals and he's dead. I'm sorry they're dead, sorry as hell, but as a practical matter, Prozini can rant and rave till the cows come home."

"He's worried about Osstrum and the complaining investors."

"They ain't gonna find shit either. Prozini took all the files with anything to do with the auction. You said they ended up in the dump. What's he going to do? I can swear in court that we did everything right! And, we did!"

"I hope you're right. I don't want any adverse publicity just now," Rose said. "Not while the Bar Association considers my appointment."

"Sounds to me like Bone's stirring this up."

"Prozini said as much. Milty and the chief said the same."

"He's a trouble maker," Caleb said.

"I don't want the son of a bitch to screw up my appointment."

"Careful with the language, Daniel No profanity, remember?"

Chapter 21

Vivaldi played on my outside speakers while I read the paper and watched afternoon shadows creep over my little spread. All things considered, it was as good as it would get for me. I missed Kathy. Hell, I had to work hard to keep her out of my thoughts, but if she made a decision, I had to accept it. That son of a bitch, Ray Cooper! Or, maybe I was the son of a bitch. I picked up the phone.

A young woman answered. "This is Bishop Bone. Could I speak to Kathy?" Soft, feel good music played in the background. That's not the way I felt.

"Oh, Mr. Bone!" she said. "Mom isn't here right now."

"Do you expect her back soon? I can "

"Umm, I don't know. She went out. It might be late."

Shit! That's what I thought. Dinner with Ray Cooper.

"Tell you what, I'll call back … maybe tomorrow." I wouldn't, but I could hang up without cursing.

"I'll tell her you called."

Don't bother, I thought. Vivaldi's "Seasons" stirred the outside air. Shades of evening cloaked the woods. Night birds sang and lightning bugs lit the dark with amber glows. Nocturnal creatures felt secure enough to creep to the edge of the creek for a quick drink, then vanish into the darkness. And, I fumed.

"To hell with it. I'm going to the Pub!" I needed a distraction from my stupidity.

* * * * *

Cars filled the slots in front of the Pub, and people filled the entry alcove to wait for a table. Another aggravation. The gremlins were after me in full force. I cursed and drove on. With that many people around, there was bound to be somebody in there I knew and I sure as hell didn't feel up to a social visit. I pressed the accelerator and passed an assembly of motorcycles, Skinny's, now Caleb's, among them. Next to his was Jimmy Pitts' brightly chromed cycle.

"Doing the Pub crawl," I mumbled. They should be home with their wives. Don't be cynical I told myself. For all I knew, their "birds" rode in with them. I'd go to the Fire Hole for a beer, maybe have a basket of catfish fingers, hushpuppies and fries. It could be a rough place, but the food was good.

I almost missed it. Was that Cooper's red Corvette? Couldn't be. He was in Sante Fe at dinner with Kathy. It pissed me off to think it. Maybe somebody else had one. Maybe he loaned his to a friend. I had to find out. I parked and walked back.

I eased past those waiting in the alcove and picked a seat at the bar with good visibility. The Pub was crowded, with lights turned low for effect. Candles flickered at the tables. People huddled over tables to laugh and exchange stories. Recorded music played through speakers. Yeah, everybody was having fun. Except me!

Caleb and Jimmy nursed beers and swapped wisecracks with a waitress at a table in the bar area. Their shiny helmets sat on the floor. They didn't see me. Black leather windbreakers lay draped over their chair backs. The chrome studs glistened in the soft Pub light. Jimmy looked stiff and uncomfortable from the fight. I imagined his face still showed the consequences of his bad judgment, but it was covered in shadows.

The bartender took my order for a mug of their best. I resumed my search. Ah, there! Cooper! Cooper? It was dark except for the candles, but there was enough light for me to see the shadowed smile on his face and that of his young dinner companion. So, the son of a bitch wasn't in Sante Fe after all. I didn't know what happened, but I was glad, whatever it was. I could hear my gremlins stomp off to look for another victim to harass. About damn time!

I felt better in a flash. I had my beer and a spicy catfish plate at the bar. Nobody bothered me, and I didn't bother anybody. I went home a hell of a lot happier than when I left. The security lights were on and my doors were closed. I bounded up the porch steps to hurry inside. Hell, I was happy enough for another beer, just on general principles. My answer phone beeped.

"Bishop. This is Kathy. Sarah said you called. We finished early. Paul wanted me to look at some inventory a gift shop needed to unload. Turned out there was nothing he wanted." Sarah and Paul were her children.

When I called back, she picked up the phone on the first ring.

"I walked outside to watch the creek run past, and I thought of us. Thought I'd call to see how you are."

"I'm fine. I had a good flight. At the last minute Ray cancelled. I almost called you to take me to the airport, but one of the girls in the library dropped me off."

"I would have. "

"I know."

"Sorry I raised a stink about Ray," I said.

"I thought at first you were jealous, or rumor mongering. You didn't need to be concerned. However, Ray came into the library a few minutes after you left. Suggested dinner at the Pub."

Asshole, I thought.

"When I asked if that wasn't where Chandra Patterson had worked, he practically turned green. Needless to say, we didn't have dinner, and he didn't fly to Sante Fe with me. I was relieved. I dreaded it."

"Me, too."

She laughed.

The view out back looked better than usual that night. Crickets and frogs and evening birds filled the night with music. Bats yo-yoed up and down over the creek to catch bugs. A coyote howled in the woods, and a flock of deer pranced by for a quick sip. And Ray Cooper was shit out of luck.

* * * * *

Milty and the chief told me to back off, but I had a couple of questions for Washington before I turned it loose.

"Is Caleb around?" I asked the guy who answered the phone.

"No, he's, uh, let me see. The sign out board says he's out with Jimmy Pitts. The Pitts are harvesting lumber in the Crosby Community. He wanted to scale some of the logs as they were cut."

The community was named for the first family to settle there or perhaps for whoever opened the first "filling station" or grocery store.

"Where is it?"

"Not too far." He gave me detailed directions. "Watch out for the log trucks. They get paid by the load and try to make five loads a day. They don't mess around."

It threatened rain. Lawton could use a two or three day steady rain to cool things down. The hot, dry weather was good to harvest timber, but not good for crop farmers and people with soft topped jeeps and bad air conditioning.

I passed three fully loaded log trucks, all scraped up here and there. I never saw one that wasn't. In the old days, before the law got tough, some were without doors. Men with tired, lined faces hunched over steering wheels and drove as if their lives depended on one more load before time to quit. Shirts with ragged holes for arms; unkempt beards and stringy dark hair twisted in the wind that poured through open cab windows. They either had no air conditioning or what they had didn't work.

I spotted Jimmy's Harley and pulled off the road. Beside the Harley were two tractors, one with a front shovel and another with a grappling hook that dangled at its rear. A yellow cooler sat on the ground in the shade. Jimmy stared at a yellow tractor fitted with massive, circular arms; his face shaded by a straw hat with a broad brim. His short sleeved khaki shirt, pants and boots looked as if the heat had not touched them. He turned as I parked and came toward me with an outstretched hand. Both his eyes were still black. He bent forward with each step to show he favored his injured midsection.

"What are you doing out here?" he asked through clenched teeth of his broken jaw.

"I wanted to ask Caleb if he had Skinny's survey notes on some of the parcels sold at the TRS auction."

"Uh huh. He's down the road yonder to do a little spot scaling. We'll log here next. Maybe not today, though." He looked at the sky. "Looks like rain."

The cooler air was filled with the fresh smell of moisture. There was no thunder, however, and no imminent turbulence.

"Yeah," I said.

"Dry is better for logging and hauling. Trucks slide all over hell on wet blacktop."

I pointed toward the yellow tractor with stubby vertical arms and a glass protected cockpit. "What's that?"

"That's a feller buncher," he said and winced as he turned.

What the hell was a feller buncher?

He must have seen the look on my face because he said, "It grabs a tree with its arms, cuts it off just above ground and fells it where you want it. Depending on size, it can hold onto more than one. We call that bunching. A feller buncher."

Descriptive to the core. Something to tell my grandkids.

"In the old days, when a tree was cut, it fell pretty much the way it leaned. We knocked down lots of young trees that way, some older ones too. With the feller buncher, we can lay the trees in an open spot!"

"Automation?"

"Damn right." He talked like a bad ventriloquist. "Took me awhile to convince Burl of that. Hell, if it wasn't for me, he'd still cut logs by hand and drag them out of the woods with oxen."

My eyes drifted to the tractor with the grappling hook.

"That's a skidder. The driver grabs hold of a log with that grappling hook and drags it to a collection point where it's loaded onto a truck. That shovel," he pointed toward the other tractor. "cleans up the slash so the land can be re-seeded."

He waved at a stand of hardwoods. "You can cut an oak and it'll send out new shoots the next spring. Don't have to re-seed them. Pines, you have to re-seed."

"I'll be damned," I said.

"Takes a lot of capital to get into the timber business these days. We've got a machine down the road that strips limbs off trees. Saves a lot of time. Guess what it's called?"

"A de-limber?"

He laughed and immediately winced. "You looked at the answer."

"I suppose you heard about Morgan Reynolds' problems?" I asked.

"Yeah, a prime example. He went in on a shoestring. He should sell and get out of the business."

I didn't know how to respond since I wasn't sure Morgan wanted it known that he had an interested buyer, so I kept my mouth shut.

I did say, "Didn't Burl consider buying Morgan's mill, to shut it down?"

"That's right. He hates competition. He never liked to be told what to do even when we were kids."

"But he took a crew down there and helped Reynolds clean up the mess."

"Now and then Burl lets the Bible get between him and his bottom line. It doesn't happen a lot."

"I heard you two got into it," I said.

"Uh huh. I had to teach the big bastard a lesson." He didn't say more. Well, in the eye of the beholder, even if the beholder's eyes were black.

Caleb drove up in his gray van and got out with a clipboard. He was in jeans and boots. When he saw me, he threw the clipboard back into the van. He called my name by way of acknowledgement and extended his hand for the customary greeting. "Surprised to see you out here," he said. "This is wilderness country."

He turned toward Jimmy and said with a jerk of his head, "'Bout finished what you'd set out to do down yonder. If the rain holds off, they'll be able to get a few more loads before the end of the day."

"Good," Jimmy said.

I told Caleb that I needed information.

"I'll help if I can."

"I need copies of Skinny Dearman's appraisals of some land you guys sold at auction."

He shook his head before I'd finished.

"Can't help you, Mr. Bone. That black guy from Chicago told Daniel he wanted every thing that had to do with the auction. Something about a lawsuit."

"You turned everything over?"

"Daniel said we weren't to keep anything. I even bundled up my, well, Skinny's survey notes. Hell, I don't know what fuckin' good they'd do anybody, but Daniel said everything, so I cleaned out our files."

I cursed to myself. "Let me ask you this, then. You know the parcel Morgan put the straw bid on?"

"Sure do. Jimmy and Burl bid on it. Theirs was low."

"You worked for Newsome when the Pitts sold the land to TRS, didn't you? You must have helped Newsome do the appraisal."

"Not really. Tommy did his thing and I did mine."

"Some people say his numbers favored the Pitts."

"Bull shit. The numbers were on target," Jimmy interjected. "That was good timberland. Still is."

Caleb shrugged. "Newsome's appraisals were good when he signed them. Not a better forester in these parts, no two ways about it. However, anybody will tell you an appraisal is only an estimate and only good for when it's made. Prices change over time. A buyer can always get a second opinion."

"How many do that?"

"Not many," he said. "But, most people in the business come to have a gut feel for value."

"The TRS investors think that Newsome's appraisals cost them a few million dollars. Or Dearman's."

"Shit happens," Jimmy said. "TRS might have dumped some of that land before the auction. Logged some. Like as not recouped some of their investment before the auction."

"That wasn't the case," I said. I wasn't certain, but said it like I was.

"Uh, huh. Like I said, market conditions change," Caleb said. "TRS got caught in a squeeze. Timber market turned soft. Why do you think they had to liquidate?"

"Some people think it was more than the market." I bluffed to get a reaction.

"What's that supposed to mean?" Caleb's face reddened with an angry frown.

"There's talk that the bids were rigged. Judge Chancellor said as much to me. The investors—"

"Yeah, They lost money, so it must be somebody else's fault. How many times have we heard that, Jimmy?" he asked.

"More than I can count on my fingers," Jimmy said through his teeth.

"Were the parcels marked for inspection before the auction?" I asked. Surely the boundaries were marked with ribbons or stakes so interested parties could see what was up for bid.

"Of course they were. What do you think?" Caleb said. "We tied ribbons at every change in direction. Put up markers. Followed the legal descriptions Prozini sent us. I doubt you'd find them now though. Last time I checked the markers and ribbons were torn down. Some survey stakes are still in the ground, but you'd need a surveyor to find 'em."

That sounded like a dead end.

"Skinny was worried about the descriptions." I threw that out to see if it'd catch anything.

"What do you mean?" Caleb asked. "If Skinny was concerned, he'd 'a told me. He didn't." He took off his cap and ran a hand over his silver hair. "Sorry, Mr. Bone, you must have misunderstood … or somebody did."

Damn. It was like fishing without bait.

Jimmy half waved at the "feller buncher" and said, "Bone wanted to know what it was."

"It cuts trees and lays them in a bare spot on the ground," Caleb said.

"I told him. Hell, Caleb, I think I'll show him how it works. I haven't been on one of these things in awhile." He turned to me. "You want to see how it works?"

"Sure," I said.

"I'll cut that one," he pointed with his head at a twisted pine with knots and limbs. "That's the kind Reynolds cuts. Not worth taking to our mill."

He went toward the machine, but paused when he reached for the door handle.

"Damn ribs," he cursed. "Caleb, get that fuckin' brace off the back of my cycle. Can't breathe with it on, can't work with it off." Jimmy eased into the machine's cabin and slid into the seat with a loud grunt.

He pushed at something and the diesel engine jumped to life. With obvious difficulty, he maneuvered it in the direction of the rejected pine. When in place, he raised out of the seat, opened the door and shouted, "I'm gonna cut it and lay it over there." He pointed to a bare spot ninety degrees away from where I figured the tree would fall.

As he sat down, his face pained. "I need that damn brace, Caleb!" The massive metal arms at the front of the tractor closed tightly around the tree as Jimmy yanked levers. He pulled another lever and a saw whirred and cut into the tree's trunk below the yellow arms.

Caleb hustled around the tractor and climbed into the cab with the brace. Jimmy held up while Caleb wrapped the cloth brace around his midsection. Yellow sawdust sprayed outward as the saw ripped through the wood. Within seconds it was cut clear through and yet, except for a slight tremor, the tree was held upright in the tractor's arms.

When Caleb pulled to tighten the brace, Jimmy grunted loudly and fell to one side. At that, the tractor lurched and twisted around and took the tree with it. The metal arms held the tree upright, but it swung in my direction. I didn't want to run, but it crossed my mind.

I wished I had. As Jimmy righted himself, his hand flew up and the metal arms that grasped the tree opened. Both men grabbed at the controls, too late. That damn tree dropped directly at me.

In one of those split seconds, I looked right and left and spotted a massive oak to the right of where the pine would fall. I got there about the time the limbs of the pine raked through the limbs of the oak in a downward sweep. I hugged that oak like a new layer of bark. Even so, pine limbs scraped my arms and shoulders, and left cuts and bruises as they whipped past. My shirt was in shreds.

The tree hit the ground with a loud thump and sent shock waves under my feet. A plume of dirt, leaves, and bark flew everywhere like debris from a bomb blast. I didn't move. I wasn't even sure I could. No matter where I looked, all I saw were pine limbs.

"Son of a bitch!" I heard Jimmy say.

"Is he dead?" Caleb asked.

"Don't know," Jimmy answered. "Help me off this damn thing."

I wasn't dead, but if I had followed my instinct to try and run away from the tree's fall, I would have been. Instead I ran into the fall and saved myself. A few cuts and bruises were far better than a mashed skull or at the very least, broken bones. Seconds later, I saw their faces peer through the mesh of tangled limbs in search of my body. "In here," I shouted.

Caleb got a chain saw from his van and sawed a passage way for me through the limbs. Minutes later, I stood outside the tree's crown and stared at the tangled mass, thankful to be alive. I ripped off the remains of my shirt and threw it into a pile of trash.

Jimmy apologized. "When Caleb tightened this damn thing, it was like somebody'd stuck me with a knife and my hand slipped. We grabbed for the controls, but that tree was already falling."

"I noticed."

"Can we buy you a drink or something?" Jimmy asked.

I declined. My arms and shoulders itched all over and had red streaks. I wanted to get home and take a bath and paint my wounds with Mercurochrome.

"I'll take a rain check," I said. Hell, I didn't have a shirt to wear anyway.

A loaded log truck passed and honked to signal his last load of the day. Jimmy waved. Just as well. The sky was a mass of dark clouds that churned and exploded with white streaks. I'd be lucky to get home before they let loose the water they brought with them.

"At least you got to see how the feller worked," Jimmy said.

"In spades."

Chapter 22

I reached my top step as the first drops of rain fell. Before I was out of the shower, pile driver sized drops of rain rattled the roof. The steady thump had a relaxed rhythm to it. I went onto the porch to witness nature's tantrum. Thunder and lightening sent echoes through the woods. Sheets of rain whipped about by the wind, whistled through the screen of my back porch. The icy sprays felt good on my face. Before it was over, a small tree from someplace up stream floated past to shoot over the falls and lodge down stream, an obstacle to floaters and canoeists.

I reflected on the near miss with death. Not accidental, my cynical side said. Yet, I'd witnessed Jimmy's obvious pain, before he got into the tractor and afterwards. He should not have attempted what he did with broken ribs. Had Caleb deliberately yanked too hard on the brace?

Hell, I didn't know. I was lucky to walk away. The twenty-two I'd carried since Otis' attack was useless against a tree. The day ended on a high note though. Kathy called from Sante Fe. I didn't tell her about my encounter with a tree. Perhaps the real reason I kept it to myself was that she wasn't here to "oh" and "ah" and to soothe my wounds. It was her night to baby-sit for both sets of grandchildren, she told me, so her children could enjoy a night out before she came home. No, she hadn't seen her ex, in case I wondered.

I'd meet her at the airport.

* * * * *

When Kathy looked me in the eyes, fresh off the plane and flashed her special smile, it warmed my soul. I knew we were okay. I wanted to celebrate her return with a bottle of wine, but she was tired from the trip and needed to see her mother.

"Saturday night, though," she said with a smile and touched the tip of my nose with a finger. "Get fresh croissants for Sunday coffee."

* * * * *

"Prozini threatens to hold up final distribution until our complaint is settled," Jonas Osstrum told his stepson as they sipped cocktails before dinner. "Blackmail to make us drop it."

"Can he do that?" Fitzgerald asked.

"Not only can he, he can use the money to defend the lawsuit," Osstrum replied.

"If you win, you'll get it back won't you?"

"If anything's left."

"He has assets, doesn't he?"

"I expect he hid anything we could get at. Our lawyer isn't even convinced we have a case. You heard anything helpful?" Osstrum asked.

Fitzgerald shook his head. "The news around here is the big fight between Burl and Jimmy Pitts. It was a real brawl. Both ended up in the hospital. If Jimmy hadn't hit Burl on the head with a piece of wood, Burl might have killed him. They say Burl gave him, as they like to say down there, a real ass whoopin'."

"I'll be damned. What was it about?"

"Nobody says. If they know. A few days before, Burl called me up to do a 'special job.' He didn't say what, just 'show up.' He took me into the vault, where they keep their daddy's moonshine money. I told you about it."

Osstrum recalled that he had.

"'Count it, every damn dollar,' Burl said. He picked up a notebook that I took for a logbook, and put it under his arm. If either took money out, they had to enter the amount and date. I don't know how they accounted for it as between them."

"Offsets to bonuses, you think?"

"Who knows? When Burl started out the door, I told him I didn't feel comfortable counting the money by myself. He pointed to a camera. 'You won't be alone,' he said.

Osstrum laughed. "Sounds like a hard man. How much was there?"

"You won't believe it. There was over three million dollars in that safe. Mostly hundreds and fifties. Three million, eight hundred and fifty three thousand, four hundred and eighty dollars."

"He say anything when you told him?"

"Just snapped his head like he knew it. Later I heard about the fight. I wonder if that money might have had something to do with it?

"They don't get along. Jimmy's in charge of the kiln and little else. People at the mill answer to Burl. Jimmy chases around. I suspect he taps the moonshine money to support his habits. Has a reputation. I don't think Burl likes it. Probably what the fight was about."

"Is he married?"

Fitzgerald said, "Yes. I don't know how his wife puts up with it. He's been after a girl in the office, Mae Belle in the accounting section. Once I saw them in front of his office. He had his hand on her behind. Old Burl saw them too and hollered, 'Mae Belle get in here!'"

"What happened?"

"They sure as heck quit. Last time I was out there, Mae Belle wasn't at her desk. I don't know if she was fired or what."

"Almost four million dollars! Whew!" Osstrum said and drained the last of his glass. "That daddy must have made some damn good moonshine." His eyes searched the restaurant for their waitress.

"There's no way for one to keep track of what the other takes of the money. All one of them has to do is grab a handful of bills and log in whatever amount he wants."

"How would anybody know?"

"From the look on Burl's face when I told him how much was left, he looked like he suspected Jimmy had cheated."

"Ah, here come our steaks," Osstrum said.

* * * * *

On Labor Day, Kathy and I drove to the Campbell's farm for their annual celebration. Some people in Lawton judged their social standing by whether or not they were invited. My invitation came from the time I worked for Seth. Political speeches were made around noon to make the evening news. I timed our arrival for later in the afternoon. It wasn't August hot, but warm enough to make short sleeves and shorts feel comfortable. We parked in a bush hogged lot that sloped down to a lake where guests stood and talked. Some sat on picnic benches. Kids raced about.

Smoke curled up and into trees from cookers worked by men in aprons and tall hats. Tables heaped with food sat near the cookers. Ice filled barrels beside them held drinks. People lined up with plates all over to get some of everything. The sweet smoky smell of barbecue and strains of live music from a group on a platform filled the woods.

I took a deep breath and said, "Smell that barbecue!"

Kathy said. "Makes my mouth water."

We walked toward the nearest cooker. Passed, as we did, the Campbell's weathered log cabin that overlooked the lake. In the style of a Cajun shack, it had a tin roof and a wrap around roofed porch furnished with a number of padded rocking chairs, most occupied. Rose and his wife were on the porch in a conversation with what I took to be a group of lawyers and their wives. I don't know why, but it surprised me that Rose had a wife. How in hell could any woman put up with him?

We grabbed plates and lined up. I asked Kathy to go first. I didn't know what to take, it all looked so good, barbecue chicken, pulled pork, ribs, barbecue beef. Was I hungry enough for some of all? Kathy took a side of barbecue chicken, coleslaw, spicy baked beans, thick and creamy and fresh baked French bread.

I took a pile of pulled pork heaped onto a huge bun, a slab of ribs, the spicy baked beans and potato salad made with crunchy celery and onions. Pies and cake and bowls of fruit and buckets of homemade ice cream a lady spooned up waited on a dessert table. I'd be back. We took small bottles of wine from the ice-barrel and found a table in the shade where we devoured our food to the tunes of the country western band on the music platform. The spices in the barbecue and the beans were the best ever. Sauce from the ribs crawled down to my elbows, but how else can you eat ribs?

We had to make a choice, seconds or dessert. We took dessert. "Ice box pie," somebody said. A country favorite. Kathy was sensible and passed, but I pigged out. It'd take some extra jogging to work off the calories, but I had no regrets.

Rooster stopped by our table. His wife went to Knoxville to visit their son. Bank business kept him in town. Neither of us had suggestions to solve Morgan's problems. As the sun dipped behind the trees and covered the lake and cabin in shade, guests began to wind their way to the parking area. Kathy and I stopped by the cabin to thank Seth and Beth for their hospitality. Inside the rustic living room, Chief Jenkins and his wife were giving their good byes to Seth and Beth. Kathy and I moved toward them to add ours. We were the last.

Seth said, "Wasn't this great?"

"Best ever," We replied.

"Beth did a fantastic job." He pulled her to him and gave her a big squeeze. He got a big smile in return. Beth urged the four of us to stay a little longer.

"Anything new on that timberland you asked me about?" Seth asked.

"I meant to call you. I think I found the judge's loophole."

"You did?"

"I think so. I think somebody might have used one set of legal descriptions for the auction but attached the correct descriptions to the recorded deeds."

"Come on! Switched legals? That's a mouth full. Was it deliberate?" Seth asked.

"I think so. It's possible bank negotiations made it look like a switch. But, I'm convinced it was a switch. A three million dollar fraud. The appraisals, Newsome's and Skinny's, back it up."

Seth asked. "How could you switch legal descriptions without somebody noticing?"

"Who reads metes and bounds legals?" I asked. "Bidders likely relied on site identification markers and ribbons and on liquidation appraisals for their information. Ribbons and markers were torn down after the auction so there's no way to tell if a switch was made."

Jenkins cleared his throat and said, "Uh, before y'all get too carried away, Bishop told me and Milty about this switching business earlier and we couldn't find any evidence of fraud. We've talked to anybody and everybody who had a hand in the auction, even Mrs. Kitchens and Mrs. Gibbs. Looks more like bank negotiations, pure and simple than anything sinister."

"You didn't tell me," I said.

"I meant to," the chief said. "Both ladies said they'd negotiated with the bank to keep some of that land free and clear. Available to sell."

If the legals were altered, they benefited and had to be in on it. So, what would they say?

The chief said, "Prozini told us we wasted our time. He wants to put his losses behind him, move on to his next investment. Milty wants a call from the bank, but doesn't expect much without a court order. That's why I hadn't called you, Bishop."

Seth asked the thought I'd had. "If the bids were rigged, the women, Kitchens and Gibbs, would be part of it? They had to know what to bid, to be the high bidders?"

"And if they did, I doubt they'd admit it," I said.

"Do they have any to link to the auction, other than their bids? Without a link, I don't see how you can show fraud," Seth said.

"None we can find," the chief said.

Seth said, "If the whole thing is a mistake, a screw up, maybe somebody found out and decided to cover it up. Might beat the hell out of admitting it."

"Yeah," I said. "Same result, two murders, but without the fraud. Somebody with a reputation on the line might be motivated." A Supreme Court appointment, say?

"The two women didn't sound like killers," the chief said, "but you never know."

"They didn't have to be killers, just greedy," I said. "Somebody calls and says you got windfall acres. Pay me some bucks and you can keep it. Then the judge and Skinny stumble onto it."

"Glad it's not my problem," Seth said, then asked, "What about the mill? Is Morgan going to survive?"

"Even with all the help he's received," I said, "he might still be short. Prozini has a buyer for the mill. Morgan doesn't want to sell, but what choice does he have?"

If it got close, Seth said he'd kick in more money or guarantee a loan from Rooster's bank. "Morgan's worked too hard to lose the mill for a few bucks."

On the way home, Kathy said, "Kitchens and Gibbs borrowed money from the same bank, didn't they?"

"Their families had dealt with the bank before, they said."

"Maybe they lived here at one time, got married and moved away," she said. "What were their maiden names? That might show a link."

"Good idea! From the way they sounded, I'd say that they were in their mid-thirties so, if they got married when they were twenty or so, that'd be close to fifteen or so years ago," I said.

"Our archives might have something. I'll search in my spare time," she said. "It'll take awhile. Lots of people get married every year."

I kissed her.

"Sampsonville has a weekly. You said the parcels were near the county line. Could be they lived in Sampson County. We don't keep any of those papers, but I'll check around."

"That'd be a big help," I said.

* * * * *

A flatbed truck loaded with "Reynolds' Lumber" passed me at the mill gate, headed out. Morgan was still in business. He stood under a canopy at one end of the portable mill and sent logs along the conveyor belt. Yellow sawdust sprayed out. Scooter and a couple of hands worked the other stations.

A log truck rattled into the yard with logs. Yet another came in behind it.

When he saw my jeep, Morgan motioned Scooter to take his position. I followed him inside. His face had the gaunt look of a refugee who'd had no food for days. He said they cut logs until ten every night and started again at six.

He reached into the small refrigerator behind him for a root beer. I declined.

"Scooter's finished his course work. He'll graduate next January," he said. "I'm so damn proud, I can't tell you. He works here all day and does his correspondence work at night after we lock up."

"He's tough like his dad," I said.

"A lot smarter. He has job offers, but turned 'em down. Says he wants to work with me. I haven't paid him a dime since we started up." He turned his face and wiped his eyes. "I'm emotional. Must be tired."

"Heard from anybody?" I asked.

"No, not a soul," he said. "Could be the buyer, if there was one, got cold feet. I wouldn't put it past Prozini to try to make a buck peddling the mill through a broker."

"Me either. Can you survive?"

"Not a chance. We work day and night to cut as much timber as possible."

"What about the portable mill?"

"The owner called a couple of days ago. Says he needs it. Didn't say when exactly, just pretty soon, so I figure we've only got a few days. We'll cut as much as we can before he comes for it."

"Has the insurance company made a decision?"

"The check came this morning. I've beat the bushes for outdated equipment. I can get it and we can cut timber, but we won't be competitive, and sooner or later it'll catch up with us. Pitts'd beat us on price even if Scooter and me work for minimum wage. "We don't even get that right now."

I was sorry, but he knew that.

"I got a call from an outfit in the northwest. Job as assistant manager for a good sized mill. A decent salary. I'd make money at least." He shrugged. "I said I was interested. You get interested when you get beat down. They want me to fly up for an interview."

"You going?"

"Don't have a hell of a lot of choice, do I?" His voice cracked. "The way things stand now, I'm not sure this mill has a future under the best of circumstances."

I thought of Seth's comment about helping, but kept it to myself. Morgan still had other options, slim as they were.

"What we need down here is a mill that can produce plywood. The average house uses six thousand feet of plywood. The housing market's picking up now and plywood's in demand."

"You'd need capital."

"Unfortunately. Another product that's gets a lot of attention is a board made from strands or flakes sliced from small logs—lots of 'em around here—bonded under heat and pressure. The other thing might be to add a treatment facility. Pressure treat lumber to protect it from the elements."

"That service could be offered to other mills, like Pitts," I said.

"Yes, then we wouldn't be competitors anymore, but, as you say, all that takes money. Right now, I want to get a shipment out before the man drives up and takes his mill."

That determination is what I saw the first time we met. Morgan hadn't changed.

* * * * *

My feet had just hit the floor the next morning when the phone rang. It was Morgan.

"That New Orleans lawyer called me a little while ago. He wants me to come to his office to talk about the sale of the mill. I told him if he wanted to talk, it'd have to be here. I can't spare the time to drive down there. He'll be here his afternoon. You mind sitting in?"

I'd be there.

Chapter 23

We watched Swegman pull up in front of Reynolds' trailer. He drove a new Mercedes. In his early forties, average height, slender with a narrow, intelligent face. His shoes glistened in the afternoon sun as he reached the office. A briefcase dangled by his side. He walked with the confidence of a lawyer trying to convince a client that he has everything under control. One of the first bits of trade craft a lawyer picks up after law school.

Morgan welcomed him at the door.

"Julian Swegman," he said, and stuck out a hand first to Morgan, then to me.

"Morgan Reynolds, but I guess you know that." Swegman said he did. "Come on back," Morgan said.

"Bishop Bone." I introduced myself.

"Yes, we talked on the phone," he said. "Mr. Reynolds said you might be here. I take it you represent Mr. Reynolds?"

"For this meeting," I said.

"Good," he said.

Morgan offered him something to drink. He took a can of coke and sat down.

"You represent?" I asked.

"My client wants to remain anonymous until we reach an agreement," he said.

"We can only go so far on faith," I replied.

"Of course. I understand. But, don't get the horse before the carriage." He smiled. "I'm here to negotiate and I have the authority." He pulled a note pad from his brief case and opened it.

"What is your offer?" Morgan asked.

He said. "My client has authorized me to offer you three hundred thousand dollars, payable fifty thousand at closing and the balance in equal, annual payments over five years, conditioned on being able to assume your loan. You would hand over the keys and walk away."

Morgan glanced at me. I had a hunch that sounded pretty good after his days in the hot sun at the portable mill. Actually, considering the condition Morgan and his mill were in, it wasn't a bad offer.

"Four hundred thousand" I countered. "All at the close, conditioned on the bank's release of his home."

Swegman chuckled. "My client felt the offer was more than generous considering the state of the mill. I understand that work has been done, but under the best of circumstances, it's still old equipment. So, I came to negotiate, but you can't expect me to negotiate with myself. If you make a realistic counter offer, we can proceed."

"We have," I said.

"I see," he said, "You must understand that my client is faced with substantial up front costs, millions, to modernize the mill with state of the art electronic imaging systems, computer controlled curved saw gangs to improve recovery. The mill has to be competitive with the Pitts' mill. You're familiar with their mill, I understand."

Morgan said, "Very."

He said, "My client is committed to the mill. The mill can be profitable and you'll get paid. The client should have no trouble getting your home released after improvements are made. The bank will be well secured."

"If it's all the same to you, Mr. Swegman, I'd just as soon get everything up front. Then, I wouldn't have to worry about it," Morgan said.

"You insist on a cash out deal?"

"I'd consider it," Morgan said, with a glance in my direction.

"I can recommend a hundred seventy five thousand dollar cash payment to you. We'll request the bank to release your house."

I said. "That wouldn't do it."

Morgan shook his head in agreement with what I'd said. I didn't know, but I bet he had substantially more in the mill than that.

"Mr. Bone," the attorney said, "it's not like Mr. Reynolds has much leverage here. I don't like to be blunt, but what does he have that's so valuable?"

"This mill has been here over a hundred years. The location is good, good interstate and railroad access, available labor and good access to timber. It has the support of the community. Morgan has built up a good relationship with customers. He has a basket full of contracts. Bankable profits."

"To sell lower grade lumber, I understand, at low margins, not what my client would pursue. When the mill is upgraded, it will have a new identity, new customers. The past will be gone. Support for the mill will be enhanced. Those items have little or no value as far as these negotiations." He dismissed their significance with a wave of his hand.

"That's it, then," I said. I closed my note pad and stood.

"You're saying the meeting is over?" Swegman asked.

"You said it was over, didn't you? I agree with you."

He put his pad into the briefcase on the floor and closed the lid.

"You may wish you'd been more flexible," he said with a tilt of his head.

"You may wish you had," I said.

He breathed noisily and said, "I'll consult with my client to see if there's any reason to continue. Let's see where we stand? Mr. Reynolds wants a cash settlement of four hundred thousand dollars. Is that your final offer?"

"He might accept less if he stays on as mill manager with a good contract," I said.

"That will never be considered. My client has a manager in mind for the mill." He stood. "Thank you for your time. I'll present your offer to my client. If there's any room to negotiate, I'll be in touch."

"Until you do, I'll advise Mr. Reynolds to pursue his other offers," I said.

"I doubt there are others, but, yes, pursue them, please. I'm confident no one will make you a better offer."

Our bluff was called. A sense of loss swept over me. Had I just screwed Morgan out of the best deal he could ever hope to get? I was afraid I had.

"Gentlemen," Swegman said. "Why don't we leave it like this? If you don't hear from me by the close of business tomorrow, you can assume my client has no further interest."

A glimmer of hope.

When his taillights were no longer visible, I said to Morgan, "Basically, all he was offering was a hundred and seventy five thousand to cash you out. Maybe get your house released."

"Might be better than nothing," he said, "unless I get some equipment in here soon. It'd give me enough to pay Scooter some. Won't cover what I have in it, time and money." He turned his head and looked out the window.

"Look, somebody's interested enough to send a lawyer up here from New Orleans. You can bet you haven't heard their best offer yet." I wished I totally believed that.

"It didn't sound like that to me."

"It wasn't supposed to. Swegman did a good job. I bet you'll get a call tomorrow with a better offer, maybe more cash up front, and a shorter pay off time."

He hoped I was right. Not as much as I hoped it. I recalled a professor in law school who told us not to take a client's problems personally. I had and it felt damned uncomfortable.

I said, "I can call Burl Pitts to see if he's interested. With your permission of course."

"Burl Pitts! Why do you think he'd want to buy it?"

"He once told me he should have bought it and torn it down."

"It's a thought, Bishop, but Burl is as tough a businessman as I've run up against. Do you think he'd offer much for this mill, knowing I might have to shut it down?"

"Would he want a competitor mill in here, with state of the art equipment and financial backing?"

"Let's see if I can keep it before you offer it to Burl. I'm not certain I have to sell just yet."

On the drive home, I reflected on what Swegman said. He was right. The only leverage Morgan had was flexibility. If Morgan sold the mill, Swegman's client would gain immediate control. Otherwise, they had to wait until the bank shut him down and who could say when that would be. Morgan was current on his loan.

Morgan called near six o'clock.

"Swegman says his client will pay two hundred and twenty five thousand dollars, one up front. The rest over two years. Good faith effort to get my house released."

"We're making pr—"

"There's more. He wants me to have signed contracts for twelve million board feet of good quality timber, grades one and two, high yield timber, at the bottom end rate, in effect, below market."

"Not good, huh?"

"No, I've gotten by on verbal deals to buy grade three stuff."

"In effect, he wants you to squeeze your friends for part of the pay out."

"Yeah," he said. "I'd get paid out of the profits generated from sympathy contracts. I can't do that."

"How'd you leave it?"

"I didn't. He said if I was interested, call him. Didn't seem like he gave a damn if I did or didn't."

"Call him back and say that you'll take three hundred thousand dollars plus release of your house. Two hundred up front, the rest at ten thousand dollars a month. Promise your best efforts to get signed timber contracts. That's like a promise to smile and say hello … nothing."

"I suppose it's worth a try."

From the weariness of his voice I could tell that he was ready to toss in the towel. He was worn out from working long hours in the scorching heat and humidity.

Seth called minutes later. "I just ran into Rooster at the bank. Can you go over there and meet with him? Something's come up with Morgan's loan."

I knew about what Rooster wanted to tell me. It had been in the back of my mind. Not good news.

* * * * *

Rooster and several men in banker blue emerged from the boardroom with copies of a memo. Few words were exchanged. I watched from a chair in the upstairs lobby.

"Bishop," he called from the door. "Can we talk in here?"

Like many boardrooms I'd been in, it had a long oval table surrounded with comfortable chairs. A Bible lay in the center of the table on a silver tray. The Bible struck me as ironic, if you consider a bank's propensity to be coldhearted when it came to foreclosures.

"Morgan's loan," he said and stared down at a sheaf of papers he placed on the table. "An attorney, Julian Swegman, sent in an offer on behalf of an unnamed client to buy it for cash with a thirty day escrow, and the Board agreed to accept it. We were a little surprised that anyone would want to buy the loan at face value, considering the favorable interest rate we gave Morgan. It's not that great an investment."

"Unless they mean to foreclose."

"That's what we decided. A board member suggested that Morgan might file for bankruptcy protection, so the bank should get out as swiftly as possible. For what it's worth, I opposed the sale. We agreed to back him. A sale means we abandon him. It goes against my grain."

"Is this confidential? Can I tell Morgan?"

"Hmm, I suppose it is confidential. If you tell him, he's likely to rush out and file bankruptcy."

I said, "A new owner should be able to get the mortgage released by the court. I doubt there's any equity in the mill above the mortgage. What's a shutdown mill worth?"

He answered, "Not much. Morgan is the only thing of any value out there and we can't foreclose on him. You know what? Why don't you suggest to Morgan that Swegman 'might' offer to buy the mortgage? I didn't tell you to do it."

I understood.

"Interesting thing, if Morgan can step around and keep the loan current, Swegman's client will end up with a loan that yields less than the going rate," he said.

"I doubt he'll be able to hang on much longer. He's at the end of his rope, physically and financially."

If the judge's murder and that of Skinny Dearman were related to the acquisition of the mill, Morgan might live longer if he handed over the keys. That possibility just popped into my thoughts.

Rooster looked at me and said, "The board asked me to honcho the sale. I'm not certain the letter to Swegman will go out right away. We're busy around here. In fact, I'm going to be out of town for at least two days."

"Thanks." I told him what Seth had said at the farm, about helping. I didn't know if Morgan would accept, but it would save him.

"Hmm. Might be too late now. We've approved the sale. I could call a special meeting. See if they want to change their minds. Most just wanted to get rid of it. Seth's got a lot of clout though. Let me know what you want me to do."

I drove back to the mill. The little portable mill shot out two by fours like a machine gun, Morgan on the trigger. Nightlights were on even though it wasn't yet dark. They cast the mill in tarnished silver shadows interspersed with twilight and patches of sheen. Otis loaded lumber on a tractor for the kiln and planer mill. At the other end, Scooter rolled logs onto the conveyer belt. Morgan ran the saw carriage head. Their clothes were black with sweat and covered in sawdust. I could see that they were ready to drop. Bodies moved in and out of the kiln and planer.

Morgan called for a break and walked toward my jeep.

"I hope you have something good," he said. "My ass is dragging."

"Afraid not." I got out and leaned against the hood. I suggested that Swegman might negotiate with the bank to buy his loan.

"Can he do that?"

"Banks do it all the time."

"You said might."

"It's a premonition you should take seriously."

"What can he do?" he asked.

"Nothing so long as you make your payments."

"Hard to do if the man comes for his little mill before I can get the big mill up and running," Morgan said.

"If you don't make your payments they'll foreclose," I said.

"Get it for nothing. They won't have to pay me a dime," he said. "My friend in Jackson said I should file bankruptcy."

"That'd buy you few months. Costs money to file, unless you know a bankruptcy lawyer who'll work on credit?"

"You're the only credit lawyer I know. Can you handle a bankruptcy?"

"I've filed some Chapter Sevens, straight liquidation. A debtor takes what he has and puts it on the table for the creditors to divide up. Used to be anyway, before the law changed. Simple deals. I've represented banks in Chapter Elevens, but I've never filed one. A good lawyer would chew me up. I hope it doesn't come to that, for both our sakes."

"It doesn't look good, does it, Bishop?"

I couldn't tell him it did.

While I worked with a strip shopping center developer in Meridian to improve his occupancy, below fifty percent then, Rooster left two messages on my machine. Swegman had called three times to inquire about the bank's decision. The bank's letter to Swegman was written but wouldn't be mailed until Saturday. The board members Rooster called weren't warm to the idea of changing their minds in favor of some kind of guarantee by Seth, even with Seth's clout.

I called Morgan the next day. "Have you heard from Swegman?

"He called to say the best his client will pay is two hundred thousand over four years or one hundred thousand cash. Good faith effort on my house. Take it or leave it. We're going backwards," he said.

"They're confident they can buy your loan from the bank," I said.

"Maybe we negotiated too hard," he said.

I took that to mean "me" though I knew he didn't intend it that way. If he had to sell, he wanted as much for the mill as I did. That didn't mean he wasn't right, however.

"Will you be able to make next month's loan payment?"

"I'm okay there, but based on our bookings, unless something new comes in, I'm short on the one after that. I spent the money that came in from our public plea and the insurance proceeds on used equipment. I may lose the mill before I get the equipment installed."

"So, we have a month before you're in default. After that, the bank can foreclose."

"Or whoever buys my mortgage."

"Before that happens, I'll call Burl Pitts and see what I can negotiate with him. I could also call Seth Campbell. He might be willing to make you a personal loan for what you need."

"Charity, Bishop. Pure and simple. Hell, I appreciate that he might. I do! He's a good man. Like you. But I hate having to take charity. Saw too much of that when I was coming up. Sometimes nature, in this case the business world, tells you something. If you can't make it, you just have to die. I may just have to die."

"Lots of people around here disagree."

He sighed. "I fly to Portland tomorrow to interview for a job. I'll be back Sunday. Scooter will run the mill while I'm gone. His buddies from Jackson State came down to help. I'm on my ass tired and they act like it's a holiday! We'll talk when I get back."

Chapter 24

I tried to put Morgan's problems out of my mind for my dinner date with Kathy. We had reservations at the restaurant on the river. She greeted me in an outfit that showed enough cleavage for me to consider a dinner postponement. I liked the way her eyes caressed my face. She smiled and kissed me on the lips. A whiff of her perfume made it hard to let her go.

The waitresses wore pink and green outfits, with sixties styled caps and not a sad face among them. We sat outside on a deck over the river. I had a chilled bottle of champagne. The waitress brought glasses.

"I've been bursting to tell you my news!" Kathy said. She reached over the table to touch my hand.

"What?"

"I called Ruth Cranston who runs the library in Sampsonville and asked if anybody had copies of their old weeklies. She did and said I was the first ever to ask to see one. They're in stacks, arranged by year in an old corncrib in back of her house."

"I'll go over and dig around. Want to help?" I said.

"No need. When I told her what I wanted, she laughed and said she could save me the trouble. Alice Kitchens and Barbara Gibbs are Jimmy Pitts' daughters! She went to Alice's wedding. She's the oldest."

"Jimmy Pitts!"

"In fact, they were here when Jimmy was in the hospital. Did I do good?" She smiled.

"Good doesn't half cover it! I'll be damned! We have a link." I kissed her over the table. The tables on both sides broke into applause. I did it again, an encore performance.

"There are so many implications I don't know where to start. They were straw buyers for Jimmy! Had to be!"

Kathy saw the frown that came onto my face. "What's wrong?"

"With Jimmy in the picture, it does change things however. The bank might very well have released the lopped off acres for extra collateral Jimmy put up. No rigged bids, just back door deals to spite his brother."

"You're still frowning," she said.

"We still have two dead men and appraised values that were too low."

"You'll work it out."

About then, I began to think I didn't know enough about the timber business to feel comfortable. I'd caused a lot of trouble and had nothing to show for it. Were the deaths accidental after all? I'll have to leave town.

To hell with it! Kathy had arranged a sitter for her mother. The dinner was also great.

* * * * *

I called Swegman and said, "There's a rumor around town that someone offered to buy the bank's loan. I assume that would be your client."

He didn't answer right away then said, "I can't say, but suppose you're right."

"You must know that Morgan will fight any foreclosure. You might want to tell Mr. Pitts that also." It wasn't too far fetched to suggest that Jimmy was the "interested buyer." Thanks to the auction, Jimmy owned, or controlled, thousands of acres of high-grade timberland and he hated Burl enough to go head to head with him.

"Pitts? What does … I don't know the Pitts. Is this some kind of game? What do you mean? My client is a listed company."

The smart bastard gave nothing away. Or, was I wrong? Was Swegman's offer real? I felt like an idiot. Had I been wrong about everything? Gibbs, Kitchens and now Swegman.

I tried again. "Come on Julian, you know Jimmy Pitts pulls your strings."

"No one pulls my strings, Mr. Bone. I get paid fees for legal services."

"Am I to take it that your client is no longer interested in negotiations?"

"They reached the 'nuisance value' stage after Mr. Reynolds' last refusal. My client will pay something to get rid of Mr. Reynolds, but not the numbers you threw around. Reynolds will be lucky to get a hundred thousand, maybe a hundred and a quarter, over time, to effect a smooth transfer of ownership."

"You'll get notice of a Chapter Eleven filing as soon as the escrow on the loan closes. It'll take months before you can foreclose, maybe never. What will happen to your client's interest?"

"My client is very patient," he said, adding, "If you'll excuse me, Mr. Bone, I have a call."

It seemed cold to call Morgan with Swegman's response, so I drove in to tell him in person.

When I drove up, the mill wasn't running. In fact, I didn't see anyone around. Morgan's truck was parked in front of the office but no other.

"Morgan!" I called at the door.

"Come on back, Bishop," he called. There was no joy in his voice.

He sat at his desk, stared at a pile of logs through the window, held a beer in one hand. It wasn't yet lunch and he rarely drank.

"Bad news?" I asked.

"The worst. The portable mill owner is coming for it. We cleaned it up. He apologized, but said he needed it. I understand. I was glad he left it as long as he did. Right now, I am out of business. It's gone. Get a beer if you want one." He motioned in the direction of the refrigerator on the floor behind his desk.

"I, uh, talked to Swegman," I said.

"I called him, too. So far he hasn't returned my call."

"I doubt he will. I think they'll go the foreclosure route unless you take a nominal amount and walk."

Morgan stared out the window. "A nominal amount is better than nothing. I need a job."

"We could file for Chapter Eleven protection, but without an operating mill, I don't think we'll have a business to reorganize under the law." I wasn't even sure a loan by Seth would help. Morgan needed the equipment in place and operating. I wondered if a court would give him time if the equipment were being installed.

Morgan interrupted my thoughts. "I'm at the point where I have to admit I ain't got a pot to piss in or a window to throw it out, Bishop. We fought a good fight, but we lost. I'll take the nominal amount, unless you can get more out of Burl, then sneak out of town with my tail tucked between my legs, another sorry, no count, nigger."

"That's not true and you know it!"

"Hell, I'm a damn good manager. I know that, but I don't have an answer for that damned screwdriver. It ruined me. The rest of the shit, I could handle. That screwdriver killed me."

"What about the used equipment you bought?" I was thinking about a bankruptcy plan.

"Yeah! Some good news for a change. Can you believe it? The broker got a better deal than I first thought. I can get enough equipment to get the mill up again."

"When?"

"Uh, that's the bad news. A couple of weeks, three at the outside. Then I have to get it installed. I won't ship lumber anytime soon. No way to make next month's loan payment or the one after that. If I were a betting man, I'd say the odds were against me. Scooter says we'll make it. That boy won't give up."

"How'd the interview go … in Portland?"

"It went okay. They're interested. I'll get an offer. I hope to hell I won't have to take it."

Add me to the list.

My next stop was the chief's office. Irene's music filled the corridors of City Hall. As usual, as soon as she could place my face, she told me to go on in. I couldn't wait to close his door behind me.

"Morgan Reynolds might lose the mill," I said.

"So I hear. You've done the best you could do, Bishop. Sometimes a man's best isn't good enough. Being a good man isn't worth much without money."

I told him that Kitchens and Gibbs were Jimmy Pitts' daughters. "Kathy tracked it down."

"I'll be damned! I bet Burl found out. My guess is that's what caused their fight. Burl wouldn't stand still for that kind of double dealing shit."

"Uh huh," I said.

"Mystery solved!"

"Not—"

He waved me off. "Don't start with your gut feelings, Bone! You've caused a lot of trouble. Pissed a lot of people off, as usual."

He only called me Bone when he was pissed.

"That just about slams the lid shut on your theory, doesn't it?"
I didn't have an answer. Wished I had, but didn't.

"Pretty much confirms what Rose said might have happened. Jimmy put up extra collateral to free up some of that land to sell, if he needed to. No doubt it pissed Burl off, but so what. That's not a crime. If it were, you'd be in for life. Two good men are dead, but no proof of anything but accidents. I don't want to hear any more about it."

I agreed with him. I'd tilted a lot of windmills and all I had to show for it was a busted lance and a sick feeling that I was dead wrong. But, I wasn't ready to admit that to the chief. He'd never let me forget it.

I asked. "The bank confirm that's what happened? Extra collateral for the release?'

"The bank's not saying a damn thing without a court order. The president over there told Milty the loans were more than secured. Milty talked to a judge about an order. Short answer—no court order without more proof."

"Skinny's appraisal was too damn low, Chief! Jimmy's daughters, hell, most likely Jimmy, ended up with a big-assed profit. Sure as hell smells like proof to me."

"That's it, Bone! Milty went to the wrong judge. He should have gone to one that went by smell. It's not stare decisis anymore it's stare de-smell. I'll tell Milty! Listen, Bishop, the bank says it's secured. Milty's satisfied that the bank released acres for additional collateral. No fraud. That's the bottom line. Any number of reasons why Skinny's appraisal came in low. Investigation closed."

"Two men were killed."

"Give it up. Both accidents. Like everybody thought before you started stirring things around."

"Three million dollars is plenty enough motivation to kill."

"Motivation is not evidence."

"Why did TRS only lose big money on the four tracts?"

"You don't listen, Bone. We have no proof the damned auction was rigged. Losses are proof of bad judgment, not fraud. How would Jimmy's daughters know what to bid? Bids were sealed. Under lock and key before the auction. No way!"

"Something's not right."

"I know it by heart! Those guys lost three million dollars. Two men are dead. Maybe accidents, maybe not. Somebody sicced Otis on you. Coincidences! Too damn many to suit me. Milty sees it too, but what the hell can we do?"

"I don't know."

"At last, something we agree on."

"It sticks in my gut to let somebody walk away with three million that doesn't belong to them."

"If they are? If? We don't have any damn proof!" He sighed. "Okay, who do you want me to arrest?"

"I don't know."

"Well, neither do I. I'm worried. That's the second thing we've agreed on."

Irene's music hung over me like a dark cloud all the way out the door. I felt an imminent depression.

The chief was right. I didn't have a damn thing to back me up. I wished for my old RV. I'd get in it and leave town for a month. Give the stink I created time to blow over. And the minute I was out of town, Cooper would call Kathy. I went home and sat on the porch. The beavers were busy. Looked happy. Lucky bastards!

Later, I heard a car door slam beside the back steps and got up to check. Chief Jenkins got out of his car. "I'm gonna fish," he called up and said. He waved his fishing gear. "If you want to hear what the bank said, you'll have to come to the creek. I called."

I followed him.

"So?"

"I told Ben Crowell, that's his name, that Kitchens and Gibbs were Jimmy's daughters. He said he knew that, but still would not discuss customer business without a court order."

"You mention the possibility of fraud?"

"I did. He laughed at me. 'Not on this bank!' he said. I tried, Bishop. Can we put the damn thing to bed and be friends?"

"Thanks." I walked back for my tackle.

We fished with the crickets he brought. He caught three good pan sized bream. With my two, he had enough for a decent supper.

* * * * *

Burl sat in his easy chair to catch the early news. One hand held a beer. Blended smells of fresh greens and fried chicken floated into the living room. The telephone rang. He picked it up.

"Burl," he said.

"This is Ben," the man said.

"Anything the matter? You don't sound all that good." Burl switched off the television set.

"I thought you might want to know that Chief Jenkins over at Lawton called about the loans we made Jimmy's girls. Milty called the other day about the same thing. They suggested some funny business at that TRS auction. Something about switching legal descriptions."

"Switched legal descriptions? You call Jimmy?"

"I tried. He was out. I left a message, but figured I ought to let you know in case you see him first."

"You see anything wrong with the loans?"

"No. We relied on the appraisals done by Caleb's man, Skinny Dearman, to make the loans, but in an abundance of caution and because time was short, we took Jimmy's stock in the mill as additional collateral. He guaranteed both loans."

"Loans are well secured then. What'd you tell Jenkins?"

"I told him if he wanted to invade the privacy of any of our customers, he'd have to get a court order."

"He say he was?"

"He said, 'if that's what it takes.' It bothers me some because Judge Chancellor and the Dearman boy are dead."

"Accidents, Ben. Both of 'em."

"Yeah. Can't say I see a connection anyway, but you can't be too careful these days. Milty's no fool, Burl. If he says the legals may have been switched and all that, I have to listen. I can't see how it'd involve the bank, but you think we should call a special board meeting to consider an investigation?"

"I don't think the bank has any reason to worry, Ben. Caleb's bought timber for us as long as I've run the mill. I'll stand behind what he says. What that dead young man, Skinny Dearman, said. Caleb wouldn't let an appraisal go out in error. If the timber was worth what they bid, how in hell could there be fraud?" Burl asked.

Ben said, "Switched legals, Milty s—"

"Somebody's feeding Milty a line of bull. Call a meeting if you want to, but I think it'd be a waste of time."

"If you say so, Burl," the banker said. "Just wanted you to know about the call. It's your bank too."

"Thanks."

"When will you start to chair meetings again?" Ben asked.

"You're doing a good job, Ben," Burl answered. "Damn suits make me uncomfortable, especially neckties. How in hell can anybody think with a noose around their neck?"

When Burl hung up, his wife came into the room. She rubbed her hands on her apron. Her gray hair was wrapped in a white scarf. Like Burl's, her face showed signs of age.

"Who called?" she asked.

"Ben, down at the bank. Had to do with Jimmy."

"What'd he do now?"

"Jimmy took a pile of daddy's moonshine money to back his bid on some timberland, used a lot of his own too, then put the property in his girls' names to hide it. I should have gone to the auction, but Caleb said he'd watch out for us. He didn't. I think he's gone to hell, too. Much more of this crap and I'll be looking for a new appraiser."

"Is that what y'all had that fight about?"

"Yeah. I took one look in the safe and knew money was missing. Stacks of bills were gone. Big stacks. The log showed two hundred dollars was taken. That's the same as stealing! I had it counted by the new guy. I told Jimmy he's not to take any more money out of the safe, unless I'm there."

"What'd he say?"

"Oh hell, he stomped and cursed, but I don't give a damn. If he wants to act like a damn thief, I'll treat him like one. I've changed the combination and the lock on the door."

"He's never gotten over the way your daddy left the mill."

"Daddy knew he could never run it."

"What's he going to do with the timber?"

"I reckon he thinks the mill will buy it … pay top dollar. Rose says if I want to make a stink about it, I can legally force him to offer it to the mill for what he paid. I'm not going to do it. He can hold it forever for all I care. Rose said he should have asked for approval before his bid. I'm still thinking about what to do. No need for the bank to get involved in my business though."

"I reckon you'll handle it, Burl. You always do. Supper's almost ready."

"Smells good," he said. "Ben sounded worried. Unusual for him."

"What do you make of it?"

"Don't know. He said Lawton's District Attorney and Chief of Police complained about that auction. Something to do with switched legal descriptions on that auctioned property them girls of his bought," Burl said.

"That Bone man was on the television awhile back saying that dead judge was suspicious of something wrong with the auction."

"Nothing ever came of it. I wonder if that's what this is all about. I won't worry about it. Ben says the bank's secured. If somebody switched a legal description, I don't see what it's got to do with the bank, or Jimmy come to that."

"Come help me set the table."

Chapter 25

Once, in California, I bumped into a friend of mine who had just retired. I asked him what he did with his time. He said, "I've taken up gazing. In the afternoon I take a pitcher of martinis out to the patio and gaze at guys playing golf to escape the pressures of the office. That's all I do now, Bishop. I gaze."

I thought he sounded depressed. I understood that.

I sat on the back porch and "gazed" across the creek. It had been awhile since I'd felt that low. Everything I'd touched since the auction had turned to shit. Three beavers entered the pond with limbs between their jaws. Two swam directly to the dam. One hesitated, then headed to the mouth of the little branch that fed the pond. "Wrong direction," I said. "Bass akerds." Colloquial slang. Felt good to say it.

A thought hit me like a bucket of ice water. Like that damn beaver, had I been at this thing "bass akerds?" It was the Holdcorp piece, not the others! Had to be! Big loss and no bank backing like Gibbs and Kitchens. I went to the mill to run an idea past Morgan. When I arrived, the portable mill was gone. Morgan, Scooter, and Otis and a couple of men wandered along the catwalk inside the mill. Morgan saw me drive up.

"Morgan," I said as I approached the steps to the catwalk.

"I guess you can see. The man came for his mill, Bishop," Morgan said. "I don't suppose you have good news." He came down the steps. Scooter and Otis moved along the catwalk out of sight.

"No," I said.

"It's around town that the bank sold my loan. I can't cut timber and I can't make my payments. I'm dead."

"What about the equipment?" I asked.

"Yeah. Once the new heads are installed, I can saw logs. We'll have to haul lumber to the planer and kiln till we get the rest of the mill working. Take two shifts to ship what we could ship in one, but—" He shrugged with a palms-up gesture.

"Will you be able to make your loan payments?"

"I don't know. I have orders. I just need time. You thought anymore about bankruptcy?"

"Some. Swegman's client will ask the court to allow foreclosure. If you're shipping lumber, we have a decent chance to stop it. Buy time to get the rest of the mill up and running."

"If not, we're up shit creek. Is that the bottom line?"

"That's about it."

"I've got to find where that damned equipment is. The man's says it's on its way, but nobody knows exactly where it is."

"Burl—"

"I appreciate what the man did for me, more than I can say, but it'd stick in my craw to sell to him. I don't think I could sleep nights knowing he beat me."

"I have an idea. Could even things up a little, if I'm right." I explained what I had in mind.

"What can it hurt?" Morgan said. "I'll get Scooter in here. When do you want to do it?"

"How about tomorrow? I need time to work out the details."

The next day, I briefed everybody as to what they had to do.

"Let's do it!" Scooter said. "Get some offense going!"

He stood at the far end of the trailer to wait for my signal. I stood in the front door and dialed Swegman's number on my cell phone. Morgan watched from the doorway of his office.

"Law offices of Julian Swegman," a woman answered.

"This is Bishop Bone. I represent Mr. Reynolds and I need to speak to Mr. Swegman on an urgent matter."

She put me on hold. Seconds later, Swegman answered. I waved at Morgan and Scooter and stepped outside to continue.

"Mr. Swegman," I said. "I understand the bank has sold Mr. Reynolds's loan to your client, Holdcorp."

"I thought the matter was confidential, but since you know, yes, Holdcorp will buy the loan. Obviously, we intend to foreclose."

"That's why I called. I will file for Chapter Eleven protection so Mr. Morgan can reorganize the business."

"I can get the property released by the court immediately," he said. "You know there's no equity above the loan. In any case, Mr. Bone, what's to reorganize? There's no business."

"Not true," I said. "Mr. Reynolds bought a used carriage head and enough equipment to get him cutting timber next week." He wasn't, but Swegman didn't know. "He has contracts to sell lumber and contracts to buy timber. That's a going concern. In fact, he'll make loan payments. No default. Your client may have bought an investment." Hell, Seth'd make a payment without Morgan knowing if it came to it.

"We'll see about that. You will get a lesson in bankruptcy, my friend."

By then, Morgan had Prozini on the line. "Bishop says I can convince the court to stop foreclosure until my reorganization plan is approved."

Prozini replied, "If you file bankruptcy, Morgan, you can kiss your career goodbye. Nobody will hire you ever again, and no lender will extend credit to you! You'll pay cash to your suppliers for ten years."

"I have nothing to lose, John. Bishop thinks there's something funny about the outfit that bought my loan. He's going to flush out who's behind it."

"Bone's on an ego trip, Morgan. Take the offer and walk. Your credit will be intact and you'll have a few bucks in your pocket."

On cue, Scooter called Swegman.

"Hello, this is John Prozini," he said, with his best Yankee accent. "I need to speak to Julian, now!"

"He's on the phone."

"This is important! Urgent!"

Swegman asked me to hold while he took another call.

Per the plan, Scooter coughed as Swegman answered, to further disguise his voice.

"Julian," Scooter said. "Prozini here. Sorry. Got choked. Reynolds's on the other phone. He says that guy Bone's filing bankruptcy for him. What will that to do to me? I don't want my name known. Bad for business."

Swegman said, "Reynolds will run the mill as a debtor in possession, business as usual. I'm on the phone with Bone right now. They'll have about four months to get a plan approved to reorganize the company. I'll oppose it. I'll win. There's no way you'll be involved. I'm Holdcorp's CEO. I've told you." About that time Swegman became suspicious. "Can I call you right back, John. I need to get rid of Bone."

Swegman got back on line with me, and said, "Sorry, Mr. Bone. I have to keep you on hold for just another minute."

He dialed Prozini's number.

"Is John available?" he asked Prozini's secretary.

"He's on a call to Mr. Reynolds."

Satisfied, he returned to his call with Bone.

"Do what you have to do, Mr. Bone. My client's last offer was more than fair. I'm sorry Mr. Reynolds didn't see fit to accept it. He may look back and wish he had."

All calls ended.

Scooter was excited. "I did good, man!" he said and recited his conversation with Swegman. "That dude just knew I was Prozini! I sooo convinced him! Hollywood, here I come!"

Morgan patted him on the back. "Good job, son."

"Prozini used you to bid on prime timberland," I told Morgan. "Now, he wants the mill. He must have a buyer for it. Wants to turn a quick profit. Sell the mill and land."

"He sure as hell couldn't run it. He can't sit still long enough to run anything."

"Nothing illegal about any of that as far as I can see," I said. "However, Osstrum might see it as a breach of a fiduciary duty. Prozini makes a profit at the partnership's expense."

"Sounds good and all that, Bishop, but how does it help me?"

"I'll threaten to expose Prozini to Osstrum if he starts to foreclose. Has to make him stop and think."

"We hope."

"Find that equipment. You need to cut logs."

"If I have to truck it in myself, Bishop, this mill's gonna hum."

"Damn right!" Scooter said.

"What?" Morgan asked me. I'd gone silent. "Where'd you go?"

"Oh, nothing to do with the mill," I said. "Just something else that's been on my mind. Hattie Brown told the chief that Chandra was seeing somebody on a motorcycle. We thought it was Skinny. She rode with him to school."

"Jimmy Pitts has a Harley," Morgan said.

"Right. He's after every woman he sees and the Pub's his regular watering hole. It's speculation, but I never liked the man. Unless the chief finds Chandra's cell phone, we may never know."

"I could tell Otis," Scooter said and laughed. "He wouldn't care about the cell phone."

"Forget it, Scooter. It'd get Otis in trouble and wouldn't do us any good," Morgan said. "As you say, Bishop, there's not a lick of help in any of it for the mill. I need to hear some cuttin' noise. The sound of note payments!"

"Get the equipment, Dad. We'll get it installed," Scooter said.

Morgan's phone rang. "Reynolds Mill," he said then listened. "When? We'll be waiting!"

He looked at us with tears in his eyes. "The equipment will be in here by the end of the week."

Scooter let out a "whoop."

I slept soundly for a couple of hours that night. But, around midnight, I woke up. How did Prozini kill the judge and Skinny? Bigger question was did he? I didn't have an answer for either question. I couldn't sleep much after that. Since I was stewing, another question popped up. The bankruptcy? I hoped my bluff would work. If it didn't, I'd have to file to buy time. Damn.

* * * * *

Morgan, Scooter, and Scooter's friends from Jackson State wrestled the equipment onto a forklift to get it into the mill and installed. After he helped unload, Otis left to check linkages in the conveyor belt for breaks.

Scooter bragged to his friends about how he flushed Prozini out. "I cooled that lawyer! He just knew I was Prozini! Dead on. 'Julian,' I said, with Prozini's Yankee accent. He called me John. Man, it was like we were old friends."

Morgan's attention was on the place the equipment would go. Would it hold up? Would it work? He bought it 'as is.' And, could they saw enough lumber to make loan payments? What if his customers didn't pay on time?

Otis returned in time for the tail end of a laugh as Scooter completed his story.

"What's up, Dudes?" he asked. "What's funny?"

Scooter repeated the blow-by-blow of how they tricked Swegman.

"That's funny alright," Otis said.

"Yeah! And Mr. Bone thinks it was Jimmy Pitts doing Chandra," Scooter said, then immediately regretted it.

"What? Bone thinks Jimmy Pitts did Chandra?" Otis asked.

Scooter knew he'd made a mistake and began to distance himself. "Uh, it crossed his mind? More guess than anything. The dude owns a motorcycle. Mr. Bone didn't really know anything for certain."

"I knew it wasn't that other one with a motorcycle, Skinny Dearman. Chandra wouldn't look twice at him. Sure could 'a been that Jimmy Pitts, I reckon. One of them flashy types Chandra went for. He was on my list." His brow furrowed. He remembered his promise to his grandpa.

* * * * *

I resumed my education in the pitfalls of bankruptcy in case my plan to expose Prozini didn't work and Morgan needed time to get the mill productive. Swegman's threat to teach me a lesson lurked like a dagger. I pulled my old books off the shelf and began reading. Next, I went to the Internet. All told, I learned how much I didn't know. How to prepare a reorganization plan, the creditor's committee, cram-downs, too damn much. I could hire a friend. How much was it worth not to be made a fool of? I opened my checkbook. I'd have to take my chances.

I stopped studying long enough to meet with a borrower in Jackson, a heavy equipment dealer. Like Morgan, he was in default, and threatened to file bankruptcy if the bank didn't renegotiate his loan. The bank wanted to avoid that delay, but needed concessions. The borrower agreed to pledge six hundred acres of good farmland to support the loan. He'd sell the land over time to pay the loan down.

Afterwards, he told me, "I was bluffing about the bankruptcy. Hell, I wouldn't do that."

He wasn't the only one to bluff about bankruptcy.

I arrived at the cabin around four. The chief's car was at the rear. I'd rather it be Kathy's. I changed and walked down.

"Got four already," he announced with a gesture toward his fish bucket. "Haven't heard from you. Thought maybe somebody had up and shot you."

"I keep moving. Harder target to hit."

"I hear Reynolds might get the mill up again. It's also around town that he may take bankruptcy to gain time … thanks to you."

"You're right on both counts," I said. Something silver yanked my red and brown fly under. I jerked to set the hook and began to crank. The tip of my rod bent to the point of breaking. I had a big one.

"You carry your pea shooter these days?" he asked. "You tell people they can't do something, kind of pisses 'em off."

I said, "I have been since Otis got after me with his baseball bat."

"He and Willie still cut your grass?"

"Every week. I ask them not to, but they still come. It makes me lazy, but hell, I'll adjust."

"You give up trying to prove the auction was rigged?"

"Right now, I have to concentrate on saving Morgan's mill. You remember Holdcorp?" My fish tired and I reeled him in, a plump trout. The Jenkins would eat "good" that night.

"The outfit Morgan bid for," he said.

"It bought Morgan's loan from the bank and intends to foreclose. I don't think the deal's closed yet, but it's just a matter of exchanging money for the mortgage. Morgan needs time to get the mill running. Bankruptcy buys what he needs."

"A high stakes poker game," he said. "That kind of pressure'd cut into my sleep."

"It hasn't helped mine."

"I didn't know you did bankruptcies." He worked his catch in. It flipped out of the water with a splash. He grunted with satisfaction and reeled him in.

"I don't. Swegman says he'll rip me a new one in court."

"Glad it ain't me. I don't need a new one."

"Me either. Tell you what we just did." I said told him about the telephone scam Morgan, Scooter and I pulled on Swegman and Prozini.

"If the bankruptcy doesn't work, I'll threaten to tell Osstrum about it if they don't back off their foreclosure."

"Be damned. No wonder people get after you with baseball bats."

"It's a gamble, but I think Prozini would rather deal with Morgan than Osstrum."

"Holdcorp's bid was more than the appraised value. TRS benefited. How do you answer that?" He asked.

"I don't."

He hooked another one. It cleared the water with a leap. "Damn!"

He shrugged. "What if Prozini calls your bluff? Says take your best shot. Not illegal to bid on land or buy a mortgage or, come right down to it, to broker a deal for the mill. Where does that leave you?" He lost the fish and cursed.

"Gone. Like your fish."

"Yeah. You may end up hitless for all your work. Sounds like dandy Jimmy and his daughters wiggled off your hook too?"

"You could say that. Looks like the only thing he did wrong was buy behind Burl's back."

"Old Burl made him pay for that."

"Pitts Lumber may have a claim on any profits Jimmy makes. Not my problem. I have to wait for Prozini to make a move."

"Takes patience," he said as he packed his gear.

"Lots," I said.

Otis and his grandpa showed up in the old man's pickup truck after five to cut my grass and to weed. I recognized the sound of their truck. The brakes squealed when Willie stopped.

I continued to work on a draft plan of reorganization for Morgan's mill. It assumed the mill was fully operational or would be. Morgan called that morning to say the equipment was almost in place. He also had another bit of good news. His insurance agent had found a carrier to insure the mill, another thing I needed for the bankruptcy plan.

Otis and Willie cut and pruned and weeded. It was still hot and humid when they started on the back yard. I went out to speak to them.

Both were covered in sweat and grass clippings. The old man's head was protected by his hat; Otis' wrapped in his sweatband. Even so, sweat poured off their faces.

"How about some ice water?" I asked from the back steps. I caught the smell of fresh cut grass. Birds came out to peck and scratch.

Willie removed his hat and swiped his face with a sleeve. "Naw suh, Mr. Bone." He pointed to the hose at the corner of the cabin. "This be all we needs, right here," Willie said. He turned the handle and drank from the end of the hose. He took off his hat and let the water run over his head. "Uh huh. That feels good." He wiped his head and face and said, "How you been, Mr. Bone?"

"Fine," I said. "How about you and Elsa?"

He said they were okay and that Otis worked hard at the mill and stayed out of trouble.

They worked to make a pile of the brush and clippings from the yard. I felt guilty so I grabbed a pair of work gloves to help load it into the back of Willie's truck. He said they'd dump it in his pasture to burn. It was a three-load effort with a wheelbarrow. I worked up a good sweat.

When the last of it was cleared, I rolled the wheelbarrow back to the shed and headed to the back steps. Otis shoved the lawnmower in behind me. He still hadn't said a word.

Willie threw his hoe over his shoulder and turned to the truck. Otis grabbed his rake to follow.

The phone rang. It was Jimmy Pitts!

I said. "What can I do for you, Jimmy?"

"I need some legal advice," he said.

"Why not call Rose? Isn't he your attorney?"

"He is. That's why I can't. He's represented the mill since Daddy ran things. As far as I'm concerned, he represents Burl and the mill. I damned sure ain't going to him with my problem. It's about Burl."

"I'm listening."

"Tell you the truth, I hoped you'd come out here. I have all my papers and stuff out here."

"You mean now?"

"Yeah."

"You can bring them here," I said. A drive to Sampson County at that time of evening didn't appeal to me.

"I'm stuck on kiln duty tonight. One batch is ready to come out and I've just unloaded a batch. I've got loads backed up."

"What's it about? Is it so urgent it can't wait until tomorrow?"

"It's about me and Burl. You know about the fight."

"Yeah."

"He got pissed 'cause I used some of daddy's moonshine money to bid on that timberland. A lot of it when you get right down to it, I have to admit, but hell, that money is half mine anyway. I used mine, too. I guess you know my girls did the bidding."

I did.

"Burl said I went behind his back. I told him to stick it up his ass. I'd do whatever the hell I wanted with my money. That's when he blew up. Said the land belonged to the mill."

"He may have a point," I said.

"That's what Rose told him. Said I needed company approval before I bid. That's bullshit, Mr. Bone. Me 'n Burl sat in here and went over every one of those parcels of land before we decided to bid on the one Reynolds fronted for some outfit."

"You know about that?"

"I heard about it. The way I see it, the company had a chance to bid on the other tracts and didn't. That left it open for me. I'll pay your fee on this."

"I don't practice, Jimmy. You'd be better off— "

"You're the one I want. I told you I'd need a favor. I'm calling it in."

He might think I owe him a favor, but I didn't.

"It wouldn't be a favor. I don't have the clout you need."

"It's important to me, Mr. Bone. I need to talk to somebody. I just got off the phone with Burl. Told him I was calling you."

"That must have scared him." I laughed. "What'd he say?"

"He told me to go ahead. He was calling Rose. He said they were going to teach me a lesson. You too."

"Not me. I'm staying out of it. I've already learned lots of lessons. One is not to stick my nose in where I don't know what I'm doing. Get a name lawyer, Jimmy. I've—" I was ready to hang up. The conversation wasn't going anyplace. It wasn't my problem.

"But Mr. Bone, Burl wants to squeeze me out! I swear. I need some help! He's acted funny since the auction. Didn't like it one bit that Morgan out bid us on that piece of timberland. Even when he found out he wasn't bidding for himself."

"He helped Morgan out," I said. "Must not have been too upset."

"That's what I mean. Acts like he's going nuts. Cursing the man one minute, working his ass off for him the next. Burl's always been kind of crazy anyway. Now he's really gone over the edge."

Still not my problem. I did have a question though. Good time to ask. "How'd you guys pick the piece you did bid on? Morgan's piece."

"Burl knew the land. He knows timber rightly enough. It's one we sold to TRS years ago, prime and close to the mill. We walked it before we put in the bid. That n … Reynolds guy didn't log more 'n a few trees in there."

"The appraisal was low. How do you account for that?"

"Caleb appraised low to get buyers interested. Prozini told him to."

"TRS lost a million dollars on that tract. I thought Skinny appraised those parcels for the liquidation committee, not Caleb."

"Yeah. I guess Skinny did, but Caleb reviewed it. Thing is, me and Burl went over all the appraisals with a fine toothed comb and decided to bid on that one big piece. Our bid would have been high except for the

Reynolds bid."

"Why didn't the company bid on the other parcels, the ones you had your daughters bid on? They were close to your mill and from what I understand, good timberland."

"Skinny said there was evidence here and there, mostly on the far side, of beetle infestation. And, it looked like somebody'd clear cut and left it. Didn't re-seed. Topsoil eroded."

Morgan told me there'd been no logging on the parcels. Had a crew logged the wrong property? Was it deliberate? Theft? I knew that happened now and then.

"But you bid. Weren't you troubled by the infestation and the logging?"

"I walked the tracts with Caleb and didn't see a hell of a lot of infestation and there was plenty of prime timber trees left."

"Does Burl know you walked the property after you guys decided not to bid for the company?"

"Hell no! I didn't tell him shit. What's that got to do with anything?"

"Well, when you and Burl decided what parcel to bid on, you both were mistaken about the timber in the tracts your daughters bid on. An argument could be made that you had a duty to let Burl know what you found when you walked the land with Caleb."

"That's what I wanted to talk to you about. I've got the old appraisals for all the tracts of timber around here. I'd like you to take a look at them. You'll be able to see what I'm—"

"You have the old appraisals?" I asked. I thought all of them had been thrown away! Damn!

"Hell, yes! I've got the one we used when we sold the tract to TRS way back when, Newsom's appraisal, and the ones the committee sent out with its bid packages on all the tracts. Thanks to Caleb, I have copies of the ones the committee kept in the conference room. On every parcel sold at auction. Don't tell Prozini. Information like that can come in handy down the road."

That changed things. I knew I'd never completely get that damned auction out of my head until I compared the legals in the Newsom appraisals with Skinny's auction appraisals. "Tell you what, Jimmy, I'll be out there in, say, thirty or forty minutes."

I wasn't going to represent him, but maybe I could convince him to get somebody else … after I'd looked at the appraisals.

He'd leave the pedestrian gate open.

I flipped my phone shut. Mr. Patterson and Otis waited a few feet away to say goodbye. I'd forgotten they were there. I thanked them for their work, again offered ice water and money. They refused both.

They drove away and I headed to Sampson County; my twenty-two in my pocket.

Chapter 26

"Grandpa," Otis said, "I want to talk to that Jimmy Pitts. Just talk. I ain't gonna hit him or nothing. Scooter said he was the one. According to Mr. Bone."

"What you want to go cause trouble for, boy? All that business about Chandra's settled now. Ain't gonna do no good for nobody if you stir that pot again."

"I have to ask him if he done her. I ain't gonna rest till I know."

"Boy, I ain't liking to say this, but Chandra was … she was loose like that. What all did Scooter say about it?"

"Mr. Bone told him somebody with a motorcycle'd been picking Chandra up at that Pub. Maybe Jimmy Pitts. Ain't no way she'd mess with that skinny dude. He was double plain. Jimmy Pitts is the only other man with a motorcycle around here who could 'a done it. Please Grandpa. I'll ask him one question and leave. Just want to settle my mind. Mr. Bone'll be there. What can it hurt?"

The old man sighed.

"Boy, I guess I know how you feel. It's stuck in your craw and won't come out, but we ain't going nowhere. Let's go home see what your Granny's cooked for supper."

* * * * *

The pedestrian gate at the Pitts' mill was ajar. Lights were on in the main office, but I couldn't see anybody inside. Jimmy's motorcycle was parked in it's usual spot. I didn't see Jimmy. I didn't see anybody. It was spooky. Made me glad I had my little automatic.

He likely meant for me to meet him where he worked, the kiln shack, I decided, so I went there. A load of lumber sat outside one kiln, a tractor coupled behind it. It's sliding door was open. The smell of cooked pine hung in the evening air. The door to the other kiln was closed. Steam rose from its exhaust vents and through a loose seam in its tin siding.

The shack office door was closed but lights were on. I went inside. Monitors tracked the dryness of the lumber. The display cycled. Some numbers stayed the same, some changed. I checked my watch. The drive took me thirty-five minutes. I was right on time. I looked outside, but saw no one. The only sounds were those made by gasses as they escaped from the kiln.

Jimmy's desk beckoned me to have a look inside. I didn't like the man and I didn't trust him. There were two places a man kept his secret stuff, his wallet and his desk drawers. The center drawer had nothing of interest, except a forty-five automatic. As I thumbed through files in a drawer, I heard footsteps on the gravel outside. I shut the drawer and sat down.

Jimmy came in, dressed in his leather motorcycle getup. "Ah, Mr. Bone. I waited for you in the office."

"I wasn't sure which office you had in mind. I didn't want to barge in on Burl."

"I don't blame you." He rubbed his jaw with the back of his hand.

"You said you had all the appraisals," I said.

"I've got 'em all. Which ones you want to look at first?"

"Let me start with the parcel in Sampson County. After that, the ones in Lawton County."

"Sure. Let's take a look."

"I'd like copies, if that's okay with you?" I planned to check the legal descriptions on the deeds with ones on the appraisals.

"If it gets Burl off my ass, take 'em with you. Just bring 'em back after you copy what you need." He opened the drawer of a file cabinet behind his desk and lifted out a pile of bound appraisals and wrinkled sheets of handwritten notes.

"The valuations between the old appraisals and the most recent ones differed because of logging and infestation?" I asked.

"That's what Skinny said. Caleb and I didn't see enough to get concerned." He put the appraisals and notes on the desk in front of me and gestured for me to have a look.

"Burl's been all over me since he found out. Him and Rose. They say they'll take me to court to force me to sell my shares in the mill. Does that make sense?"

"Some. I don't know how far they'll get, but they may force you to sell your interest if your dispute with Burl puts the company at risk. The secret bids you made won't help."

"Uh. With Rose about to be appointed to the Supreme Court, I expect the judges around here will try to kiss his ass. What chance will have if I go to court without a damn good lawyer?"

"Has a ring of truth," I said.

"Will you take my case?"

"I'm not a trial lawyer. You need a big name firm. I can only give you an opinion." I reached for the appraisals. He'd get my opinion after I'd had a look at the appraisals.

He stood and said, "Tell you what. Before we get started, I have to load the kiln. Can you give me a hand? Only take a couple of minutes."

I followed him outside.

He cranked up the tractor behind the load of lumber and asked me to go inside the kiln to watch when the lumber touched the door at the far end. A small, wall mounted light filled the inside with a dull yellow glow. My nose crinkled at the smell. Like burnt rags.

When the lumber was an inch or so away from the door, I raised my palm for him to stop. He did, hopped off and looked inside. The tractor motor continued to run.

"Stay there for a minute," he said. "If the load starts to move when I disconnect, holler out. I may have to pull it back a little."

I stood where I was, some twenty or so feet at the rear and watched the load. I didn't see how in hell it could shift, but I wasn't familiar with the operation.

There was a loud metal clang when he uncoupled. The load didn't move.

"Let me back out," he said.

As he did, I noticed a slight tremor in the load of lumber but no movement. It looked secure, so I turned toward the door. That's when it began to slide shut.

"Hey!" I shouted. "Wait a damn minute!"

The door closed to within a foot before I could get around the load of lumber. I grabbed it with my hands, but it was too heavy and the force behind it too strong. I turned loose.

"What the hell's going on?" I shouted.

"I'm going to dry you out good, Bone. And when you're shoe leather, which won't take long, I'll dump you onto the conveyor belt and grind you into hogging chips. Maybe you'll do some good for once in your miserable life."

"People know I'm here!"

"No, they don't."

"Burl and Rose—"

He laughed. "You got shit for brains? I didn't call them! Anybody else you told. Well, they may know you headed in this direction, but hey, you didn't make it. I waited 'round here for hours. Too bad. I don't know how your jeep ended up in the creek like it did. Maybe you had an accident and got washed away."

Shit!

Steam poured into the enclosed room, hot, dusty steam. I grabbed my cell phone and punched in the chief's number. The call failed. No signal could penetrate the sides of the metal building. Damn it. The dim light of the kiln quickly clouded over with swirling steam and dust. I'd be dead within minutes.

I began to cough. I ripped off my shirt to cover my mouth and nose. The sensors! What did he say when I was here before? When the sensors on both sides of the stack read about the same temperature, the kiln shuts down. I fumbled for my twenty-two. I thought I heard another voice but couldn't tell.

Breathable oxygen in the room was about gone. My body was drenched in sweat as I slid a bullet into the chamber and aimed it at the first sensor. Two bullets later, the light went out. I fell twice as I stumbled to the other side. At the door, I stopped to shoot at where I thought the clasp might be, but the door didn't give.

My head spun so from the heat and dust, I could barely see. I passed out for a second. I thought there'd be air near the floor so I crawled toward the other side. When the red dot of the other sensor panel showed through the haze, I pulled my self up and put my last three shots into the panel. The sensor light went out, but not the hot dusty air. My knees buckled. I grabbed for the lumber, but sank to the concrete floor.

I lapsed in and out of consciousness. I waited for the computer to shut down the hot air and prayed it would. If both sensors were out, the computer should interpret it to mean the temperatures on both sides of the stack of lumber were the same and shut it down. Jimmy could manually override the computer, but I'd have a little time. To do what, I didn't know.

The hiss of steam stopped! It was still hot as hell inside, but got no worse.

Muffled voices and sounds came from outside. Curses and thuds. The door shuddered under the impact of something thrown against it. More thuds and curses. A fight?

My head cleared enough for me to search for a way out. With some effort, I broke a two by four off the top of the stack of lumber to use as a battering ram against the metal seam of a tin wall panel. I was able to force a small crack until my two by four splintered. I broke another piece from the stack and pushed at the crack until it became an open slit. Fresh air poured in! I could breathe! Nothing ever felt so good. I wedged the board in the hole and jerked the tin sheet back enough to slide out.

I stumbled out to see Otis on the ground. Caleb and Jimmy stood over him. Jimmy kicked him in the ribs. Otis groaned and rolled away. Jimmy kicked him again. Blood ran from Jimmy's split lip.

"Hold it!" I shouted and fumbled for my weapon. It wasn't there. I grabbed the cell phone on my belt and pointed it.

Caleb laughed. "Look Jimmy! He's gonna shoot us! Go ahead, shoot! Never been shot with a cell phone."

He came toward me with raised fists. "Get your gun, Jimmy! You gotta kill 'em both now. Damn it to hell! We'll roast 'em later."

I shoved my phone into my pocket and raised my fists to do battle with Caleb. His body was outlined in a silver-fuzz. I blinked to make it go away. It didn't. Caleb staggered me with a hard right hand I didn't even see until it hit me. I fell against a stack of lumber but stayed on my feet. He hit me again, poked out lefts and rights. I bobbed and ducked and used my elbows as a shield, but that was all I could muster. My arms grew numb and my legs felt like rubber bands.

I lunged and wrapped my arms around his waist. He pounded my back with his clinched fists. I was finished. My knees buckled as I heard a sharp crack. One I'd heard before. With a second crack, Caleb screamed and fell. His fingers clawed at his throat to free it from Mr. Patterson's whip. Jimmy's mouth dropped open. Mr. Patterson reeled in his whip to drag Caleb along the ground.

Jimmy turned to get the automatic from his desk, but Otis grabbed his leg and pulled him down.

I had reception on my cell phone. I punched in the chief's number and told him where I was.

When Jimmy tried to pull free, Otis popped him one. Willie stood behind Caleb with his whip ready should Caleb make a move. The chief said he'd get "hold of" the Sampsonville Sheriff and be there in twenty minutes, full siren.

When they showed up, Jimmy claimed that "Bone and that nigger barged in here and started to tear up the place. When I tried to stop 'em, that one swung on me." He pointed at Otis. "I held 'em off, then Caleb showed up to help. Thank God for that. Saved my ass. Then that other one showed up with his whip." He pointed at Willie.

"That's right," Caleb said.

But, there was another witness.

Willie and Elsa Patterson waited in the truck while Otis went to have his "say" with Jimmy, the first voice I heard. As they argued, Caleb drove through the pedestrian gate on Skinny's motorcycle and parked next to the kiln. He hit Otis over the head from behind. That's when the fight started. It distracted them while I tore a hole in the kiln wall.

Willie worried that Otis might have gone beyond "his say," especially with Caleb there. So he got out of the truck and made his way to the commotion. Elsa followed in case "Willie needed me." She stayed out of sight but was close enough to witness it all.

Caleb and Jimmy were hauled off to the Sampson County jail.

"There's a bunch of appraisals and notes on Jimmy's desk," I told Jenkins. "Take 'em with you and lock 'em up."

He helped me open the kiln door to get my twenty-two. I showed him what I'd done.

I was still groggy when I got home, but called Kathy to tell her what happened. It'd be all over town the next morning. I slept late the next morning. Even then it was hard to get out of bed. My head felt like a three-day hangover. Hadn't had one that bad since my army days. I had coffee on the back porch. The sun was out and, the birds were in full song. A good start to the day. After breakfast, I tried a slow jog to the falls and back to get some adrenaline into my blood stream. Later I felt recovered enough to look at files and do reports.

Kathy called. I told her I was okay. She said she'd be there after work. It looked like the day would start well and end better.

Jenkins called. "They're out on bail," he said. Jimmy and Caleb retained a big gun lawyer out of Jackson. "Bo Stringer's the guy's name."

"Don't know him," I said.

"He's good. He once got an acquittal even though his client confessed. Told the jury they could ignore it if they wanted to. They did."

I asked, "Have Jimmy and Caleb been charged over here?"

"Not yet. Milty wants to do his homework before he makes an arrest. The last case he lost was four years ago to Bo Stringer. Milty calls him Bullshit Slinger. He told me this morning he won't lose this time."

"What are you doing?"

"Milty got a judge out of bed this morning to sign search warrants. We're all over Caleb's office, his house, his car and van. We got his credit card records and his bank records. My men are talking to Claire Dearman, Willie and Elsa Patterson and Otis and the help at the Pub. Same for Jimmy's."

"I doubt that'll make Burl happy. He likes to be left alone."

"Apparently he's cooperative."

"Have you looked at the appraisals?" I'd bet my cabin they'd show that the legal descriptions used for the auction of the Gibbs and Kitchens parcels had been switched.

He said, "We've got a guy on them. If I hadn't picked them up, they'd have been in the burn barrel five minutes after Jimmy got out of jail."

"No doubt."

"By the way, Bo Stringer's called a press conference for three. That's really why I called. I thought you'd want to see what he has to say. It'll be on local news."

* * * * *

News Break at Three opened with the story of the arrest of Jimmy Pitts and Caleb Washington for attempted murder.

"The men were released on bail, but our News Team has learned that the Lawton County District Attorney plans to file additional charges against the men. Their attorney, Bo Stringer, had this to say."

The camera panned past the hole I made in the kiln to an enormous broad-faced man with thick silver hair in a dark, double-breasted suit, in front of the kiln door. Jimmy and Caleb were by his side.

"Last evening, my clients surprised Otis Patterson and Bishop Bone vandalizing the kiln and were attacked. Mr. Patterson had previously attacked my clients in Lawton and has been in trouble with the law on numerous occasions."

"Witnesses claimed Mr. Pitts and Mr. Washington were the attackers!" a reporter said.

Bo scoffed. "The grandparents of Otis Patterson? What would you expect them to say? Not exactly without a vested interest, are they?"

"Bishop Bone claims Jimmy Pitts attempted to bake him in the kiln," the reporter said.

The lawyer dismissed the charge with a flourish of his hand. "Mr. Bone, I'm told, has spread rumors of wrongdoing, even murder, since the TRS auction. If memory serves, the man has been linked with scandals in the past, a real troublemaker. All that will be brought out at trial. My clients did nothing more than defend themselves."

The story ended with another shot of the damaged side of the kiln.

Not five minutes later, my phone rang. It was a News Team reporter. He asked if I had seen the story. I told him I had. He wanted my reaction to Mr. Stringer's charges.

"If I cause Mr. Pitts and Mr. Washington any trouble, I'm glad. Jimmy Pitts tried to bake me."

My rebuttal made the evening news along with Willie Patterson's.

* * * * *

That evening, Kathy brought steaks and a bottle of wine. She kissed me at the steps. We threw the steaks on the grill, opened the Chianti and listened to creature noises in the woods while the steaks sizzled. To her it was a done deal. Jimmy and Caleb were guilty. Most people around town thought so as well. No smoke without fire. "You're a hero around town," she told me.

I told her I'd considered a vacation out of town until the stink blew over.

"Nonsense. Take your credit." She leaned over to kiss me again.

I turned down the grill for awhile.

Later on, I said, "Rooster called to say that Swegman cancelled the purchase of Morgan's mortgage. His client didn't send the money."

"The bank still owns the mortgage?" she said.

"It does. Morgan was tickled to death. He says they'll soon be shooting out two by fours and, 'Good Lord willing,' will make their next loan payment. One of his college friends sent a check out of the blue for enough to get the rest of the mill up. He says they'll be back to one shift in no time."

Chapter 27

Chief Jenkins called to say they'd made progress. "Milty sends his congratulations. You stuck with it when the rest of us were ready to throw in the towel."

"Until Jimmy tried to bake me, I was reaching for mine," I said.

"We found your computer and printer in Caleb's shed before he made bail in Sampson County. You wouldn't want 'em back. 'Been exposed to rain and covered in spider webs. Your files too. I arrested him on suspicion of burglary. No bail."

"That was a break."

"Yep. We got another one when we searched his van. We found a little rainbow colored cell phone in its glove compartment. Chandra's phone."

"I bet that knocked you out of your chair."

"It did. We've ordered the phone records. The legal descriptions for the appraisals we took from Jimmy's office were different from the ones used for the auction. Like you said, somebody switched them. That made Milty smile."

"Somebody?"

"We figure Caleb. He and Jimmy were buddies and Jimmy stood to gain."

"What about the Holdcorp piece, Prozini?"

"It was switched too. We arrested Jimmy on suspicion of fraud and added the same charge against Caleb. Milty said we'll work out the details before we go to the grand jury."

"Lots to work out. Prozini had to be in on part of it?"

"As I said, lots to work out before we go to the grand jury."

"Stringer have anything to say about that?" I asked.

"He ranted and raved that we'd offered no proof that his clients had done anything. He told the court that all we had shown was that Rose had made a mistake with the legal descriptions. He said, 'My clients are just as upset as anybody by this gross mistake. And, obviously restitution is in order but nothing criminal was done by my clients.' The judge denied bail. Stringer will appeal."

"How'd the mistake charge sit with Rose?"

"He was too red assed to sit," the chief said. "He swore to the news people that no mistakes were made by anyone in his office. Milty says the Bar Association will likely hold their recommendation until the mess is cleared up."

"I don't like the man, but mistake or deliberate, it happened in Rose's office. However, it wasn't a mistake," I said.

"We want to nail it down before Stringer's appeal gets heard."

He'd call me if anything else turned up.

Son of a bitch, I thought. Could those bastards wiggle off the hook? I didn't sleep much that night. It was getting to be a habit.

I analyzed a borrower's financial statements the next morning and sent the bank a report. I was so distracted by the possibility that Jimmy and Caleb might get off, I had to do everything twice. That afternoon, I walked to the creek to keep from going crazy while I waited for news. The creek was up, its green waters rippled with a clean, fresh smell. The last rain had brought it back to life.

"Bishop!"

I looked back. It was Milty holding a six pack and a fishing rod. The chief was a step behind with his rod.

"It's all over but the shouting," Milty said as they came down the slope. "Caleb confessed."

"No shit?"

"No shit," the chief said. "Jimmy's been charged with murder."

"Celebration time," Milty said and handed me a beer.

"What happened?"

Milty said, "The last call made on Chandra's cell phone was to Otis Patterson, the night Otis went after you his baseball bat. I added attempted murder to the charges against Caleb."

"They're adding up," I said.

"There's more. Somebody called Jimmy on her phone the day she died."

"Chandra?" I asked.

"More like Caleb," Milty said. "Based on the time of death in the autopsy report, the coroner said when the call was made Chandra might have been alive, but more likely than not, unconscious."

Jenkins said, "Within minutes of the call, Caleb and Jimmy met at the Pub for a beer. A waitress remembered both men. They had a serious discussion. And Jimmy paid with a credit card."

"So, I charged Caleb with negligent homicide," Milty said, "and hinted that charges for the murder of Chance and Dearman were coming."

"What was Stringer's reaction?" I asked.

Milty said, with a grin, "Strangely, he didn't tell me, but Caleb did. He said he hadn't killed anybody and wanted another attorney. Said his interests and Jimmy's weren't the same anymore. His new attorney said Caleb wanted to cut a deal. I told him to come on in."

"No shit!"

"Caleb told us everything. It was Jimmy's idea to switch legal descriptions for the auction. Caleb was promised a hundred thousand when the dust settled. After the auction, Caleb reattached the correct legal descriptions. He and Jimmy had to open and reseal a lot of bids to find out what to bid on the parcels his girls bought. He'd bootlegged a set of keys off Rose's."

"The judge must have figured it out," I said.

Milty said, "Almost. Chance asked Caleb if they'd checked the legal descriptions sent by Prozini with the ones attached to the deeds. Chance thought that was the loophole. He was close. Caleb assured him they had. He figured that was the end of it, but when he told Jimmy at the mill, Jimmy went crazy and told him that they had to do something before the judge figured it out. Caleb told him he'd done all he was going to do and left. Jimmy left on his Harley seconds later."

"That was the day the judge was killed," I said.

"Yep," the chief said. "The next time Caleb saw Jimmy, he said Jimmy was all smiles. 'The judge won't cause anymore trouble,' Jimmy said. We charged Jimmy with murder and Bo Stringer about had a stroke."

"I imagine he'll sniff around for some kind of deal," Milty said. "He won't get it."

* * * * *

I told Kathy the rest of Caleb's confession over a blackened catfish dinner at Cowboy Jim's. We sat outside on the deck. I even tossed a piece of bread over the rail to the rail to the squawking ducks.

"Caleb didn't know if Jimmy killed Skinny or if he put the screwdriver in Morgan's driver head assembly, but felt he did both from the way he acted. Jimmy was the one behind Holdcorp's offer to buy Morgan's mill and when that failed, his mortgage," I told her. "He had Caleb run the offer through Prozini so his name would be kept out of it. It would have been his money had the deal gone through."

"I thought it was all Prozini," Kathy said.

"Only on the Holdcorp parcel. The mill was Jimmy's. Caleb said he tried to talk Jimmy out of it, but Jimmy hated Burl so much, he wouldn't listen. Jimmy wanted the mill to go head to head with Burl. That's what drove everything," I said. "Jimmy told Caleb to pick up anything the judge left at the office. It ended up in his burn pile."

"What a mess," she said.

I told her the rest. Jimmy told Caleb to pass the word to Prozini that a listed company contacted him about a mill. Burl's wasn't for sale, and Morgan was in trouble. Prozini was more than willing to broker the deal through Holdcorp for a three-percent commission plus expenses. Holdcorp would in turn sell the mill to Jimmy. The land too, for the right price.

"That means—"

"Yeah. Two scams," I said. "Jimmy and Caleb worked one. Prozini the other. Independently."

"I'll be," she said.

"Prozini's was first. He sent a short legal description to the auction committee and planned to deed himself the omitted acres after TRS dissolved."

"But he bought the entire piece, didn't he?"

"That's right. Caleb told Prozini that Burl and Jimmy were low-balling a bid on timber land they had earlier sold TRS. That was the one Prozini had shorted acres from the legal description he'd sent the liquidation committee. So, to make sure nobody began to wonder what had happened to the shorted acres, Prozini put in a slightly higher bid through Morgan. He re-added the shorted acres to the legal description on the final deed."

"Will he be charged with anything?" Kathy asked.

"Fraud. He agreed to deed the Holdcorp property back to TRS. Milty expects he'll get a suspended sentence and probation. For sure, his career as a promoter is over."

The singing troubadour in his cowboy hat plucked his guitar along the back wall of the restaurant and sung of lost loves. I put a couple of dollars in his jar on the way out.

* * * * *

A couple of weeks later, the chief told me that lab tests proved Jimmy was the father of Chandra's baby.

"I figured it was Jimmy or Caleb," I said.

"Jimmy's trial's next week. I'll be glad to get it behind me," he said. "I hear Morgan's selling lumber as fast as he can load it on trucks."

"Oil business is booming and drilling companies want hardwood for pallets they lay down as haul roads in marshy areas."

Willie and Otis didn't come back to cut my grass any more and I didn't expect them to.

The End